Praise for Kate Johnson's
I Spy

5 Stars "I absolutely LOVED the story. Sophie is an awesome character, full of life. She has a quick and sarcastic sense of humor that made me laugh out loud. Did I tell you how much I liked her?"

~ *Anne Chaput, eCata Romance*

4.5 Stars "If you like the Stephanie Plum series, I believe you will like I, Spy? ...This book is modern, quirky, ironic and sassy. I can easily see how this will spin out into an excellent series."

~ *Janet Davis, Once Upon A Romance*

"This book has everything! Kate Johnson has created a wonderful set of characters. This is one book...I would have on my keeper shelf!"

~ *Jan Crow, ParaNormal Romance*

4 Stars "...an outrageously funny story... I Spy? was one laugh after another. It is good to see that a ditsy blonde can save the day and when Luke and Sophie finally hook up readers will just not believe where! I Spy? is one hot read and too funny for words. Readers enjoy!"

~ *Alisha, TwoLips reviews*

A is for Apple

Kate Johnson

A Samhain Publishing, Ltd. publication.

Samhain Publishing, Ltd.
512 Forest Lake Drive
Warner Robins, GA 31093
www.samhainpublishing.com

A is for Apple
Copyright © 2007 by Kate Johnson
Print ISBN: 1-59998-658-2
Digital ISBN: 1-59998-605-1

Editing by Jessica Bimberg
Cover by Scott Carpenter

First Samhain Publishing, Ltd. electronic publication: September 2007
First Samhain Publishing, Ltd. print publication: November 2007

Dedication

For the teachers who inspired, frightened and bullied me into learning. Especially Auntie Sheila. I wish you were here to read this. Although you'd probably have to correct my grammar.

Prologue

Basically, I've been spending a lot of time lately drinking too much and eating nothing but Pringles, thinking about sex and my gun. The reason for this is pretty much because I'm about two thousand miles away from both, on an island paradise that's boring as hell. I don't speak the language, I don't understand the currency, and although it was supposed to be a getaway, what I really want to do is get back to my job, which is dangerous, unpredictable, frustrating and unbelievably cool.

My name is Sophie Green, and I'm a spy.

"*Esto es un robo*," I said, and the little blonde in front of me looked slightly alarmed. "*Manos arriba. Dónde está la caja? Ábralo.*"

"You're holding me up?"

"Do I sound convincing?"

"Very," she nodded admiringly. "I think you even convinced the people in the apartment downstairs."

I looked over the balcony, where there was indeed a Spanish family looking rather alarmed.

"Sorry," I yelled. "I didn't mean it. I can only speak the Spanish I learnt from *Butch Cassidy and the Sundance Kid*."

I looked over at Angel, who was giggling uncontrollably. "Can you say that in Spanish?"

She took a sip of margarita and called out, "*Apesadumbrada, ella no lo significó. Ella cotizaba de una película. No es realmente un robo.*"

They yelled something back up, and I caught the words "Sundance Keed" and Angel yelled down, "*Sí!*"

"I think you're forgiven," she said to me.

I smiled and sat back against the white wall and looked out over the street and the dunes and the sea.

"You know, this might sound insane, but I'm actually kinda missing England."

"You'd rather be in grey Essex than Fuerteventura?"

I made a face. "Last time I went abroad someone tried to blow me up."

"And the time before that you made out with my boyfriend."

"He wasn't your boyfriend then. You didn't even know him then. In fact, I should get Brownie points for introducing you."

Angel looked at me over her margarita. "You didn't introduce us so much as crash your car with him in it and get me to visit."

"Well, it still worked," I said placidly, far too relaxed to argue, and slightly too pissed, too.

"Have you heard from Luke?" Angel asked.

I scrunched up my nose. Luke was my boyfriend and had officially been so for just under two months. I'd told him not to call me while I was on holiday because it'd make me homesick to hear his voice, but I was starting to wish he had anyway. Harvey, Angel's perfect boyfriend, had called every day, just to hear her voice, and every night to wish her sweet dreams (while I held back my nausea).

"You know Luke. The most unromantic sod there ever was."

"I think he's pretty romantic," Angel said. "Remember when you were hurt and he lent you his entire collection of *Buffy* DVDs?"

I smiled. Luke and Angel were the only people who understood my *Buffy* obsession.

"It was his fault I was hurt anyway," I said.

"How so?"

Actually, it had been totally my fault, I'd run into a building site and it had sort of collapsed on me, but I usually managed to come up with some excuse as to why it was Luke's fault.

"He should have gone in first," I said, and sucked some green ice up through my straw.

"Do you miss him?" Angel asked, and I brought up a mental picture of Luke Sharpe. Six-foot-one, blond hair, blue eyes, cheekbones you could cut diamonds with, long, lean muscles, a package so sexy I had to guzzle a lot of ice to cool myself down.

"That bad, huh?" Angel asked.

"I can control it," I lied.

"So what's SO17 got lined up for you when you get home?"

I sighed. I didn't want to think about it. "You know I couldn't tell you even if I knew," I said.

"Which you don't?"

"Not a Danny."

She looked puzzled, and I smiled and explained, "Danny la Rue? *Clue?*"

She laughed. "You've been hanging out with Macbeth."

"He sort of rubs off on you."

We looked out at the view for a while longer. The sun was sinking over the sea. It was simply one hundred percent beautiful.

"It'll only be something boring," I said, inaccurately as it turned out.

Chapter One

Taking off from Fuerteventura at nine p.m., we soared upwards through a glorious sunset. The air outside the terminal had been so hot I'd nearly choked when I left the air-conditioned departures lounge. I was wearing a halter top and a little flippy skirt that showed the Spanish ground crew exactly what colour my bikini bottoms were.

When we landed at Stansted it was just after one in the morning. And it was *cold*.

"Jesus Christ," I gasped as the Stansted ramp boys got a view of my underwear, "don't they get summer here?"

"This is England," Angel said. "So of course not."

Between us, we knew pretty much everyone at the airport, the dispatchers and luggage loaders, the gate staff and baggage agents. By the time we'd got through saying hello to everyone, and by the time they'd all finished complimenting Angel on her perfect all over tan, and asking me if I'd perhaps been to another island—say, Greenland—it was nearly two in the morning. We grabbed our baggage and stumbled out into Arrivals.

Where a tall, handsome man with shiny hair and great teeth was waiting, holding a dozen long-stem red roses and looking right at us. I nudged Angel. She spied him, abandoned her case and rushed into his arms.

"Harvey! My God, I've missed you so much!"

This was true. Pretty much all she'd done was sit around going, "I wonder what Harvey'll be doing now? I wonder if Harvey misses me? I wonder if he'll be at home when we get in?"

But Harvey, all-American wonder-boy, had gone one better and turned up. At two in the morning. With flowers.

I looked around. I checked my mobile. No Luke.

"Hey, Sophie," Harvey said, when he'd unsuckered himself from Angel. "Good trip?"

I smiled. Harvey really was just so lovely. "Great," I said.

"Did you stay in the shade all week?"

I scowled. "I have Celtic ancestry," I said. "I don't tan."

He grinned. "Well, it's bad for you, anyway."

I don't care. I still want to be brown.

"Do you need a ride home?" he asked, and I shook my head.

"Ted's in the car park. I'll speak to you tomorrow, Ange?"

She nodded and spied someone over on Baggage. "I'm just going to say hi to Aletta," she said, tugging Harvey after her, and he grabbed her suitcase and followed like the good boy he is.

I hefted my big case, which had seemed somehow lighter before I saw Harvey, and trudged to the lift, searching in my bag for my car keys. I get a staff parking place because my day job (or sometimes my night job) is being a passenger service agent at the airport, just like Angel. We check people in, board them at the gate and generally pander to their whims.

I need this day job because my other job is slightly unpredictable. I'm a spy. I work for a very small, very secretive government agency called SO17, along with my boss and three other agents. Luke is one of those agents. Only two people

12

outside the British government know of our existence, and I've just waved goodbye to them. Angel's parents were agents, and Harvey is on secondment from the CIA.

I spied Ted waiting for me, stumbled up to him gratefully, feeling unbelievably cold, and had a small panic attack about where I'd left my car park pass. And then I saw it in the door bucket, and felt quite stupid.

I collapsed into him, running my hands over him appreciatively, and sighed. I was home. So long as I was with Ted, nothing bad could happen to me.

Well, apart from when Luke and I had that massive break up in the front seats. And that time someone got in the car and pressed a gun to my head. And there was the crash incident. But we survived, me and Ted, we're resilient.

I looked over Ted's big bonnet. He's a Land Rover Defender, my jolly green giant, big and solid and utterly cool, and I adore him. He's got me out of a lot of trouble, has Ted. I started him up, and he rumbled happily, glad to see me again. I put him in gear and pointed him homewards, and off we went, round the roundabouts, along the little back roads, nearly home by the time my mobile started ringing in my bag.

Luke, I thought, and picked it up. But the display read One, and I clicked onto the call gloomily. One is our boss—we have numbers according to seniority. Luke is Three. I'm Four. I'm not allowed to put anyone's real name in my phone directory, so I just entered them under their numbers.

"Hello?" I yawned.

"Sophie?" Her voice was clipped and cool. "You've landed. Good. Where are you?"

"On my way home." Yes, I know it's illegal to use a mobile when driving. Who's going to catch me at two in the morning?

"Can you call into the office? I have something for you."

Why did I get the feeling this "something" was not going to be of the present variety?

Our office was in the airport business park, a couple of hundred yards behind me, so I turned around in a lay-by and swung back on myself. There was a blue Saab parked outside. Karen Hanson's car. The boss was in.

I swiped myself in and went through to her little office. Our headquarters are really small—two offices and a secret lab. The offices are made up to look like ordinary, boring pre-fab offices everywhere, with hessian on the walls and dying potted plants scattered about. The lab is subterranean and accessed only with a swipe card pass, PIN code and voice recognition.

It's really, really cool.

Karen was waiting for me, looking her usual immaculate self even in the middle of the night. "Good trip?" she asked curtly.

"Yeah, great," I said. "Really relaxi—"

"Good," Karen said. "Now it's back to work."

"I haven't even got home yet!"

"This is not an issue. You are aware, are you not, Four, that Five is currently working in America, tracking a businessman with bad connections?"

Five was Macbeth, who started at SO17 the same time as me, and fast-tracked his way to Competent Agent in about half a day. I, on the other hand, still usually need someone to baby-sit me. "What kind of bad connections?"

"Mafiosi. His name is Don Shapiro—short for Donald, but not many people know that. He's actually British and we're trying to, shall we say, discourage him from coming home."

She looked up at me and I, feeling something was needed, nodded seriously.

"Where do I come in?"

"Bait."

Oh, Jesus. I hate being bait. Luke is always making me do this. Just because I'm blonde and have big boobs, I'm always the decoy. We never seem to investigate women. Or gay men. I would so love to see Luke making a fool of himself the way I usually do.

"The case is in Five's hands, but I presume you know the drill by now?"

I nodded disconsolately and she handed me a file. "I suggest you familiarise yourself with this."

"Now?"

She gave me a penetrating look. "Do you have a more pressing appointment?"

Yes, with my bed. I was knackered.

"No," I sighed, and took the file out to the outer office, kicked off my sandals and flumped down in the desk chair to read.

Don Shapiro was of Italian-American descent. He had been brought up in the UK. His wife and his son were British. Well, actually, she was his ex-wife. They'd been divorced for ten years and the kid only saw his father in the school holidays. He went to boarding school in Scotland.

Mr. Shapiro was officially in the import/export business. I say officially, because I once had to shadow a banker who turned out to be trying to rule the world. People are never what they seem.

I can personally vouch for that.

I read the file through about four times, but I hardly absorbed any information. My brain was broken. Words were swimming. By the time Karen breezed through the office, on her way home, the sky was getting light and my eyelids were getting very heavy.

"Shouldn't you be on your way?" she said, and I blinked.

"Yes. Tired. Very tired."

"Not home," she said. "To the airport."

I stared in horror.

Karen flipped to the last page of the report. There was an airline ticket tucked in there. British Airways, Heathrow to JFK. In two hours.

"Best get a move on," she said briskly. "Don't want to miss the flight."

Wouldn't that be a tragedy?

I'd like to say that my job is all about glamour. Fast cars, slinky dresses, lethal cocktails... But in reality here I was, trundling down the M11 in the skinny hours of the morning, wiping sleep from my eyes and shivering in the cold. Ted's heater had never been particularly efficient, and since I crashed him a couple of months ago, keeping warm has meant wearing a jumper. Or a boyfriend.

And right now I was a bit short on both.

I was halfway round the M25, trying to remember how to get to the hell that is Heathrow airport and suspecting I'd gone the wrong way, when my phone started bleeping and buzzing in my lap. I jumped, nearly swerved into the middle lane and managed to get the hands-free extension in before I answered with a very sleepy, "Hello?"

"Where the hell are you?"

I blinked tiredly at the road signs and started the overcomplicated procedure of changing lanes. Well, it's complicated for me, anyway. I'm not terribly bright.

"Hello, Luke," I said.

"Where are you?"

"On my way to the airport."

There was a pause. "You'd better not mean Fuerteventura airport."

"Of course not."

"Oh, good."

"I mean Heathrow airport."

Another pause. "*Why* are you on your way to Heathrow?" Luke asked wearily.

"Because that's where my flight's going from."

"What? *From*? Sophie, you're not making any sense."

"I'm going to New York."

This time the pause was longer. Then the man I'm sleeping with asked me, "Are you on drugs?"

"What's that supposed to mean?"

"Why are you going to New York?"

"Karen sent me."

"Something wrong with Macbeth?"

"Apparently Don Shapiro isn't partial to fifteen stone black men."

"She's sending you out there as bait?" Luke asked incredulously, and I scowled at the Mondeo in front.

"That's the impression I got."

Luke was silent a bit. Then he said, "How long will you be?"

"I don't know." I hoped not long. I wanted to see the Big Apple, but something told me I'd not have much time for sightseeing. I'd been bait before, and it had never ended well. "Not long. Probably Macbeth just wants to get Shapiro out of the way so he can scope out his hotel room." I yawned and nearly missed my exit. "Shit!"

"What?"

"*Four Weddings* moment."

"Tell me you didn't just reverse into the traffic?"

"Do you want me to? I think Ted could take it."

There was a longer silence. I could imagine a lot of expressions on Luke's face, none of them very complimentary.

"I'll let you concentrate on your driving," he said eventually. "Call me when you get there?"

"I will," I said, touched.

"Just so I know you're not in Johannesburg or something."

I wrinkled my nose, less touched.

"I'll speak to you later."

"You better."

When I first met Luke Sharpe, he gave me a false name and pretended to be Italian. It wasn't really his fault—he was undercover at the airport. He was sexy Luca from Roma, and everyone fancied him.

And then I found out who he really was, he washed out the dark hair dye and took away the coloured contact lenses and there he was, my blue-eyed boy, sexy as hell, the image of the man I'd always wanted.

Five days later we had sex in the rubble of an abandoned building site. It probably wasn't the best way to start our relationship, but there was a nice quality of drama to it. We bounced around for a while (no, not like *that*. Well, okay, yes, a lot like that), trying to figure out how we felt about each other, if we felt anything at all. I think a large percentage of what I feel for Luke is pure lust. The jury's still out on what he sees in me.

I don't mean that masochistically. There are days when I look in the mirror and think, damn, I'm hot. And there are days when I look in the mirror and it breaks. Luke must have caught me on a good day the first time he saw me, because the main SO17 hypothesis is that he hired me because he wanted to shag me. That's really the only explanation anyone can think of. I'm a rotten spy. I make mistakes, I forget things, I'm quite terrified of my gun—

Dammit, my gun! It was still at home. I was going to New York and I didn't have a gun. That's like going to church without a hat, isn't it?

I picked up my phone again as I navigated the complex route Karen had told me would take me to the staff car park, and called Macbeth. The line wasn't good, and I could only hear about half of what he said, but I told him my ETA and asked, somewhat hopefully, if he had a gun I could borrow.

He laughed. "Darlin'," he said, "I got plenty."

I ended the call hoping he'd been talking about what I'd been talking about.

Chapter Two

Despite being knackered and grumblingly pissed off, there was still a part of me that was excited about going to America. I mean, I'd never been outside the EU before. France, Spain, Italy, I have the T-shirts. (No, I really do. I'm a geek as well as stupid.) I was going to go to Prague with a couple of old school friends a while ago, but it fell through. I've always wanted to go to Australia. Maybe I still will. Who knows where the work of an international spy will take me?

'Cos it's usually not much further than my local chipshop.

But America. New York, the Big A. That's exciting, right? All those shops and bars and beautiful people. Maybe I'd finally get to find out what all those cocktails they drank on *Sex and the City* actually were. I'd see my first Jimmy Choo up close and personal. Although, probably only in a shop window, because I'm far too scared by posh shops to actually go in them.

I parked up and found my way to Terminal Four. The BA check-in desks were right ahead of me and I tugged my case up to the front of the short queue. It weighed twenty-two kilos, and I was glad Luke wasn't there, because twenty-two was ludicrous for one week's holiday somewhere hot. I still wasn't sure what had made the case so heavy. I mean, all my summer clothes were really tiny and thin. I hoped New York wouldn't be too cold, because I had one fleece sweater and it was buried under all my sarongs and bikinis.

Security was stupid. I mean, it probably isn't any more secure than the regular question-and-scan routine we use at Stansted. Hell, some days I'll check in six flights to Belfast—and meet six flights coming back—and believe me, they know about terrorists there. The endless rounds of confusing questions (Why was it necessary to know how I'd arrived at the airport? *Why?*) and dragging my case from one place to another just served to annoy me. And, you know, if you're trying to stop people bombing you, then annoying the hell out of them probably isn't the way to go about it.

Blah. I was just bitchy because I was tired. No sleep and no coffee makes Sophie a mean girl.

I finally made it through to regular ol' fashioned security, where I made the scanner bleep and had to be searched by rather unamused woman, a contrast to the cheerful Stansted guys, who all knew me anyway. When I'd been allowed to put my shoes back on (remind me not to travel in DMs), I turned to find someone holding up my bag, asking whose it was.

"Mine," I said gloomily.

"Do you mind if I search through it?"

"Would me saying 'no' make any difference?"

Boy, these staff really needed a sense of humour. My tightly packed shoulder bag was emptied, my two wallets (one euros, one pounds—dammit, I'd need dollars, too) both swabbed for... I dunno, what the hell do they swab for? Explosives? Drugs? Did I look that wrecked?

"That's fine." The euro wallet was handed back to me, and I was left to try and fit everything back into my bag. James Bond never has to deal with this shit.

I got myself some coffee and slumped down by the gate, idly watching the staff print out load sheets and make phone calls, mentally picking on their performances. I was tired, really tired—I hadn't slept since yesterday morning and what I really wanted to do was go home and curl up in my lovely soft bed with Tammy, my little tabby cat. Or Luke. Either would be good.

They called the flight and I shuffled down the jetbridge and found my seat. Oh, joy and rapture, they'd given me a bulkhead seat! Now I could stretch out my unfeasibly long legs (yeah yeah, but you try buying jeans) for the seven and a half hours it'd take to get to New York. Of course, sleep on public transport is impossible, that's just a law of the universe. As soon as I dropped off, my neighbour shuffled past, or the hostess rattled by with a trolley, or they'd make an irritatingly perky announcement. How dare they be perky when I was a zombie? I started wondering in my delirium what the US policy on the walking dead was.

A thousand years later, we started descent and I hurried to fill out my customs declaration and visa waiver. The customs declaration was easy. I wasn't carrying any food apart from a choccy bar and I wasn't sure that counted. The green visa waiver was another matter. I filled in the front with no problem—name, date of birth, passport number, etc., and then I turned over.

Oh.

I had no communicable diseases, had never been convicted for a crime, wasn't on drugs or looking for work. It was point C that got me. The one where they asked if I'd ever been involved in espionage activities.

Oh. Dear.

Ahem. I had the feeling this was a trick question.

I ticked no, and hoped I didn't look guilty.

The queue at Immigration was long enough to make me want to cry, but when I got to the little desk, a woman looked me over, asked how long I'd be staying (crap, how should I know?), stamped my passport and waved me off.

Right. All that anxiety for nothing.

I collected my bag and switched on my phone. "Macbeth," I called him, "I've landed. What do I do now?"

"You're staying at the Hotel Philadelphia," he told me, "on Seventh between 32nd and 33rd."

"In English?"

"That's the address."

"Oh."

He laughed. "Go to the Ground Transportation desk in arrivals and get the hotel shuttle. It'll take you right to the door."

"Where I will...?"

"Meet me, and I'll fill you in."

"Okay. Philadelphia, shuttle—got it."

But evidently I hadn't, because I had to call him back when I got to the desk, to get my hotel name. I kept thinking of the Hotel California. See what I mean? I'm useless. It's a wonder I didn't end up in actual Philadelphia.

The shuttle was a minibus and it took me right to the door of a massive hotel. I'd been dozing on the bus so I didn't take much in of my surroundings, but as soon as the door was opened a wall of heat and sound hit me. Hot town, summer in the city.

In total contrast, the huge, grand Art Deco lobby of the Philadelphia was air-conditioned to Arctic conditions. I was shivering as I met Macbeth. He took one look at me and took over the check-in procedure.

"You're in room 1316A," he said, handing me a little green credit card of a door key. "Want me to show you where it is?"

I nodded feebly and he dragged my suitcase off to the bank of lifts. Oops, I mean elevators. I was in America now.

Inside was a small TV screen showing CNN news. Swanky. Businessman Don Shapiro had made a massive donation to the ASPCA, following his adoption of two hideously ugly hairless puppies. I was confused. Was our bad guy a good guy?

"Don't let that fool you," Macbeth said. "He's a real piece of work. He wants the dogs to guard his new apartment."

"Where does he live?"

"In a hotel until his apartment is finished, but it's on the Upper East Side. Very expensive."

Of course.

"What do I need to do?" I asked, as the lift doors opened and Macbeth kindly towed my huge case out into the thirteenth floor lobby. I averted my eyes from the window—heights make me very nervous.

"He hits the hotel bar most nights. You sit there, look pretty and show some skin and keep him and his goons occupied while I go through his room. Tomorrow I need you to do the same again while I check out his apartment."

Marvellous. I knew all that training would come in handy.

It was about two in the afternoon, but to me it was seven in the evening and I'd been awake for two whole days without taking off my makeup. Thank God I'd got a tub of green gunk to clean my skin up—Angel and I had spent the week in Fuerteventura pampering ourselves. I scoured my face, took off my clothes and fell into bed.

I was woken in the late afternoon by my phone trilling out the Darth Vadar theme tune. There was only one person who made it ring like that.

"Hello, Luke," I yawned.

"Am I keeping you up?"

"Mmm. What time is it?"

"Eleven."

"Shit!" I bolted upright. "I'm supposed to be at a bar—"

"Are you, now? I meant eleven my time. It's about six where you are."

I squinted at my watch and relaxed. He was right. "Don't scare me like that."

"Right back at you. I thought you were going to call me when you landed? Which should have been ten hours ago."

"You're counting?"

He didn't answer that. "Was your flight okay?"

"Mmm. I got to watch *Charlie's Angels*. Again."

"And did you rant, again, about the plane decompressing when they open the door and jump out? And how they'd suffocate from lack of oxygen at that altitude?"

"Yep."

"Glad to hear it. What's Macbeth got you doing?"

I told him about Shapiro, the hotel and the apartment, and Luke asked what I was going to wear.

"I don't know," I said, nonplussed. "Something out of my case."

"Do you have anything in there that looks remotely expensive?"

"I don't have anything anywhere that looks remotely expensive."

There was a pause, such as might be made by someone trying hard not to add a comment to that.

"Go out and buy something."

"With what?"

"Got your company credit card?"

Oh, God, yes. I'd almost forgotten about that. I'd been with SO17 nearly five months now, and I'd only just been allowed a credit card to cover things like flights and emergency clothes.

"I can't go in expensive shops," I said, "I'm intimidated."

Luke muttered something I didn't catch.

"Try Bloomingdales. They have nice stuff but it's not too scary. And don't forget shoes—Manhattanites set a lot of store by their shoes."

"I know, I watch *Sex and the City*."

"Hmm."

I looked at my reflection—crumpled clothes and mussed greasy hair sticking to the face mask I'd forgotten to take off. Good job Luke hadn't got a vid phone.

"Do you miss me?" I asked nervously.

"Course I do. Place is all quiet and tidy."

"Ha ha."

There was another pause, then Luke said more quietly, "I do miss you. Things are just...less fun without you."

A little tear trickled through the green gunk on my face. How adorable was that?

"I miss you too," I gulped.

"If you're not home soon we're going to have to try phone sex."

I rolled my eyes at my green reflection. So much for adorable.

"I have to go," I told him, before he started really thinking about it. "I have to get a dress."

"Something tight and short... How's your tan?"

"You'll laugh at me." Luke's one of those annoying people, like Angel, who walks under a streetlight and goes a lovely golden shade all over. Well, nearly all over, ahem.

"That bad?"

"I got sunburnt on my shoulders. The rest of me is Persil white."

"Well, I'll just have to check that out for myself when I see you."

"Hmm."

"Oh, Soph—when you filled out the immigration form, did you tick the espionage box?"

"I'm not stupid."

"Questions still stands."

I stuck my tongue out. "No."

"Okay, good."

A pause. "Well, bye then," I said.

"Bye."

So there was nothing for it. I had to go shopping.

The only thing was I didn't know where Bloomingdales was. I didn't know anything about Manhattan, except for where the *Friends* and *Sex and the City* characters lived. Which wasn't very helpful.

I wandered down to the lobby and went to the information desk, where there were some leaflets about the city. One of them had a map, and I scanned it for department stores. There it was.

I also saw an ATM, and wondered if my cash card would work there. Yes, my friends, I truly am an innocent abroad. The card worked, and I got fifty dollars out, hoping that was a reasonable amount of money. I really had no idea what the exchange rate was. I was fresh from Euroland.

Armed with my little map, I set off across town. I wasn't brave enough to try the subway yet, and anyway, it couldn't be very far from 32nd and 7th to 59th and Lexington, which was next to Third. Couldn't be that hard, right?

Right?

By the time I'd got to Central Park, I was knackered. It had taken about forty minutes, and I still had to make my way across to Lexington, which was five blocks over, because somewhere around the chaos of Times Square I'd taken Broadway instead of Seventh and ended up a block over...

When I stumbled into the air-conditioned calm of Bloomingdales, a nicely suited man asked me cheerfully, "And how are you today?"

"Bloody knackered," I said. "Where's women's clothing?"

He gave me a once-over, like the women on Rodeo Drive in *Pretty Woman*. "Second floor."

"Cheers." And I set off, only to find that Bloomingdales is the most confusing shop in the whole world. The escalators are set up oddly, each floor has about ten different levels and I went straight up to the third floor first, because in English that's the second floor, and I was all confused...

Eventually I found the ladieswear department, flipped my scruffy hair out of my eyes and started looking for something drop-dead. Because drop-dead was exactly how I felt.

I ended up with a very cute black and white fifties-style dress, all fitted bodice and fluffy skirts, and shoes to match, and then I had to hunt down some stockings and while I was there I went for new underwear too, and a cute little handbag... Well, I was on assignment, and there was no telling how much distracting I might have to do. Besides, I didn't have to pay for it.

Which is just as well, because I'd spent hundreds of dollars.

The other thing I don't understand about American money is the tax system. If you pick something up off the rail and the label says $19.99, you don't pay $19.99. Because they add sales tax on at the desk. How this has not been rectified I don't know. Americans must all be good with numbers. What's wrong with putting the tax inclusive price on the tag?

I left Bloomingdales with my Medium Brown Bags, feeling a lot smarter, and found it was chucking it down with rain. And my bags were made of paper. And my shoes were incredibly flimsy.

So. Less smart.

There were, of course, no cabs. I trudged to the subway, a system I thought I might be familiar with since I'd used London's, and promptly got lost.

By the time I got back to my hotel, I was wet and blistered and grumpy, and there was a voice mail on my phone from Macbeth telling me to meet him in the lobby of the Park Avenue Hotel in an hour and a half. Bloody hell!

I leapt into the shower, shrieking when the hot water hit my blistered feet, and washed my hair. When I was done drying it, the room was like an oven, so I opened the window and flashed half of Manhattan in the process. No one told me New York would be this humid.

I pulled on my lovely little dress, which was even better for being a size eight (I tried on several twelves, thinking ecstatically that I'd lost loads of weight and must now be the same tiny size as Angel, before I remembered that American sizes are different to ours) and the shoes it had taken me so long to find (see above re: sizing). I made myself up with the cosmetics I'd picked up at Sephora on my way through Times Square, smoothed down my hair and braved the subway again. Yeah, I should have got a cab. But I've seen too many movies about psychotic cab drivers and, well, I'm a wimp.

I had to change twice, but I paid especial attention to the signs this time, and only got lost once. I arrived on Park Avenue feeling a little wilted, but reasonably expensive, and no one sneered at me so I must have been looking okay.

The hotel door was opened for me by a man in a fancy suit, and a dredged up memory told me he should be tipped. So I took a five from my wallet, still not entirely sure what the conversion rate was, and not wanting to be stingy. The doorman beamed.

"Thank you, ma'am. You have a splendid day."

Hmm. It was nine p.m. Not much day left.

Macbeth looked pretty impressed, too, when he saw me.

"Very nice," he said. "That new?"

"Why, it doesn't still have the tags on, does it?"

He grinned. "You look new and shiny. But stop limping."

I made a face. "My feet hurt. I'm all blistered and these things," I waved my pretty new shoes at him, "aren't helping."

"You have to suffer to be beautiful."

In that case, I must be looking really hot.

He pointed to the hotel bar, gave me a photo of Don Shapiro to memorise, and then handed me a little bag containing an earpiece and told me he'd be upstairs, listening in.

"How will you get in without anyone seeing you?" I asked. "Don't they have CCTV in all these places?"

He grinned. "And?"

Good point. There was nothing Macbeth couldn't disable.

I went to the ladies and put the earpiece in, switched on the battery and dropped it in my bag. I fastened the little mike inside my bra and said in a low voice, "Can you hear me?"

"I can hear everything," Macbeth said, and I was sure there was a leer in there. "Go get him and, remember, he likes his girls sophisticated."

I made a face at the mirror. Sure, I looked pretty sophisticated now, but after a couple of sophisticated cocktails I'd be legless.

I made my way over to the bar, hoping my overall image was one of a sexy wiggle, not a pained hobble, and perched myself on a barstool.

"Can I get you anything?" the handsome bartender asked.

"I'll have a—" A what? My usual pub drink was lager. At home I drank wine or cider (am I cool, or what?). In Fuerteventura we'd been working our way through the silly cocktail menu of Sex on the Beach and Slippery Nipples. Somehow, I didn't think any of those drinks would go down well here.

Although...

"Guinness," I said. Guinness is the Land Rover Defender of drinks. Tough and ultimately cool, no matter who's drinking it.

Plus, it matched my dress.

It came in a pint glass and I told myself to go slowly. I might look cool now, but in half an hour I'd be falling off the stool if I wasn't careful.

Half an hour came and went, and there was no sign of Shapiro. I'd sipped a quarter of a pint and was feeling pretty silly sitting there all on my own.

"Are you waiting for someone?" the bartender asked.

"Yes," I said. "He's...he's late..."

"I see that. Where you from?"

"England."

He grinned. "I see that, too. Whereabouts?"

"Uh, near Cambridge," I said, because that always sounds nicer than "I'm from Essex", and I'd rather be thought of as a toff than a Shazzer, thank you very much.

"And what are you doing here in New York?" He said it Noo Yoik.

"Business," I said.

"What kind of business?"

The mind your own kind, I nearly said, but I was too distracted, because during one of my many glances towards the door I saw someone familiar walk in. Someone very familiar.

"Excuse me," I said to the bartender, leaving money on the bar, and hopped off my stool and ran over. "What are you doing here?"

He stared at me. "Do I know you?"

I frowned. Then, "Oh, yeah, very funny. See, I do scrub up well."

"Uh, yeah. Very well. Look, who the hell are you?"

I stepped back and looked him over. Tall, good body under his jeans and faded green T-shirt, great teeth, lovely hazel eyes, shiny brown hair.

"Harvey?" I said uncertainly. "What are you doing here?"

He stared at me a bit more, and then he started laughing. And I laughed too, hesitantly, feeling slightly stupid, still having no idea what was going on.

"Are you here on—" I looked around, "—business?"

He grinned and nodded. "Business. Yeah, I like that. I guess I am."

Bloody Karen sending someone out to get in my way. "Is it—is it the Shapiro thing?"

He frowned and took me by the arm to a further away corner of the plush bar.

"What do you know about the Shapiro thing?"

"Duh, it's why I'm here. Didn't Luke tell you?"

"Well—"

Of course, Luke and Harvey don't really get on. Luke thinks Harvey's as useless as a Ken doll, and besides, they started badly when I met Harvey and, er, sort of snogged him before I got together with Luke, and now Luke still thinks there's some sort of spark between me and Harvey. Whereas Harvey's a lovely bloke and all, and undeniably cute, but just... I don't know, just a little too nice. Maybe there's something wrong with me that I prefer Luke, who is admittedly a bit of a bastard.

And then someone came up to us, unctuously dressed in the hotel uniform, and asked Harvey greasily, "Excuse me, sir, are you a resident?"

"Well, no, but—"

"It's just that we do have a dress code here in the Houston bar," the uniform gave a little sneer, "a tie, and no sneakers or jeans for gentleman."

"Oh, just for gentlemen?" Harvey said. "The ladies don't have to wear a tie?"

The uniform didn't smile.

"Look," I said, "he just forgot, right, Harvey? Why don't we get out of here, 'cos I don't think Shapiro's coming, and we can go talk about this, right? My hotel's not too far."

They both looked at me, the hotel guy with a leer, and Harvey with panic.

"Listen, lady," he said, "I appreciate it and all, but—"

Jesus, did he think I was making a move on him? And hadn't he once invited me up to his hotel room? No, not once— twice?

"I'm not making a move," I hissed. "Doesn't the name Luke mean anything to you?"

Harvey opened his mouth, but the hotel guy got in there first. "Sir, I'm going to have to ask you to leave," he said.

Harvey glared at him, then me, and said, "*Fine.*"

And then he walked out.

Bloody hell.

I shuffled after him on my painful feet, mumbling to my mike, "Macbeth, can you hear me?"

"Loud and clear. I got surveillance set up outside the room, I'll holler if he's coming. You go after the Yank."

"You know why he's here?"

"No idea. Not like they ever tell us anything."

"Cheers," I muttered, and caught up with Harvey at the revolving doors. Then I got stuck and went round twice before being ejected onto the pavement and nearly knocking Harvey over as he lit up a cigarette.

"I didn't know you smoked," I said in surprise.

"What you don't know about me could fill the Empire State," he said. "Who the hell are you?"

"This isn't funny—"

"Nope. Listen, lady, I'm not who you think I am."

No kidding.

"You know Harvey, right? James Harvard Esquire. Lives in England, right?"

"Right," I said, trying to figure this out in my head.

"He's my brother."

I stared.

"My twin brother," he clarified.

"But—"

"You didn't know he had a twin brother."

I shook my head, unable to think of anything else to say.

He flicked ash off his cigarette onto the ground. "Well, here I am. I can show you ID if you want."

I nodded dumbly, and Harvey II got out a wallet and flicked it to a driving licence. Alexander Henry Harvard. State of Ohio.

I peered at the birth date, but not knowing Harvey's, it meant nothing to me. But I did know he was from Ohio. Shit.

"If you're Harvey's brother," I said, "what's his girlfriend called?"

"Angel. Sweet little thing. Tiny and blonde." He studied me. "So who the hell are you?"

"I—I'm Sophie. I'm a friend of Harvey's. We sort of work together."

"Sort of, huh?" Alexander Henry said, and I wondered how much he knew about Harvey's work for the CIA and SO17.

He started walking, and I stumbled after him, wincing. These shoes might be pretty, but I wasn't altogether sure I'd worked out the sizing right and they were pinching and rubbing like a bad Swedish massage.

"So what's your business with Shapiro? And what's my bro got to do with him?"

"Um," I said, "I'd rather not talk about it."

"And who's Luke?"

"My boyfriend. Look—"

"Where is he?"

"England. Look, Alex—"

"Xander."

"Xander, right—"

"Is he cute?"

"Who?" I was confused now.

"Your boyfriend."

"Yeah, he's gorgeous."

"Got a picture?"

"What?"

Xander stopped and turned to me. "Of your gorgeous boyfriend? Can I see him?"

"Uh—" Completely thrown now, I reached in my bag for my wallet, thinking for a moment that this odd Harvey clone was going to mug me, but he just stood there, watching me.

"I'm not going to take your wallet," he said, "I just want to know if you're after my brother."

I frowned, but pulled out a file photo of Luke looking moody. It's not the best picture of him and he doesn't even know I have it, because I printed it off the office computer once when he was out. He has his arms folded, he's wearing a black shirt, his hair is tousled and he looks kind of sallow and hungover, as well he might, because I think it was taken the morning after a pretty bad night out. But he's still damn fit.

I watched anxiously as Xander scrutinised the photo in the dark. I was still at the stage where I desperately wanted everyone to approve of my boyfriend. I thought he was pretty damn stunning, but was I being deluded?

"Nice," was Xander's verdict. "Looks pissed off, though."

I grabbed my precious photo back. "He always looks pissed off."

"Even with you?"

I scowled at him, and Xander laughed, flicking away his cigarette. "So how far's this hotel of yours?"

"Erm, I don't think—"

"I'm not going to make a move on you," Xander said firmly. "Trust me."

"Oh, cheers."

He grinned, and it was Harvey's open, friendly grin. "Where are you staying?"

I knew Macbeth was still in contact, so, feeling safer for having him as back up, I said, "Hotel Philadelphia, on Seventh."

Xander looked like he was considering this. "We'll take the subway," he said, and I followed after him slightly helplessly.

My Metrocard was still valid, so I followed him down onto the platform. He seemed to know exactly where he was going.

"Where exactly on Seventh?" he checked as we went down to the platform.

"Between 32nd and 33rd."

He nodded and switched lines easily, me following along like a little hobbling dog.

We got off at Penn Station and waited for the Walk sign to turn to our advantage. Xander hesitated outside a grocery, then went in and bought a bottle of vodka.

"You want anything?"

"Erm..." Getting drunk with a complete stranger would not, I surmised, be a very good idea. "I'm supposed to be working."

"Am I in your way?"

"Well, no, but I shouldn't really be drinking..."

"Tell you what, I'll drink and you can watch." He added some Coke and then started shovelling junk food into a basket, proper Homer Simpson junk food that we just don't get. Lay's potato chips and Hershey bars featured in large quantity. I spotted some Jolly Ranchers and lobbed them in for good measure. I love Jolly Ranchers, but no one seems to sell them in England anymore.

We got to the till and Xander looked at me hopefully.

"Nope," I said, "you picked it out."

Scowling, he dug out some cash and paid for it. Then he followed me back to my hotel. I know I could have protested, could probably have got one of those scary guys by the elevator lobby to have kicked Xander out for me, but I was pretty sure he wasn't going to attack me. I had a hunch. Well, okay, more than a hunch, but that sounds cooler.

I stopped off at a drugstore (which always sounds shady to me, because I'm a good girl who Says No To Drugs) and bought some fat sticking plasters and waterproof tape for my feet. I chucked in a bottle of water, feeling very virtuous, and off we went again, Xander slouching moodily ahead, me hobbling behind.

We got back to my room and Xander looked around. "Jesus," he said, "did something explode in here?"

I wrinkled my nose. "I don't feel at home unless I've made some mess."

"Then you must be planning to live here." He got out another cigarette, and I took it off him. "Hey!"

"This is a no smoking floor," I told him. "There are smoke detectors all over the place." I wasn't sure if this was true, but I didn't want my room stinking of smoke.

Xander scowled at me and stalked into the bathroom for one of the plastic cups by the sink. He threw himself down on the double bed and tore open the bag of Lay's crisps—sorry, chips—and sloshed out a strong measure of vodka. No Coke.

"So," he looked up at me, "how do you know my brother?"

"We sort of work together."

"Uh-huh. What do you have to do with Shapiro?"

"It's business."

"Business my brother's involved in?"

"Well, kind of," I hedged. "What do you have to do with Shapiro?"

"Asshole owes me five grand."

I blinked. "What for?" I asked, praying it wouldn't be drugs.

"I'm an artist," Xander began earnestly, and at my disbelieving look, sighed. "He commissioned a portrait. I did the portrait. He took the portrait. Now I want my money."

"Shouldn't you have got your money before he took it?"

"Didn't know he had. Came home one day and it was gone."

"So he stole it?"

Xander shrugged and opened up the Pringles, his eyes averted from mine. "Could have."

"But..."

"But nothing. What's your business with him?"

"I work for a bank," I said. "We have a few deals with him."

"Deals that involve you wearing Anna Sui and Beverley Feldmans?"

That sealed it. I knew I was safe.

I flumped down on the opposite side of the bed and began unstrapping the glorious foot-torturers. There was a patch on one side of my left foot that had been rubbed raw and was bleeding slightly and I hobbled into the bathroom, ran some water in the sink and stuck my foot in.

"Very impressive," said Xander.

"I used to do yoga." When I was five.

"Bet your boyfriend loves that."

"Oddly enough, he's not turned on by me washing my feet."

"Got the shoe size wrong?"

"...Maybe."

I bathed my poor feet, dried them off, then sat down on the bed to parcel them up. By the time I was done my feet looked vaguely mummified. Xander poured me a shot of vodka and I took it. For the pain.

"So what do you really do?" he asked, and I sighed.

"I work for a totally secret British government agency and I've been sent here to investigate Don Shapiro."

I was expecting him to laugh. Usually people do.

"What's he done?"

I stared at him. "I was joking!"

"No, you were talking into a mic when you followed me out." He grinned at me. "Artist, see? I'm very observant."

I scowled and reached inside my bra for the mic. Then I took out my earpiece and switched off the battery.

"I can't tell you what he's done," I said.

"Why not?"

"Because I'm not entirely sure."

"You're not a very good secret agent, are you?"

"Nope."

"Bet ol' Harvey pisses you off."

I gave him a sharp look. He grinned again, and it was the same charming smile Harvey often gave.

"Oh, please. We grew up in a small town, everybody knows everybody's news. The whole town knew when Harvey went to Princeton. The whole town knew when he joined the SEALs. And then the whole town knew when he started working for the CIA."

"Does the whole town know about you, too?"

"The whole town despaired of me. I was the evil twin."

"I'll bet." I drained my vodka. "More, please."

"Hey, if you're gonna drink it, pay up. I'm five thousand dollars down."

I fetched a twenty from my wallet and held it in front of his face. "Why did you come to see Shapiro this evening? Did you have an appointment?"

"Did you?"

"Answer the question or you don't get your vodka money."

He made a face. "I went to get my money. Figured I could talk to him about it."

But he still looked shifty. Maybe I'd wait until I got him more drunk to ask him again.

Chapter Three

I was woken by the sound of doom pounding into my head. Der, der, der, derder*der*, derder*der*. Der, der, der, derder*der*, *derderder*.

"What the fuck," Xander groaned, "is that noise?"

"My phone," I mumbled, mouth full of pillow. I fumbled for the hellish device, wishing I'd never agreed to a triband phone, and groggily answered the call.

"Hey," Luke sounded peppy, "good morning."

"Meh," I said.

"Don't tell me I woke you up?"

"Blegh."

"Sophie, it's four in the afternoon here. Which makes it eleven in the morning where you are. How did it go with Shapiro last night?"

"He didn't show. My feet hurt," I moaned, to no one in particular.

"Poor baby," Luke said without a trace of sympathy. "Are you going back there tonight?"

"I don't know. I haven't spoken to Macbeth yet. How's it going where you are?" I added, proud of myself for thinking to ask.

"Okay," Luke said boredly. "Listen, Karen said you might want to keep an eye out for Shapiro's kid. Uh, his name's Marc-Paul. Want me to send you a picture?"

"Yes please. Is he cute?"

"I wouldn't know."

"I thought he was in Scotland?" I glanced over at Xander, still sprawled beautifully across my bed.

"He was, but not now it's summer. He came out to see his pa a week or so ago. Only just found out. He's staying at the Park Ave. with his old man."

"How old is he?"

"Seventeen."

"Right." The most unreasonable age there is. "Send me the pic and I'll keep an eye out."

"Okay. Let me know how tonight goes."

"Bye."

I switched off and checked to see if anyone else had left a message. They hadn't. I rolled over and looked at Xander, who appeared to have gone back to sleep.

"It's a good job he doesn't have a video phone," I said, and he opened one eye.

"That was your boyfriend?"

I nodded.

"Could he tell I was here?"

"Don't think so. He didn't yell or anything."

"He's a jealous type?"

"Yep."

"Oh well. You're safe with me."

"I guessed that."

He got up and wandered into the bathroom, looking unshaven but not too bad. I knew I'd look awful—hangovers made me pasty and puffy. My head felt heavy and swollen, my stomach squished uneasily and my feet were still killing me. I looked at my careful plasters. Half of them had come off.

I heard water drumming in the bathroom and deduced, super sleuth that I am, that Xander was in the shower. Great. I wasn't sure if I could face all that water without accidentally drowning, so I hung up the beautiful, but somewhat wrecked dress that I'd thrown on the floor last night and pulled on jeans and a T-shirt proclaiming that men made great pets. I guzzled all the water that was left, along with some ibuprofen and Resolve left over from Fuerteventura—was that only two days ago?—and flopped back on the bed, waiting for Xander to come out.

We'd sat up drinking and trying to get answers out of each other until about three in the morning, when the vodka had run out and we were both too drunk to get any more. Xander had asked me all about Luke, and I'd got drunkenly tearful about missing him and sobbed in Xander's arms and I must have eventually fallen asleep, because the next thing I remember is the phone ringing.

Xander wandered out, wearing only a rather small towel, and I felt my mouth go dry. I really needed to get close to Luke, and soon.

"Does this place have a laundry?"

I shook my head, trying to find my voice. It couldn't have gone far. "I don't think so," I croaked.

"Damn. Okay. Want to go shopping?"

I stared.

"You seemed to find the Y.E.S floor in Bloomies all by yourself," Xander went on, scratching the back of his neck, "but did you find Saks?"

I shook my head.

"Or Barney's?"

"No."

"Boy, we have some educating to do."

He bullied me into taking a shower, telling me Saks would chuck me out if I was too scruffy, and when I emerged, feeling slightly more human, he threw some prettier clothes at me.

"Get dressed and put on your makeup. And do something about your nails."

Bloody cheeky. I spent hours clipping and shaping and buffing each talon to perfection, messing about with my cuticles, painting them in a pretty shade of pink, then daubing on makeup very carefully. I hung the dress in the bathroom with me to steam out the wrinkles, spritzed it with perfume, and it looked respectable enough to wear again.

When I emerged, I looked a hell of a lot better. Xander looked me over and shrugged. "You'll do," he said.

"You're still a mess."

"Honey, I'm with you. No one will care."

Was that a compliment, or not?

I repackaged my feet and gingerly put on a pair of soft mules. I took a few cautious steps. Yeah. Didn't seem like my feet were going to fall off.

Of course, this lasted until we got outside and it was still raining. Xander sprinted for the subway, while I fumbled with my umbrella and all my careful plasters peeled away. Damn.

On the train, while Xander laughed at me, I sat and showed the world my knickers as I tried to wrap some more tape about my poor raw feet. By the time I was done there was hardly a toe unwrapped, my feet were bound like a little geisha's, but I felt a bit better, so long as I didn't flex my foot too much and break the bindings.

"That's gonna be great for trying on shoes," Xander said, and I scowled at him.

"Don't you have a home to go to?"

He shrugged, his eyes on a subway poem. "Nothing to do there until I get my money."

Anyone else think he's lying?

We wandered up to Bloomingdales and went around picking out clothes for each other. Then shoes—on a mission to find the silliest pair we could. The mens' shoes were boring—how do they cope?—but there were lots of silly things in the women's department. Pink and yellow slippers, polka-dotted wedges, fat Spice Girl trainers with neon laces, heeled hiking boots. Xander tried to persuade me to get the Spice Girl trainers, but I wasn't biting. What was this, 1996?

At Sephora we had a lipstick fight. He sprayed me with CK1, which I hate, so I grabbed his hand and painted three of his nails pink.

"Not my colour," he said, eyeing them critically.

I painted the other two blue.

"Now you're just taking the piss."

I grinned. He might be hiding a lot from me, but he was still a large amount of fun.

It had stopped raining, so we went up to Planet Hollywood for lunch and sat looking out at Times Square. "This is so kitsch," Xander said. "Want a strawberry margarita?"

"Does Dolly Parton sleep on her back?"

So it was that we were both slightly pissed—well, pissed enough to think that my confusion over getting the "check" vs. getting the "bill" was hilarious—when we wandered out to look up at the MTV studios and my phone rang. It was Macbeth, and I may have greeted him a little merrily, because he asked in a pained voice, "Sophie, have you been drinking?"

"No! Well," I giggled, "let me clarify that. Yes."

"It's six in the afternoon."

"Well, that's eleven p.m. in England." Right? Or was I too pissed to work out the time difference properly?

"You have work to do."

"Such as? You never called me last night."

"Figured there was nothing for you to do. Listen—I've had stuff monitoring Shapiro's suite all night and all today. There's been no sign of him. He went out yesterday aftern...n...hasn't b...seen..." The line crackled, and I missed part of what he said.

"What?"

"He's vanished."

Uh-oh. "Does he have a laptop or anything you can hack into?"

"No. There's nothing here. Listen, that guy you were with yest...day—Harvey Number Two—he was after Shap...too?"

I glanced at Xander, who was watching a troupe of orange-clad dancers wriggling about up in the MTV studio. "Yes," I dropped my voice, "but he won't tell me why. Not the real reason."

"You think...s lying?"

"Omitting things."

"Try and get...of him."

"What do you think I've been doing?"

I could hear him laughing. "Is this anything Luke c...hear about?"

I deliberated. Technically, yes, but in the real world... "Tell him and I'll—I'll paint your nails pink."

Obviously this was a dire enough threat for him. "My lips are sea...ry an...et it out...him. Oh, an...ophie?"

"Yes?"

"I...go...wants...ria...p you..."

"What? You're breaking up. Macbeth?"

"..."

"Are you there? Can you hear me?"

"..."

Great.

I ended the call and looked up at Xander.

"Xander," I said, and he turned his head to me fractionally. "Are we far from Central Park?"

"Seventeen blocks."

"Can we go there? I've always wanted to go there."

He tore himself away from MTV and we started up Broadway. On the way he pointed out the Hershey's store, where I went and bought lots of junk for Luke. Hell, if he didn't like it I could give it a good home.

Central Park amazed me. I knew it was big, but Xander said it was eight hundred and forty acres and a hundred and fifty years old. There were massive bits of rock sticking up out of the grass and, after walking a few blocks in we were suddenly miles away from the city. Buying a couple of ice-cold bottles of water, we sat down on one of the rocky outcrops and I fussed over my feet again. I'd bought some baby wipes from a chemist—sorry, drugstore—and cleaned off the dust and sweat and carefully repackaged my tootsies with tape and plasters. Xander watched me for a while, then he asked, "So why are you really here?"

"Well, my feet hurt, and I wanted somewhere to sit down—"

"I mean in New York."

"Oh. I told you, business."

"Business that lets you sleep in until eleven and go out shopping all day?"

"Yes," I said stubbornly, snipping off a bit of waterproof tape.

"Wow. Great job."

"Right back at you. Don't you have work to do?"

He shrugged. "Until I get my money I can't afford any materials."

"What kind of work do you do? Do you paint?"

"Sometimes."

Helpful. "Or is it more like 3D art? Sculpture, collage, performance art?"

"What do you know about art?"

"I have an A level in it." Only just.

"What's that?"

I looked at him. He didn't really seem to know. "Like a degree."

"Oh. Well, in that case, I make life montages."

I blinked. "What's a life montage?"

"I take bits from a person's life and use them to make a montage of that life. In Shapiro's case I was making it a portrait as well."

"What did you use?" I asked, fascinated.

"Bits of fabric from old suits, T-shirts from when he was a teenager, copies of baby photos, spaghetti, 'cos that's his favourite meal, clippings of hair from his barber, lines of poetry he liked...stuff like that."

This could be very useful. "What kind of poetry?"

Xander took a gulp of water. "Shakespeare's sonnets, W.H. Auden, John Betjeman... Some others I can't really remember. Boring stuff."

GCSE stuff. Not very revealing. Probably the only poems he'd ever read.

"I had a couple of pictures of his kid in there too," Xander volunteered.

"Marc-Paul?"

Xander looked at me sharply. "You know him?"

"I know of him," I said vaguely.

"I saw him two days ago. He was staying with his pa."

Not any more, I thought. Where were they?

I got out my phone and sent a text to Macbeth. *What about Shapiro's son? He's supposed to be staying in the suite. Have you seen him? Have they checked out?*

"Watcha doin'?" Xander asked, peering over my shoulder. I hastily sent and deleted the message.

"Texting my boyfriend."

"You miss him?"

I shrugged. "Kinda." Kind of a lot. I didn't think I would, but I did.

"What's his name again?"

"Luke."

"As in Skywalker. Right."

"He is *nothing* like Luke Skywalker."

"What, you mean he's actually straight?"

I grinned, and Xander smiled too. He really was just like Harvey—same breathtaking smile. Very cute indeed.

"So do you do a lot of portraits—I mean, life montages?"

"Are you taking the piss?"

"No, would I?"

He narrowed his eyes, but said, "I do a few. Sometimes I sculpt. This is just my new thing. I'm trying to get enough together for a show—I know someone with a gallery in the meatpacking district, reckons if I get enough together by the end of the month I can exhibit there..."

"That's great," I said, meaning it. My brother was a musician and what he did was great, but I knew how hard it was for his band to get any recognition. I had a feeling the art world was just as bad.

"Will you come?" Xander asked suddenly.

"What?"

"To my exhibition. If I get one."

"You will," I said firmly, on the basis of a day's acquaintance.

"So you'll come?"

He looked so hopeful. And I guess it would be nice...like Charlotte's gallery exhibitions in *Sex And The City*. Lots of fit men. Mmm. Oh, and Luke too, of course.

"Well, I do live five and a half thousand miles away," I said doubtfully.

"Won't your 'business' be bringing you back here?"

Did he have to put those quotation marks in there?

"I don't know..."

"What kind of business is it you do again?" Xander asked me sharply.

"Why won't you go home again?" I shot back.

"Okay, fine. Don't tell me." He turned away, looking moody, and I ignored him. Why wasn't he going home? What was there that he was afraid of?

Or didn't he have a home?

Fear gripped me. What if he was trying to grift off me? What if he was trying to move into my hotel room?

Well, tough luck. I wouldn't be here for long.

Hopefully.

We got back on the subway and went down to the meatpacking district, which was basically a few blocks in the Village. I liked it. The streets were more higgledy—not like normal streets, but still less blocky than the rest of Manhattan—and the houses had character. Xander showed me his friend's gallery, which was shut down for the night, and we walked (well, he walked and I limped) to a street lined with trees where he pointed out a house with a tall set of steps outside which he said was filmed as Carrie's stoop in *Sex And The City*. I was sceptical. It did look familiar, but then so did a hundred others.

"So where do you live?" I asked.

"Oh, it's sort of Tribeca, SoHo, East Village-ish," he said vaguely.

"In a Brownstone?"

"Yeah."

Yeah, and I lived in Buck House.

We got on the subway back to the Philadelphia Hotel and stopped for junk food on the way.

"I am going to be so fat," I wailed, looking at the bags of seriously addictive Lay's potato chips that Xander was piling into the shopping basket. He, of course, was all nicely defined muscle. No fat at all.

Bastard.

"Hey, you wanna see fat, you're in the right place," Xander said. "You think you're the only one who eats too many potato chips?"

He had a point. In the hotel lobby had been a guy oozing over the sides of his wheelchair. I'd never seen a person that fat before in real life. He'd been complaining the doors were too narrow. I'd wondered if he was fat because he couldn't walk, or if he couldn't walk because he was so fat.

Either way, I felt wonderfully skinny.

We took the bag of junk back into the hotel and made our way over to the lifts. I still wasn't sure why I was letting him come with me. I guess it was the little lost puppy thing. Xander was cute and helpless, and besides, he knew a lot about junk food.

Who am I kidding, little and helpless! He was about six inches taller than me, and I'm actually the average height for a bloke.

Speaking of tall...

There was usually a security guy at a desk by the bank of lifts, and I was rummaging in my bag for my key card to show him when Xander suddenly grabbed me and said in a low voice, "Okay, don't panic, but that's one of Shapiro's goons over there and he looks pissed."

"He's drunk?"

"No, pissed *off*. I think he's—shit, Sophie, reverse, reverse!"

He started walking very quickly back towards the entrance, spotted someone else and tugged me back over to the lifts again. The goon—a big guy in a shiny suit, marching towards us and looking mad—was closing in, and then suddenly Xander took hold of me, swung me round and kissed me.

Now, I don't have a huge frame of reference here. I've really only been kissed properly by four guys, and one of them was my cheating college boyfriend Pete the Philanderer. He was a crap kisser, and I used to spend my kissing time with him wondering what the hell all the fuss was about. The second is a shady guy called Docherty who's worked with SO17 once or twice. He scared the hell out of me. I kissed Harvey once or twice, but they were sort of polite, passionless kisses.

And then there's Luke, and when he kisses me the entire world ceases to be.

Xander's kiss was definitely in the first category.

I could figure out why he was doing it, and as a distraction it worked pretty well, because through half-closed eyes, over Xander's shoulder, I could see the goon looking puzzled, saying something into a mouthpiece and retreating. But it wasn't a very interesting kiss. I was quite bored until—

Until, oh shit, oh crap, the lift doors opened, and a familiar blond head turned to face me, a familiar pair of blue eyes looked right at me, and a familiar scowl shot right through me.

"Oh shit," I said against Xander's mouth.

"What? Did it work?"

"Yeah, it worked," I said, heart sinking. "It worked a little too well."

"What do you—" Xander began, pulling back and looking around in fear.

"What the *fuck*," came a very familiar voice, "are you doing with my girlfriend?"

Luke strode across the lobby and grabbed Xander by the shoulder and punched him in the face.

The security guy rushed over, as did a lot of spectators.

"What the hell is going on here?" yelled the security guy, suddenly looking very big and threatening, and there was a bulge under his jacket I thought might be a gun. Great, *now* he turned up.

Bollocks, bollocks, bollocks.

Xander and Luke were staring at each other.

"You?" Luke said in disbelief, glaring hard at Xander.

"No, Luke, this isn't—" I began shakily, horrified. "It's not what it looks like—"

"So what the hell is it? Does Angel know?"

I think my eyes nearly fell out of their sockets. "Angel? What—? No." I began to laugh, and immediately wished I hadn't. "Luke, this isn't Harvey, he's—"

Then in the corner of my eye I saw Shapiro's goon coming over to see what the commotion was, and I had a horrible image of him getting out a gun and shooting all three of us.

"Luke, get in the lift," I said. "You too." I grabbed Xander's arm. He had his hand on his nose, which was bleeding.

"I am not going anywhere until you tell me what the *fuck* is going on," Luke yelled.

The goon was getting closer.

I made a split second decision and grabbed Luke and said in his ear, "There's man over there with a gun who wants to kill us both. Get in the goddamned lift or I'll shoot you myself." *Oh, and by the way, what the fuck happened to your goddamn spy training? Blowing up over a personal matter. Yep, that's in the handbook.*

"You haven't got your—" Luke began, but I gave him my best don't-fuck-with-me glare and he glowered back and stalked off to the lift.

I gave a weak smile to the security man and the watching crowd. "Little misunderstanding," I said, making a *teensy* gesture with my fingers. "Really nothing. Just a lover's tiff. Come on, darling," I said, taking Xander's arm and wincing when I felt Luke's eyes—and ears—on me, "let's go and sort this out."

"I could call the cops," the security guy said, and I wasn't sure if it was an offer or a threat.

"No, no need," I trilled gaily, shoving Xander into the lift. "It's all under control."

I rammed my fist repeatedly against the button for my floor until the door slid shut, and then I leaned against it, my eyes closed.

"Don't ostrich me, Sophie," Luke said, and I opened my eyes again. Damn. They were both still there.

"Look," I said, in as calm a voice as I could manage—which is to say, vibrating on the Richter scale, "this really is just nothing like it looks—"

"And how does it look?" Luke spat.

I like this man very much, I told myself. *I am sleeping with him. He has saved my life. There is a small possibility—now almost certainly expired—that he may be a little bit in love with me.*

Fuck it.

"It looked like someone was after Xander with a gun and we were just stalling," I said desperately. "Xander, tell him—"

"I think you broke my nose," Xander said.

"Good," Luke said savagely. "What the hell are you doing here?"

"Luke, this isn't Harvey. I thought it was." I tried to smile, but Luke cut me off.

"Is that why you were kissing him?"

"No! No, I was kissing him because, er—"

"A distraction," Xander muttered through the blood pouring out of his nose. "The guy in the shiny suit's been tailing me for days."

"He's what?" I said.

"He works for Shapiro. It's a long story..."

"No doubt. Xander, does he really owe you money?"

"Well, yes—"

"I don't give a fuck who owes who what," Luke broke in irritably. The lift slid to a halt and the doors opened, and yours truly fell back flat on her arse.

"Ow," I said, lying there with my knickers showing, slightly winded. "Aren't you going to help me?"

"No," Luke said, and stepped over me, slouching off down to hall towards my room.

Xander extended his least bloody hand and pulled me to my feet.

"He seems like a nice guy," he said. "Really."

"Xander," I turned to him helplessly, "look, I'm really sorry about this. I told you he was jealous." I winced. That was no excuse. "I'll try and sort this out—can you maybe go home and get some ice on your nose?"

He shook his head. "You don't think they'll be waiting for me at home?"

"They're really tailing you?"

He nodded painfully. "For two days now. They think I know something about Shapiro."

"Do you?"

"He owes me five grand. I haven't seen him since he came to pick up the portrait."

"Which was...?"

"Three days ago."

"And they've been after you since?"

"Yep."

Bollocks. This was all too much at once.

"Look, I have a boyfriend who's possibly armed and definitely really pissed off with me. And I have to try and figure out this Shapiro thing. And you being here will just—just complicate things," I said, looking up at him pleadingly. "Look," I grabbed his arm and tugged him around the corner where there was an alcove and machines vending drinks and ice, "get some ice, I'll try and get back to you..."

I left him and dashed down the hall. Luke was leaning against my door, kicking it moodily.

"Still here?" I asked, looking in my bag for my key.

"You owe me an explanation."

"I'm glad you're being reasonable." God, I'd forgotten how hot he was.

"Just while we're in public."

"You mean you can get less reasonable?" Jesus.

I was having trouble getting the key into the slot. I kept jamming it in and it kept refusing to bleep and let me turn the handle.

"I'm not going to do this in public," Luke said evenly.

"'Cos downstairs was so private." *Open, damn you!*

He eyed my efforts with the key. "You need help with that?"

"No."

I struggled a bit longer, then Luke snatched the key out of my hand, turned it over and opened the door in a second.

I stalked in without looking at him. To be truthful, I was a little bit afraid. I don't think Luke would ever get violent with me—well, not without my consent—but boy, did he look mad. He gets jealous very easily.

He followed me in and the door swung shut. I avoided his gaze and sat down on the bed to take off my shoes and give my poor, poor feet some air.

"So," Luke said into the silence.

"So," I replied stubbornly.

"Why the hell were you kissing him?"

I sighed and peeled off a plaster on my heel. "Did you see the guy with the shiny suit?"

"No."

Figures. I have a feeling he didn't see anything but me and Xander.

"There were two of them but I think one left. They work for Shapiro. They're after Xander."

"Xander? Who the fuck is Xander?"

"Xander Harvard. He's Harvey's brother."

"What, he's got a twin?" Luke snorted.

"Yes."

"A completely identical twin?"

"Apparently so."

"Sophie, do you have any idea how ridiculous—"

"Fine." I threw up my hands, which would have been a much grander gesture if I hadn't had a bloody plaster stuck to my left little finger. "Don't believe me. I'm only your girlfriend and your damn colleague. Go out there and ask him, if you think he's Harvey—ask him what kind of car he drives, or what kind of shampoo Angel uses—"

"'Cos he couldn't pretend he didn't know any of that stuff," Luke snarled.

"Ask him for ID! He has a driving licence. It has his name on it."

"You've seen his driving licence?"

"Yes! I didn't believe him either! But I was rational about it!"

"You call this being rational?" Luke yelled.

"I'm not yelling as loud as you," I shrieked.

"Fine," Luke bellowed.

"Fine," I screamed and jumped up, my feet still half-swaddled, grabbed my purse and my key card and wrenched the door open.

"Where the hell are you going?"

"Away from you," I snarled.

"Back to him?"

"No, not back to fucking him," I hollered. "Just—"

A door opened further down the corridor.

"Could you keep it down?" whined an American voice.

"No," Luke and I snapped at the same time, "fuck off."

The door shut pretty sharpish. I turned on my sore heel and stomped as hard as I could in bare feet, down the corridor to the vending alcove. It was empty, Xander was gone, although there was a bloody fingerprint on the ice machine.

I stomped past and hammered at the button for the lift. My eyes were stinging. I hated fighting with Luke. It always made me so frightened, although I don't know what of. Maybe I thought he might hit me. Maybe I thought he might leave me. I don't know. I hate confrontations. Why the hell am I a bloody spy?

"I could have been a vet," I muttered, sniffing, as I got into the lift and pressed the lobby button. "I could have been a lawyer or an architect. I could have stuck at the bloody airport, but no, I had to go and work for the sodding *government.*"

The doors opened and a middle-aged couple got in. They eyed me curiously, but I rooted my eyes on the little CNN screen in the corner and tried to focus on a news item about a car chase in Florida.

The lift doors opened and I stumbled out into the lobby, the marble floor cold under my aching feet. I made to go past the security desk, but I was beckoned over.

"Hey, lady, you okay?"

I nodded and tried not to sniff pathetically.

"I'm fine. It was just a—just a misunderstanding." I attempted a smile.

"One of those guys your boyfriend?"

"The blond one. The other one was just, er, he's a friend."

The security guy raised his eyebrows. "You greet all your friends like that?"

I blushed and shook my head. "It was a misunderstanding," I repeated lamely, and backed away. "Thanks..."

He nodded and waved me goodbye. I tripped through the lobby to the gimmicky bar by the front door and threw myself at a bar stool and whined miserably, "Can I have a—" wait, what *did* they drink over here? "—a Guinness, please?"

Eyebrows were raised but my drink was fetched, and when I tried to pay I was gently told, "We'll put it on a tab for you, ma'am."

I sniffed and nodded, and the bartender, who was quite cute, asked, "Are you okay?"

I shrugged. "Fight with my boyfriend."

Even that phrase made me perk up a little bit. I'd been boyfriendless for so long before Luke that I thought I'd never be able to use the word again.

"Were you the girl fighting by the elevators?"

"I wasn't fighting!" I turned to the couple next to me, who were earwagging. "I was *not* fighting."

"Sure, whatever."

The barman grinned. "Which one's your boyfriend?"

"The blond," I said gloomily. "Not sure how long for though."

"Hey, cheer up. He ain't gonna dump you."

"Yeah, right."

"Yeah, right. You're gorgeous."

I sniffed. "You're very sweet," I told him, "but I think you're lying."

He grinned. "If you were my girlfriend, I wouldn't dump you."

Okay, going a bit too far now. "Even if you saw me kissing someone else?"

He whistled. "That's what the fight was about?"

I nodded miserably.

"Well, I can see why he might be mad."

I finished my pint, chatting to the barman as I went, and at the end of it felt a bit better. I checked my watch—Jesus, it was nearly midnight!

"I should go," I said, slipping off my stool and getting out my purse, but the bartender shook his head.

"On the house," he said, and I smiled with gratitude. "Thanks." I leaned over and kissed his cheek, and he grinned at me.

"For that you can have another one—"

"I really should go," I said. "Make amends."

"Have fun."

Fun wasn't what I was anticipating.

I got back in the lift and checked my reflection. Blegh. Makeup all sweated off, eyes smudged all over from nearly crying, pretty summer dress creased, feet black with dirt and throbbing all over.

Yep. Gorgeous.

I hobbled back to my room and listened for a moment outside the door. Silence. I let myself in with a sigh and went straight into the bathroom, closing the door out of habit and going through my nightly toiletry ritual, ending with the new addition of peeling off the remaining plasters and bathing my feet.

I clicked off the light and went back into the dark bedroom, peeling off my dress as I did, and then got a hell of a shock when Luke's low voice came from the bed.

"Nice of you to check in."

Shrieking in surprise, I clutched my dress to me (why, Sophie, why, he's seen you in a lot less than underwear many, many times) and flipped on the light. Luke was lying in my bed with his back to me, and I stood there staring, noting objectively what a fine back he had.

The nerve of him!

"If you think I'm going to sleep with you," I began, spluttering, unable to think of a dire enough threat to finish that sentence.

"I don't give a bloody damn where you sleep," Luke said, not moving, "so long as it's not touching me."

At that I hurled something at him. I think it was my dress.

"Why are you even here?" I screeched as Luke threw my dress on the floor and rolled on his back to look at me. I tried to look dignified, but it's hard when you're wearing a mismatched pink bra and green knickers.

"SO17 can't afford two rooms."

"I mean in New York!"

He stared at me in disbelief. "Because Macbeth got recalled. You do remember that, don't you? You didn't think Karen would let you do this on your own, did you?"

Patronising git.

I snarled at him, while something in the back of my mind remembered Macbeth's garbled transmission. Was he going back? Was that what he'd said? That Luke was coming out here? Damn bloody useless phone!

I slammed the light off and threw back the covers and hurled myself into bed, turning my back to Luke when he did the same to me.

I waited all night for him to thaw, and I knew it was early in the morning when I eventually dropped off to sleep, but there'd been no reaction from Luke.

Chapter Four

My body woke up before my mind did, and what my body registered was this—I'm curled up half naked with Luke and he has his arms around me.

I snuggled closer without really thinking what I was doing, but the realisation must have hit Luke at the same time it hit me, because as I opened my eyes I heard him say in a furious voice, "If this is some plan of yours—"

"No plan," I said, heart sinking.

"So why are you here?"

"Well," I said, voice heavy with as much sarcasm as I could muster thirty seconds after waking up, "this is my room, and SO17 can't afford—"

"I mean right here," Luke squeezed me, and I paused for a second to appreciate the effect. Then I looked up at him, and scowled.

"I don't know. I woke up like this."

"Well, I didn't—"

"Don't you yell at me. It's not my fault."

He glared at me, but I noticed he didn't do anything to push me away.

"You didn't go back to your boyfriend?"

"Boyf—Luke, will you shut up? I explained that—"

"Hardly—"

"I told you—"

"Sophie, if you walked in and saw me kissing another woman, what would you do?"

I'd get out my gun and shoot the both of them.

"I'd expect a rational explanation," I said with dignity.

Luke snorted.

"Liar," he said, but there was a hint of fondness in it.

"Look," I said, "you really don't need to worry about Xander—"

"Oh, I wasn't worrying about him."

"I mean as a threat!"

"Why would I be threatened by an all-American jockstrap like him? Just because you seem to have an affection for that type—and when I say *affected*—"

"Oh, fuck off," I snarled half-heartedly. "Harvey is in love with Angel—"

"And Harvey Number Two?"

Had he been speaking to Macbeth?

"His name is Xander, and there really is absolutely no chance of him stealing me away from you. In actual fact, you're probably in more danger than me."

There was a pause, then, shaking like he was trying hard not to laugh, Luke said, "What?"

"He's gay, Luke. At least, I'm pretty sure he is."

"Pretty sure?"

"Well, yes. He knows his designers and he loves shopping, and he thinks you're really cute—"

"He *what*?"

"He saw your picture and—"

"You have a picture of me?"

I tried to gauge his voice. He didn't seem too mad. In fact, he seemed very amused.

"A small one," I said huffily.

"In your wallet?"

"No, in a locket next to my heart."

I looked up, and Luke was grinning.

"That is kind of adorable," he said, and I scowled again.

"Harvey has a twin brother and he's *gay*," Luke said after a while, his voice rich with amusement. "That is excellent. Did you know about this?"

"Not before last night."

"What happened last night?"

"I met Xander and figured out he was gay."

A bit more silence. It was nice lying there in Luke's arms, my head on his shoulder, almost like we'd never fought. Like the storm had passed.

"Do you think I really broke his nose?" Luke asked, and was it my imagination, or did I detect a hint of concern in there?

"If you did, Harvey will probably shoot you," I said mildly.

"Where did he go last night?"

"I don't know. Probably to hang himself off the Brooklyn Bridge."

"Ha ha."

"Yeah, you'll be laughing when you're named in court."

Luke flipped me over onto my back. "So," he said speculatively, and I'm afraid I couldn't keep from licking my lips. I watched his muscles flex appreciatively.

"So?"

"So...that's your best friend, her boyfriend, and his gay brother. Quite a collection."

God, when you put it like that... Okay, but I only kissed Angel because I was passing on a message from Harvey. And I only kissed Harvey because I was really drunk and he hadn't even met Angel and I wasn't with Luke then. And I only kissed Xander because—well, you know that bit.

"That's only four people in five months," I said, "if you count you as well. And you don't count Tammy—God, Tammy!"

"Angel's feeding her," Luke reassured me. "Still, four people in the space of time I've known you...two others since we got together... I think I have a right to ask..."

I braced myself.

"Who's the best?"

"You're such a—" I began, but my disgust very quickly evaporated when Luke dropped his head and kissed me.

Mmm, that kiss. I told you how the world sort of goes away when he kisses me. And there's only me and Luke left, a universe inside that kiss which I've missed *so much...*

"Well," I said breathlessly when he let me go and gave me a quizzical look, "I may need to reconsider. Maybe another example...?"

Luke rolled his eyes but he didn't protest. In fact he was showing me all the extras that came with the kissing, throwing my bra on the floor and doing very interesting things in the region of my knickers, when there came a desperate hammering on the door.

"Whoever it is, they can fuck off," Luke growled, and I agreed. It was probably only the maid anyway.

"Can you come back later?" I gasped. "Or maybe not at all..."

But then a voice was added to the hammering, and my heart sank.

"Sophie! I'm really sorry but this is *really* important."

Xander.

"Please go the fuck away," Luke snapped.

"I wouldn't disturb you, only it's really, absolutely vital. Harvey said I should get you..."

I looked at Luke. He shook his head at me, but then my phone started to ring, and we both groaned.

"I'll get that, you get the door?" I said hopelessly, and Luke, scowling, rolled off me and pulled the top blanket around him as he went over to the door.

I picked up my phone just as it went to voice mail. Excellent.

Xander tumbled into the room, looked from Luke to me, then back at Luke again, appreciatively, and said, "God, I am *so* sorry..."

"This had better be bloody good," Luke said, glaring at him, and the effect might have been more menacing if he'd been wearing more than a green fuzzy blanket.

"It's really good. Well, really bad," Xander amended, touching his nose, which was nicely swollen and a pretty shade of purple. "I found Shapiro."

Thank God. "Where?"

"In my apartment. He's—well, he's dead."

On the subway, Xander told us in quiet tones how he'd stayed up drinking and slunk back to his apartment in the early hours when he got thrown onto the street for being unable to pay his bar tab. Drunk and pissed off, he'd stumbled straight into bed and hadn't looked around his studio space until he'd got up to get some water about an hour ago. Whereupon he'd found the body of Don Shapiro, arranged into the pose Xander had used for the portrait, which was standing next to him on an easel.

Xander, panicking, had called Harvey for my number, and had ended up telling him the whole story. Harvey had told him Luke was here with me and that we were his best bet.

Kind of sweet, but what the hell did he expect us to do?

As soon as we were in the open air and I could get some signal on my phone, I called Harvey.

"What are we, waste disposal?"

"It's nice to hear from you, too," Harvey said. "Listen, look after Xander, will you? It can't be nice finding a body in your apartment—"

"No," I said shortly. "I remember what it's like."

"I told him you were with the government," Harvey said.

"Cheers."

"What else could I say? I'd be there myself, but I'm kinda far away and..."

"Yeah, I know," I said resignedly. "I'll call you back later."

"Thanks, Sophie."

I ended the call and looked up at Luke on one side of me, and Xander on the other. Boy, they actually made me feel short. Well, maybe average sized.

"This is it," Xander fished a key out of his pocket as we approached a huge warehouse door. We weren't far from the meatpacking district and the smell of dead things hung heavily in the air. I shuddered. I haven't eaten meat since I was a child, and this kind of reminded me why. Not to mention that the smell might be coming from Shapiro...

Xander fitted the key in a smaller portal and we stepped in after him. "It's a total mess," he said with what I supposed was normally cheerfulness, but now came out rather strained and horribly nervous. "Obviously I don't usually have all the blood..."

"That's okay," Luke said, slinging an arm around my shoulders. "You should see Sophie's place."

I scowled at him, but Xander managed some sort of smile.

He unlocked an inner, metal door and we walked into a big warehouse type space. The floors were thin and creaked alarmingly, there was crap all over the place—big easels and blank canvases, huge vats of paint, boxes of materials, things like bits of string and sequins on the floor. There was a curtain pulled across to just by the door; behind it was a big messy bed and a jumble of clothes, with another curtain behind that hardly concealing a little shower room.

Every wall, the whole ceiling and all over the floor, the bedspread and the curtains, and even part of the windows, were all covered with paintings and scribblings. It was like Xander had run out of canvas and started putting down his ideas on his actual apartment.

"Wow," I said. "Pretty cool."

Xander disappeared into the bedroom section and lit up a cigarette with shaky hands.

"Very nice," Luke agreed distractedly. He and Xander seemed to have come to some sort of détente on the way over, after I stamped on Luke's foot and made him apologise, and then on Xander's and made him accept.

"There is one thing," Luke went on conversationally. "Where is the body?"

71

Xander came out and stared around. He pointed at what might have been a sofa under decades of debris, an easel beside it, pools of sticky drying blood staining the painted floor. To be honest there was so much going on in the room I'd hardly had time to look for a body. Certainly the blood hadn't seemed out of place on the garish floor.

"It was right there," Xander said, going over and cautiously lifting a large sketchbook as if expecting Shapiro's body to be hiding under it.

"Well, it ain't there now," Luke said. "Are you sure he was dead?"

"He had a big slit right across his throat," Xander said. "And he was sort of bluish."

"That might give it away," I said. I walked over to the sofa, where the blood was dried and congealed. But then it could have been paint for all I knew. "Xander, how long since you've been back here? Before this morning."

He shrugged. "Three days."

"Three days without coming home?" Luke said. "Where have you been?"

"Friends. Your hotel."

Luke flashed a glare at me.

"Later," I said wearily. "Xander, this body can't just have vanished. Are you sure you saw it?"

"I wasn't that stoned," he said indignantly, and Luke cast a despairing look in my direction.

"What were you on last night?"

"It was good stuff," Xander protested, "expensive, I've been saving it..."

"How stoned were you?"

"Not very. Didn't have much left."

"You hallucinated it," Luke said flatly.

"Nah, it wasn't *that* good. Look, I know I saw it. I know it was there. I could smell it. It was like dead meat..."

Like dead meat...

"Xander," I said, "what did this building used to be?"

"I dunno, slaughterhouse probably. Some kind of storage. They swung stuff out of the big windows..." He gestured to the glass, currently covered with taped-up sketches, and I went over to look. The sketches were crumpled and torn in one corner, where the window was open on the catch to let some air in. Or maybe more than air.

God, even I'm not that stupid, and I'm blonde.

"Do people still do that? Carry stuff out of windows?"

"I guess. I don't know."

"So you often see people manoeuvring big bloody things around here? Wrapped in...what, plastic?"

"Usually," Xander said cautiously.

"So no one would have turned a blind eye if someone had walked out of this old slaughterhouse on the edge of the meatpacking district with a bloody bundle wrapped up in polythene?"

They both stared at me.

"You're a scary lady," Xander said.

"I don't like how your mind works," Luke agreed.

"At least it does work," I replied, feeling pleased with myself. "Right. Some time between you calling Harvey and coming over here, someone broke in through the window you left open—"

"It's on a closed-in yard!"

"—and took Shapiro's body. Why would someone bring him here then take him away?"

We all looked at each other, nonplussed.

"Okay," I sighed, "maybe not." My grand theories have been known to come to nothing before. At least this one didn't horribly backfire, as they also have been known to occasionally do. Ahem.

"Maybe you weren't supposed to find it," Luke said to Xander. "Maybe they figured you were out and just didn't have time to move it or something."

"Maybe—" I began, but I never remembered how I was going to go on from there, because the metal door swung open and a man in a shiny suit stood there, looking surprised for a few seconds.

The same man in the same shiny suit as the guy who'd come after me and Xander yesterday.

"Shit," Xander gasped and threw himself to the floor, just as the shiny guy pulled out a gun and fired a shot at him. Luke and I followed Xander's lead and ducked, and watched in horror as Xander grabbed a gun from under the sofa and aimed at the shiny guy, who was emptying the cartridge from his gun.

"Xander—" I started.

"No—" Luke yelled, reaching for his own gun, but Xander had already fired. There was a blast, a flash, then a sharp metal ping and a yelp from Xander.

The shiny guy ran.

I shuffled over to Xander, who was bleeding from a cut on his temple. "Ow!" he said indignantly, and I couldn't meet Luke's eyes.

"That wasn't your own bullet ricocheting back at you, was it?" I asked as sensibly as I could, trying hard not to crack up.

"Might have been," Xander said sulkily, touching the blood on his face.

"Shouldn't have shot at him then, eh?"

He scowled at me.

"Come on, we need to get out of here," Luke said, pulling me to my feet and leaving Xander to sort himself out.

"I need, like a Band-Aid or something," he mumbled, stumbling to a row of units I guessed was his kitchen.

"I have plenty," I said. "I really do. Come on."

Xander shut all the windows and double-locked both doors and we walked back to the subway station. On the way Xander stopped at a bakery and shakily bought a large box of cupcakes with fat icing on them, handed us one each and ate the rest himself. When we emerged into the sunlight again at Penn Station, Luke's phone rang with a voice mail and he listened to it with a frown.

"Bollocks," he said quietly as he deleted it.

"What?"

"That was Karen. She—" he glanced at Xander, who was lost in space with his last cupcake, and lowered his voice, "she said Shapiro's kid's booked on the red-eye tonight. Wants one of us to go home and keep an eye on him."

"You think he knows his father's dead?"

"How would he? Anyway, he's seventeen, won't he have school starting?"

"I suppose," I said. "So who's going, you or me? And can't Maria or Macbeth take care of him?"

"Maria's still in Spain," Luke said, "and Macbeth's disabling some high-tech security system in Germany. So it's you or me."

I wanted to go home. I really did. But I wanted to go back with Luke, and that wasn't likely to happen.

"I think one of us has to keep an eye on Xander," I said in an undertone.

"Yes," Luke said doubtfully, "and I'm really hoping you think it should be you."

"Homophobe."

"You know him better! And he likes you. You can talk about Harvey."

I sighed. I'd been about to suggest the same thing anyway.

"So you'll go home and keep tabs on a seventeen-year-old with a rich daddy. Mind you don't go clubbing too much."

"I hate clubbing," Luke said, and I felt cheered up.

We took Xander back up to my room, not knowing what else to do with him, and Luke kissed me goodbye in the corridor.

"Try and persuade him to leave the city," he said. "I can't think it's safe for him to go home now they know where he lives. Mafia connections are not good."

I nodded. I didn't want to let him go. He felt so lovely and solid in my arms.

"When will I come home?" I asked wistfully.

"When our Grand High Commander allows it. I don't know. We're going to have to try and figure this out. Why does every case we work on have a murder involved?"

"I wouldn't mind so much if there was an actual body," I moaned. "How can you investigate the murder of a man who's vanished?"

"Sounds like a DC comic," Luke said. He kissed my nose. "Be good."

"What are you, my mother?"

"I hope you don't kiss your mother like that," Luke said, grinning.

"Like what? Like this?"

I kissed him properly, and if we hadn't been in public it might have gone a lot further. But Luke pulled away from me before it did, and picked up the rucksack which consisted his total luggage, said, "Bye, then," and walked away.

I stood watching him until he was out of sight, then I opened the door back into my room and found Xander in the bathroom, dabbing at his temple with wet cotton wool.

"Here," I took it from him and sat him down on the toilet lid, "let me."

"So is this a girlie thing? Mother hen taking care of bleeding chickie?"

I have to be the most unmotherly person there ever was. "Don't push it," I said. "Your hands were shaking, that's all."

He glanced down at them. "I need a cigarette."

"Not in my room. The hotel police will come after you." I cleaned up most of the blood and looked critically at the cut on his face. The bullet had just grazed him, really it was a miracle it hadn't gone in. Half an inch to the right and Xander would have been dead.

"You have one too." He was touching my face, where a faint line gave away the car crash Ted and I'd been in a couple of months ago. Luke and Harvey had been with me, and I think the one to come off best was actually Ted.

"Occupational hazard."

"People shoot at you a lot?"

"Every now and then."

"You get used to it?"

I'd liked to have said yes. "No." I fetched my waterproof tape and cut little strips off it, then used them to hold the wound together, before covering it with a gauze dressing. "Now you look pretty stupid," I told him.

"Better than being covered with blood." He was still touching the scar on my forehead, running his fingers back and discovering the little rip on my ear. "Same bullet?"

"No. The cut was a car crash. The ear was a bullet."

"Close one."

"Yep." I pulled away from him and washed my hands.

"Got any more?"

"More what?"

"Scars."

I glanced back at him. He looked fascinated.

"You think this is cool, don't you?"

He shrugged, then he nodded.

"Xander, someone just shot at you and tried to kill you. There was a dead man in your apartment. You are in big trouble and you have to leave the city."

Come to think of it, that did sound pretty cool. But—

"This isn't a movie. Next time someone comes after you with a gun they might actually kill you. Or, well, *you* might kill yourself."

He scowled at me, and I realised this was like the conversations I have with Luke. Only reversed.

Hey, I was the mentor here! Go me.

"You really think I should leave the city?"

"Yes."

"What, like now?"

"Well, the sooner the better."

He nodded, looking suddenly exhausted.

"Sophie, I'm really tired. I didn't exactly sleep a lot last night. Can't I just stay here—?"

He did look pathetic. I sighed. "Okay. But tomorrow you have to go."

He jumped up and hugged me. "You're the greatest."

"Hmm."

We spent the day watching appalling daytime TV, with frequent comments from me along the lines of, "My God, you have a lot of ad breaks," and "Christ, I thought those parodies on the Simpsons were made up," and on occasion, "No! No! Turn it off!" It was like a car crash, I was totally unable to look away, addicted to the Weather Channel with its Bart and Homer programmes like *When Hurricanes Go Bad*.

BBC, I will never complain again.

By teatime I was so bored I was nearly crying. I went downstairs for some food and ended up getting a big bag of junk from the shop next door. On my way back past the bar I saw my barman friend and he waved at me.

"You better now?"

"Yes," I said, and hesitated. "Can you give me take-out drinks?"

He said he wasn't supposed to, but he would for me. He made up a pitcher of strawberry margarita and I wrapped it up in a carrier bag and took it back upstairs.

"Look what I have," I said to Xander, letting myself in. "No cream, but you can't have everything."

Xander perked up a bit with the margarita and we worked our way through some more junk food, watched a couple of really bad made-for-TV movies, and watched the sky get darker.

"Look," Xander pointed through the window, "you can see the glow over Times Square."

I stayed away. "I'm not good with heights."

"But you're so tall!"

"I know. Stupid, huh?"

Neither of us felt like sleeping. Xander had dozed a bit during the day while I read the books I'd brought from Fuerteventura, and I'd been asleep until midday anyway. We watched a couple more films and re-runs, and then Xander looked at me pleadingly and said, "We ran out of margarita..."

"So go and get some more."

"But he won't give me any. He likes you..."

I didn't really want to go down and get some more, but on the other hand, it *was* good margarita...

I heaved myself off the bed and grabbed my purse. "Don't go anywhere."

"Duh."

I got out of the lift on the ground floor and made my way across the glossy marble to the bar. But out of the corner of my eye I could see a familiar-looking figure in a shiny suit...

I walked a little faster. There were footsteps behind me and I knew I'd been spotted. If I went into the bar, he'd follow me.

I'd go outside, pop into a shop or something, take a walk around the block...

Damn, it was past midnight, there'd be no shops open. But by the time I realised this, it was already too late. I was outside, and I had only a few seconds to decide which way to go.

I was wearing trainers, my blisters covered over with plasters, but they still hurt as I started to run. I went north, turned onto 33rd Street, then past Broadway, down Sixth—I think—my lungs bursting. I'm not a good runner.

Left, right, left, left again—I kept going until I was so lost I couldn't even find myself. Panting, leaning against a shop window, I watched a few people go by, none of them paying the tiniest bit of attention to me.

Okay. Time to figure out where I was and limp back home.

I found my way to Broadway and headed north, fairly sure I was going the right way. Yes, street numbers were going up. Only a few more blocks to go. I guess that's the good thing about Manhattan—easy to navigate. How had I run all this way? Wow, I must have burned off loads of calories.

Goody, more junk food.

I was waiting for the Walk sign to change when I realised it. There was a black car—an anonymous American Ford with darkened windows—purring down the street towards me. I watched the passenger window open, and a familiar face atop a shiny suit looked out at me. And then I saw the gun he was holding, and I threw myself down behind a bank of mailboxes as two shots rang out past me.

Jesus.

The car passed on, I heard it speeding away, so I got to my feet and forced them to move faster, running back to the hotel. I had to warn Xander and get out of here.

It happened when I was crossing 31st Street. I'd glanced at the Walk sign and seen it in my favour, so without stopping I pelted over the street. Then I heard a roar and a screech and an awful crunch, and realised the car had hit me. Then I skidded onto the road, my head hit the tarmac, and everything went black.

Chapter Five

Someone with a strong Noo Yoik accent was speaking very close to me, touching my face, telling me to wake up. There was an ambulance on the way. I was to stay still.

I opened my eyes and looked up at a concerned round face, dark skin in a dark uniform. A cop.

"Hey, lady, you okay?"

I feebly wriggled my arms and legs and, having decided my back wasn't broken, lifted my head.

"Did that car just *hit* me?" I said in indignation.

"Yeah. It sped off before anyone could get the licence plate."

Not that I needed it. I had a feeling I knew who'd been in that car, and I had a feeling it wasn't theirs.

I started to pull myself to my feet, but the cop protested.

"You should stay still, you could be hurt—"

"I'm fine," I said, a blatant lie. My leg throbbed where the car had hit and my shoulder ached where I'd skidded along on it. But I pushed him away and stood up, swaying a little. "I'm good."

"You should wait for the ambulance—"

"I don't have insurance," I said, remembering this vital fact of the American health system. You've got to have money to be ill. Well, no—you've got to have money to get treated. So much for equality. "I really have to go. I have a flight in a couple of hours."

"You do?"

Not yet, but wait until I get on the phone.

"Thanks." I pulled my wallet out of my pocket and pressed a note into his hand without looking what it was. "You've been very helpful, uh, tell the ambulance I'm feeling better, erm, I've got to go..."

And I took off, stumbling, feeling like I'd just been put through a food processor.

I got on the next flight out. It was at five a.m., and I spent my time at the airport trying to clean myself up with the limited medical supplies I had in my bag. I'd bolted back to the hotel and found my room empty. God only knew where Xander might be. I was hoping desperately he'd avoided Shapiro's men (if indeed that's who they were), that maybe he'd gone out for a cigarette or something, and I'd missed him, but at the back of my mind lurked the awful fear that he was really just dead.

Throwing things into my case, I made a desperate and rather garbled call to the airport and cashed in my return ticket. I called Luke and left a message on his machine that I was coming home ASAP. I hailed a taxi—a new experience and one I should have been proud of, but I was too frazzled to think about it.

My eyebrow tweezers were in my suitcase. I knew my security restrictions, and although I really couldn't see what damage you could to with tweezers (viciously over-pluck a stewardess's eyebrows, maybe?), I stuck to them. Consequently there was nothing to help me get the bits of grit and dirt out of the graze on my shoulder, but hey, at least the pain there and from the throbbing lump on my head and the big dent in my leg made me forget about the raw patches on my feet.

I slept through most of the flight, tempted as I was by the movies on offer, ate nothing and stumbled through passport control (the joys of having a native passport!), only to find that it took twenty minutes to allocate us a conveyor belt and a further hour for them to put our luggage on it. The only explanation we got was a garbled PA announcement saying our bags were delayed because of beer bear jam. Or something. I was half dead and really just wanted to go home and sleep forever.

Finally I got my bag (I mean really, Ace Airlines pay peanuts for monkey work, but they can still get the right bags on the right belt) and tripped off to the car park, nearly getting run over twice on the way, but what kind of news was that? I gave Ted a big hug and collapsed in him, seriously doubting I'd get home without falling asleep or passing out from pain (supermarket painkillers not being much help to me), but I managed, and pulled up outside my lovely flat, almost weeping with joy.

The geranium in my little courtyard was pretty much dead, but I didn't care. I unlocked the millions of unbreakable locks that Luke helped me install (his own place is like Fort Knox) and fell inside, so happy to be home I was actually crying. Tammy sauntered up, trying to look malnourished, and pulled a face at me when I scooped her up for a tearful cuddle.

I threw all my dusty, bloody, smelly clothes on the floor (the couple in the plane seats next to me had not looked impressed—we were in Economy but I looked like I should be in the hold) and got into the shower. The hot water stung the raw patches on my skin, and there were tears streaming down my face when I got out and probed around for bits of dirt and poured half a bottle of Dettol on, but I felt slightly better for being clean.

I pulled on an old long white nightie and crawled into bed, my lovely soft warm welcoming bed, my adorable bed, my beloved bed, and sank into unconsciousness.

I woke to hear my name being called by Luke's voice, and figured I was dreaming. I let myself sink back down into blissful sleep again, but he called me once more, and then I heard my bedroom door open and Tammy, who'd curled up by my feet, squeaked in welcome and ran away, as is her wont.

"Sophie? Didn't you get my message?"

I feigned sleep, hoping he'd go away.

"I know you're faking it."

There was nothing for it but to open my eyes and squint rather unattractively up at him. He was wearing jeans and an FCUK T-shirt and he looked edible.

"What message?" I yawned.

"The one I left on your phone. Where is it?"

I tried to remember. "Bag?"

"Where's that?" Luke asked patiently.

"Sofa?"

He disappeared, and I tried to go back to sleep but he was back too soon, pressing buttons on my phone and frowning at me. "You didn't switch it on when you landed."

"Erm, no…"

He shook his head and held the phone to my ear. His own voice rang out: "Hey, it's me. Listen, if you're not too jetlagged and Karen doesn't have you filling out a million reports, I thought we might go to a gig tonight. At Funky Joe's. I'll pick you up at eight."

I looked up, and Luke was holding my alarm clock in his other hand. 7:58.

"So I'm a little early," he said, "but I did think you might be slightly more ready to come out."

I was frowning at him in confusion. Er, wasn't he supposed to be enquiring as to my health? My reason for fleeing the country? My total lack of investigation into Xander's disappearance, Shapiro's apparent death, and the goons who'd tried to kill me? My total cowardice in just running away from it all? Any of it?

Then I remembered I'd only told him I was coming home with not a single reason as to why, and realised he probably thought Karen had ordered it.

"What gig?"

"The band. Remember your brother? Well, he plays an instrument called a bass guitar, and he's in a band with three other guys called—"

"I know what they're called," I said. "How did you know about the gig? I didn't even know about it."

Luke declined to comment on the things I did and didn't know, as he usually did, but instead said, "Tom came by to drop off your Kaiser Chiefs CD. Which I have now borrowed, by the way. He said they'd be playing at Joe's and he'd tell Chalker we're coming..."

I felt slightly sick. "My brother knows we're coming?"

"Yep."

Which meant my parents would know. "We're" coming. And they hadn't met Luke. Didn't even know I had a boyfriend. I'd been single for so long before him that they'd never believe me anyway.

"Oh God."

"Come on," he took my hands and pulled me upright, "get dressed. Do that eyeliner thing you do. We don't have to stay long. I just thought," he shrugged, "it might be nice to meet your friends."

"You've met—wait, my friends are going?"

"Tom said Ella and Evie are going, and I don't know them but you're always talking about them..."

Jesus.

I stumbled out of bed and pulled my leather jeans and a strappy black top from the wardrobe. Tired though I was, I knew I couldn't let Chalker down by appearing as anything less than a full rock chick. I did the eyeliner thing and scrunched up my damp hair with gel to give it some body. It fell back down, flat. Oh well. I wrapped up my feet and put on some thick socks and gingerly zipped up my four-inch heeled black boots.

"Okay?" I said to Luke, who'd been timing me.

"Twenty minutes."

"That's a new record."

He rolled his eyes. "Got your bag? Keys, makeup, phone—switched on this time—wallet?"

"You really do sound like my mother."

"I'll find out soon enough."

I made Luke park at Waitrose so no one would see his Vectra—it's an okay car, I suppose (you can stop twisting my arm now), but not exactly what you might call cool—and stumbled up to Funky Joe's with him. It was a pleasant evening and the band and various groupies were standing around outside Joe's, waving pints of beer and bottles of alcopops and laughing at something Tom had said. Tom is the scrawny singer in the band. He was in my Drama class at school; the drummer took History with me, and I used to have English with the guitarist. These gigs are like full school reunions.

Tom spied me and waved. He's the only one who's met Luke, at a gig in April, when we had to catch a guy who tried to kill me...

Chalker, my very big big brother, noticed Tom waving, looked over and saw me. And then he saw Luke and his eyebrows went up.

And then he came over.

"Oh, shit," I said, clutching Luke's arm. "Oh shit oh shit..."

"What?"

"Chalker."

"Sophie, he's your brother, not the Grand High Inquisitor." Luke laughed, and when Chalker approached, he smiled and said, "Hi, you must be Sophie's brother."

"If you say we look alike I'll drop his bass amp on you," I muttered.

"You must be Sophie's boyfriend," Chalker said.

"So she tells me. I'm Luke."

"Charlie. Everyone calls me Chalker."

I waited for Luke to ask why, even though he knew the story about Chalker always writing lines on the blackboard, à la Bart Simpson, but he didn't.

"What happened to you?" Chalker broke the silence by gesturing to my arm.

"Oh." I glanced down at the fierce graze and wondered why Luke hadn't mentioned it. "I fell over."

"Is this like when you tripped over the soap packet in Menorca and sprained your wrist?"

I glared at him. Luke laughed.

"Sort of," I mumbled. "Can we go in?"

Luke shrugged. "Whatever you want."

First time for everything.

"Oh yeah," Chalker called after us, "Mum and Dad are coming. Should be here any minute."

"Run, hide," I said to Luke, who sighed.

"Do you not want me to meet them or something?"

I looked up at him, so strong and sure and handsome. How could I put this?

"I've only ever brought one boyfriend home before," I said, "and he cheated on me. And I haven't seen anyone since. So I'm a little out of practice."

"It's okay, I'll be nice to them."

"It's not them I'm worried about."

SO17 has this rule where we're supposed to have a couple of units of alcohol a night to keep our resistance levels up in case we need to drink a lot (I find this happening with increasing regularity), but can still drive and work things properly. Obviously while I was away I didn't want to lapse in this, so I took an entire week's worth every night in Fuerteventura.

I was sick of Guinness, didn't like the memories, so I chickened out and had a Smirnoff Ice instead. It was cold and sweet and good, and it didn't last long.

"So what did happen to you?" Luke said, gesturing to the raw graze on my arm, where a couple of stubborn bits of grit still dwelt.

"Nice of you to ask."

"I figured you might want to tell me."

Not really wanting to get into it right now, I said, "I fell over." This isn't so hard to believe, I have been known to trip over with no obvious cause. And I really did trip over a soap packet in Menorca two years ago. I blame Ella. Who leaves a soap packet on a damp floor in the bathroom when I've been drinking?

"Fell over what? You've got half of Manhattan in that graze."

"Voice down, Luke, I'm not supposed to have been there."

"Tell me what happened."

I sighed. He can always tell when I'm lying. "I—" I began, but was cut off by someone crying my name. I looked around and saw Ella and Evie, my two best friends since school, come rushing towards me. Ella was wearing tight jeans and a clingy vest with no bra. Evie had sparkly pink trainers, a top trimmed with marabou, and glitter in her hair.

I stamped on Luke's foot before he could say anything.

"I didn't know you were going to be here!" Evie said. "I texted you about it but you never replied."

"No, well, I was in Fuerteventura with Angel," I reminded her.

"Thought you came back on Wednesday," Ella said.

Bollocks. "Well—yes, but my phone's been playing up. You haven't met Luke, have you?"

They both stared. "Oh my God, he's with you?" Evie gasped, and Luke and I both tried unsuccessfully to hide smiles.

"Yeah. Luke, this is Ella and Evie. My best friends since school. Guys, this is...well, this is Luke."

"I haven't known her since school," Luke clarified, shaking hands with them. I was glad he hadn't kissed them. They might have fainted.

I know I nearly did the first time.

"You cow," Ella hissed in delight, "you never told us!"

"Well..." I began, and ran out of things to say. "Evie, I love your shoes."

"Nice try."

I scrunched up my nose. "I didn't—well, I mean...I—Luke, help me out here!"

"It's okay," he said. "She hasn't let me meet her parents yet either."

"How long has this been going on?" Evie demanded.

"Your parents are over there," Ella said.

"Well, a couple of—of weeks," I fabricated. "Not really long at all." I stamped on Luke's foot again.

"But how did you meet?" Evie asked.

"They're coming right over," Ella said.

"I—well, at work," I said.

"I just started at Ace," Luke said. "Sophie's been showing me the ropes."

"Bet that's not all she's been—" Ella muttered under her breath, then her face brightened. "Hi! Sophie, your parents..."

I spun around and froze, grinning like a corpse.

"Hi, Mum, Dad."

For a few seconds we all looked at each other, and then Ella tugged a disgruntled Evie away to the bar.

"Sophie," my mum hugged me and left a lipstick mark on my cheek, "you look so—" she looked me over. "Did it rain?"

Luke laughed softly.

"I took your advice and wore sun cream," I said, "and look where it got me."

"Better white than skin cancer," my dad said.

Hmm.

They were both looking at Luke, and Luke was looking at me.

I took a deep breath.

"Mum, Dad, this is Luke," I said, then squeezed my eyes shut and added in a tiny voice, "my boyfriend."

There was a pause, then I opened my eyes a tiny crack to see Luke shaking hands with my dad, who said, "I think we met before. Didn't you come calling for Sophie once?"

Luke nodded. "We weren't really together then."

"I should hope not," my mum said. "I'd be a bit pissed off with Sophie if she hadn't told us back then."

I winced. My parents can be kind of full throttle sometimes. You have to get used to them. Like caviar.

Only I still can't eat caviar.

"Well, we haven't really told anyone," Luke said, putting his arm around me. "It's still kind of new."

God bless him.

"So do you work with Sophie?" Mum asked, and we spent the next ten minutes happily lying to my parents and draining our drinks—at least, I did—until Tom bounced up and said hello to Luke.

"Oh, yeah," I said into the silence, "and Tom knows."

"I don't know anything," Tom said cheerfully.

"I like your hair," my mum told him. It was flattened in the centre and then twisted into spikes around his hairline, like the Statue of Liberty (damn, I hadn't seen that while I was there).

"You look like the Millennium Dome," I said, and Tom rolled his eyes.

"Oh, great. Your girlfriend's so charming," he said to Luke, who grinned and squeezed my shoulders. "I never had a big sister to tell me stuff like that. I'm so glad I've got you, Soph."

"You're the little brother I never wanted."

"Cheers." He took a swig of my nearly empty drink, then pointed to the cellar steps. "We're on in a couple of minutes, if you're coming down."

"Maybe, maybe not." I looked at my parents. "You go down, I want to get another drink."

"There's a bar downstairs," my mother said, but I shook my head.

"This'll be less crowded. Go on, get to the front, I know you can't see over people's heads," I teased, and she rolled her eyes but went off into the cellar bar with my dad.

I turned to Luke and blew out a sigh of relief.

"Never, ever make me do that again."

"Why? I thought that went okay."

"Yes, but we didn't say one true word to them. I'll have forgotten it all by tomorrow."

"Remind me why you work for SO17?"

"Because you wanted to shag me," I said, moving closer and looking up at him.

"Oh, yeah. Well, it worked. Sophie?"

"Mmm?" I could feel the heat of his body through his T-shirt.

"Fuck me senseless when we get home."

If we made it that far. "Sir, yes, sir."

We got our drinks and went down to the cellar bar, which is low and vaulted with old bricks, like the Cavern or somewhere else subterranean. I know the band love playing down here because they can pretend they're the Beatles.

Tom talks to the audience in between songs, and he kept waving at me and pulling faces. I knew he was building to something, but it wasn't until halfway through the second set that he looked straight at me and said, "Where's Sophie?"

I tried to hide but Luke, standing behind me, grabbed my non-alcohol bearing arm and raised it in the air.

"Bastard," I hissed.

"Sophie," Tom made sure everyone was looking at me, "is here with her new boyfriend. Everyone check them out. Aren't they cute?"

I haven't been cute since I was about five, and I don't think Luke has ever, ever been cute in his life.

"So," he looked around to check everyone was watching us, and indeed they were, "we're going to dedicate this next song to Sophie and Luke."

It was going to be a nasty song, I knew it. I turned and buried my face in Luke's chest. He was laughing.

"Is my embarrassment amusing to you?"

He grinned. "In a word, yes."

The band started up, and I relaxed, because it was a nice song, the closest they might get to a love song, in a totally ironic and twisted way, of course, because they're a rock band after all.

"Well, that was sweet," Luke said when it had finished.

"I guess," I said.

"I think they approve."

Hmm.

Three more songs, then they came off stage and flocked straight to the bar. Their manager has a no-alcohol rule before they go on stage, so they all bring bottles of 'water' or 'orange juice' and get creative. Afterwards, all that adrenaline needs an outlet, so they all get off their heads.

"We should probably go," I said to Luke, and he nodded. He waved to someone, and before I could figure out who, my parents came over.

"Are you leaving?"

I nodded. "I'm really tired."

"What did you do to your arm?"

"I fell over," I said. "Luke, are you ready?"

I congratulated the band on their excellent set, hugged Ella and Evie and avoided the groupies I'd been to school with and still didn't like. Even though I know I'm so much cooler now than I was then, so much cooler than they'll ever be (ahem), I still don't like them. I held my boyfriend close, out of their reach, and limped off up the steps into the cool night air.

All in all, it wasn't too bad. I mean, my parents could have taken an instant dislike to him. But my dad seemed to think he was okay and I was pretty sure my mum fancied him, Chalker hadn't said anything nasty, and my friends were totally in awe. As were all the kids I knew from school. Hah! I have leather jeans and a very sexy boyfriend. As long as they don't see him driving a Vectra I'm home and dry.

"Well?"

I looked up. How long had Luke been talking to me?

"Well what?"

"Where were you?"

"Thinking about making all the kids from school jealous."

"That knot of girls giving you evils? They wanted me," Luke said off-handedly.

"Oh, you are such a—"

"Such a what?" Luke spun me round and pinned me against the wall of the church backing onto Joe's.

"Such an egotist," I said, and he kissed me. Mmm. An egotist with good reason.

"Mine or yours?" he asked.

"What?"

"My flat," he explained patiently, as if I was a child, "or your flat?"

"Whichever," I said, feeling weak at the prospect. It had, I was being reminded, been a long time since we'd been properly naked together. "Just so long as there's a bed."

But once I sat down in the car, my shoulder throbbing, my leg aching and my feet weeping in protest, I was overwhelmed with exhaustion, and by the time we pulled up in the Pearce Roofing yard, I was nearly asleep.

Luke has a loft flat in a barn conversion above the roofer's yard, and I followed him up the outside steps to his front door where he keyed in a security code on the outside lock, turned about three keys, then disabled an alarm on the inside.

I stumbled inside and collapsed on the old leather chesterfield, unsure I'd ever be able to move again. I felt like I was wearing lead mascara and my bruises were killing me. I managed to hoik one foot up on the sofa and unzip my good leather boots, and peel off my socks and all the plasters.

Luke went over to the kitchen are and opened the fridge. His kitchen is open plan and very modern, to contrast with the old oak floors and beams of the loft. His furniture is old and well worn, like the leather chesterfield, his kitchen is modern and glossy, and his media equipment is expensive. He has lots of books and a soft white bed in the other room. It's a really nice place and I love it, not least because it frames Luke so well.

He held up a bottle. "Drink?"

"Whatever you're having," I replied, starting on my other foot.

He looked surprised. "Adnams?"

"Sure."

"But you hate bitter."

"Okay, all right, I'll have water."

Luke poured a glass, frowning. "Are you okay?"

"I'm fine. I'm just kinda wiped."

"You sound like a Yank."

"Can't imagine why."

He came over and pulled me to my naked feet, watched me sip my water, then took a thoughtful slug of beer. Unfortunately I was still swaying on my battered feet, and I swayed right into the bottle as he raised it.

"God!" Luke swiftly lost the bottle, grabbing my shoulders and touching my nose where I'd got clonked. "Sophie?"

I blinked, my eyes watering. In fact I was feeling very tearful.

"I'm okay," I said, for what felt like the billionth time. "You're covered in beer."

Luke looked down at himself. "It's okay, I'm not soluble." He grinned and pulled the T-shirt off. "Guess I'd better lose this..."

He did, and I paused to admire his damp chest and think for a couple of seconds about licking the beer off, before Luke pulled me to him and kissed me.

"Bed?" he suggested when he was done, touching my closed eyelids.

I nodded gratefully and allowed him to lead me through to his lovely bedroom with its gorgeous big soft bed. I looked at it longingly, knowing my intentions for it were quite different from Luke's, as he nuzzled my neck and made an exploratory mission under my top. But I jumped a mile when he brushed the graze on my arm and he offered me a contrite look.

"You want a cloth for that?"

"Yes please."

He disappeared into the bathroom. Do I have a perfect boyfriend, or what?

I took off my top and crawled into the welcoming bed. My eyes closed themselves, like I was a mama doll, and I fell into soft, comforting sleep.

Chapter Six

Daylight, and I could hear Luke's voice drifting in through the half open bedroom door. The bed was a lovely warm cocoon that smelled deliciously of Luke. I never wanted to leave it.

But—oh, wait a sec! Weren't we supposed to—and didn't I—?

Oh, God, I fell asleep! I was the worst girlfriend *ever*!

Luke pushed the door open and I looked up guiltily.

"Hey, Sleeping Beauty," he said. He didn't look mad.

"Hey," I said cautiously. "Erm. Did I fall asleep?"

He nodded.

"Before we—?"

"Before we."

I scrunched up my face. "I'm sorry. I really am. I didn't mean to..."

"Well, better before than during. Sophie. We have to talk."

Uh-oh.

"Look," I began, before he could go any further, "I was really tired, okay, I couldn't help it, and that time in New York we got interrupted, remember? I'm awake now and I—"

"Have to go in and see Karen," Luke finished for me.

I'm afraid my face fell.

"She wants you there in twenty minutes. So get up and get dressed and while you're doing that, tell me all about that huge bruise on your leg and the lump on the back of your head and all the road grit in your arm. I'm assuming the blisters are unrelated?"

I nodded. "Walking in too-tight shoes. And the one on my hand is from my suitcase."

"Did you accidentally drop your suitcase on yourself? Is that where the bruise is from? 'Cos I know what you're like with luggage. It weighs as much as you do."

Nothing weighs quite as much as I do.

"No." I sighed, and told him the whole story about being followed and shot at and run over.

"And you just got on a plane and came home?"

I stared. "Luke, I was totally unarmed. I was hurt and alone and I didn't even have Tammy to protect me."

This may sound like a joke, but Tammy is a damn fierce little creature. I'm thinking of asking Karen to employ her as a defence-cat.

"Okay," he said, "but what about Xander?"

"So *now* you're worried about him?"

"I'm more worried about what Harvey's going to say when he finds out the people who are after his little brother—"

"Only by two minutes."

"—have shot at him once, you twice, and run you over. Where is he?"

"I don't know," I said sulkily. "I went back to my room and he was gone. He could have just gone out for a fag..."

"Which takes on a whole new meaning when you think of Xander Harvard."

"He'll be okay. I already told him he needed to get out of the city. We were just lying low for a day."

"Apparently not low enough. Okay. Well, you need to get up and get dressed and go and tell Karen what happened in America."

I looked at him. "Well, the Mayflower went over in 1620, and then we had a war with the French over it, because I think things with France had been quiet for a while—then we had a war with America, then we had another war with them, then they had a war with themselves..."

Luke was giving me a narrow-eyed look. I knew what it meant, that he wasn't amused, but did he have to look so damn sexy when he did it?

"I'm very impressed at your knowledge of American history," he said, "but I'm sure Karen will find it less amusing. Come on, up. Yesterday's clothes."

"You want me to go and see my boss wearing leather jeans?"

"You have ten minutes left and that includes getting there."

It took ten minutes to drive, so needless to say we were a bit late. I was a mess. My hair and my clothes stank of smoke from the gig last night and my skin felt grey. I don't know how bad it looked—I'd managed to wipe away last night's makeup (yeuch) but there wasn't time to look in a mirror.

We pulled up at the office and Luke cut the engine. I put my hand on the door to get out, but he stopped me with a hand on my thigh.

"About this leather," he said, stroking it.

Oh God, what about it? Did it make me look fat? Was this a bursting-sausage look?

"Mmm?" I said nervously.

101

"Why haven't I seen it before?"

"I really only wear it when I'm feeling rock-chick. Doesn't get too many outings when I'm not at a gig."

"Then we have to go to more gigs."

He opened the car door and got out, and I sat there, stunned for a bit. Compliment!

Luke opened my door and pulled me out. "Wow, she's silent," he said, and took advantage of this by kissing me soundly. Helpless, and not really in any kind of mood to resist, I let him, and we were only stopped from jumping back in the car and heading for somewhere more private by Karen opening the door and standing there with her arms folded, looking unamused.

"Ahem," she said, and I obtained a new bruise on my back from jumping back against the car too sharply.

"What you two do in your own time is entirely your own business, but you were supposed to be here fifteen minutes ago, so kindly please step inside."

She turned on her smart heel and clipped back in. Luke shot me a look and towed me after.

"You've gone all red," he said in my ear.

"That'll be embarrassment."

"Very cute." He started nuzzling my neck. Karen had vanished into her office and couldn't see, but that didn't make it any better.

"Stop that."

"Okay, but I want a promise of future goods."

"You got it. You, me, bed, tonight."

"Who said anything about tonight?" Luke said as I yanked open the door to Karen's office.

"Shut up."

"Or a bed."

I tugged my hand out of his and tried to look respectable as I took a seat. Needless to say it wasn't a good effort.

Karen surveyed me with dismay. "What happened to you?"

"Me?" My hair, my clothes, the smoky smell...? Oh. My shoulder.

"She fell down the subway steps," Luke said. "Or slipped on a bar of soap. It depends who you listen to."

"It was a box of soap," I said. "And it shouldn't have been there."

"You slipped on a soap box?" Karen said, looking confused. She had immaculate brown hair and very piercing blue eyes and was so well-cared for I'd have put her in her thirties if I didn't know she'd been married longer than I'd been alive. She was always well-dressed. Today's outfit was a pair of perfect navy trousers and a blouse the colour of Cornish cream. Both looked like silk to me.

"I—well, yes, but it was two years ago. A year ago. Not now."

"Sophie," Karen said patiently. "What happened?"

I sighed and launched into the story again. She shook her head at me in what I chose to take as pity, but I think might have been a sort of parental disappointment.

"You didn't see the car coming?"

Pathetically, I admitted, "The sign said Walk. I was expecting it to stop."

She stared. "You thought the car containing someone who had just tried to kill you would stop at a red light?"

"I didn't know it was the same car! They all look the same. Towncars and Crown Victorias, why don't they have normal cars with normal names?"

Luke and Karen exchanged a look.

"Where did it hit you?" Karen asked, slightly more gently.

"The car?"

"No, Soph, the bullet," Luke half-snapped. "Show her your leg."

I glared at him. "My leg is fine."

"Your leg is purple." He came over and hauled me to my feet and unsnapped the button on my jeans.

"Hey!"

"Sophie, I have two children and I'm a qualified doctor," Karen said. "Show me your leg."

Scowling, I peeled off my admittedly snug jeans, trying not to let my underwear go with them, and perched on the edge of Karen's desk for her to peer at me. She and Luke prodded at the spectacular and very sore bruise on my thigh until my eyes watered. Then Karen made me lift my arms and felt my ribs. Well, it'd be closer to say she felt for my ribs. They're quite shy and like to hide under their padding.

She inspected the graze on my arm and checked my eyes with a light and felt at the bump under my hair. Luke, however, continued to feel up my leg, his caress becoming less medical by the second.

"Well," Karen said eventually, after what felt like a full medical, "you'll live."

"*Really.*"

"Take her up to the hospital," she said to Luke, who pulled his hand guiltily away from my naked thigh, "get some X-rays of that." She pointed to my leg.

"Oh, you think my leg might be broken?" I said with heavy sarcasm. "I wish you'd told me that before I ran around half of Manhattan on it."

"Head X-rays too," Karen said calmly to Luke.

"My head is fine."

Sensibly, they both ignored that.

"And when you come back, I have some work for you, Four."

Great. Writing up a report, no doubt. She must know how much I love reports.

"Look," I said, "why don't you tell me now? It'd stop me making two trips..."

She sat down at her desk and Luke handed me my leather jeans, which I pulled on as elegantly as I could. I was aiming for Darcy Bussell-esque grace. I think I hit the mark somewhere around Dumbo.

"Don Shapiro," Karen said, once I was dressed and seated, Luke in the chair beside me. "His body was found this morning—about five a.m., New York time—drifting down the Hudson. Impossible to tell how long it had been dead. At least, so far. The autopsy will reveal more, I hope."

I glanced at Luke, but this appeared to have been news to him too.

"His family have been alerted. It's particularly bad timing for his son, Marc-Paul, who is starting school tomorrow. Sophie, your job is to watch him."

"Okay," I said cautiously. Why did I have a bad feeling about this?

"He left his former school in a blaze of glory," Karen went on, rolling her eyes. "And in the absence of anywhere else, has re-enlisted in his local comprehensive, where he was until the age of..." she checked her notes, "...until year eight, when his parents divorced and he was sent to boarding school instead. This will be his final year—year thirteen, is it now?"

"Upper sixth," I said helpfully.

"Thank you, Sophie, for those of use too old to understand this new-fangled system," Luke said with a reasonably restrained amount of sarcasm. Of course, he went to public school, where it's all lower fourth and prefects and casual sodomy. "Back in my day we did A levels in the sixth form, but I suppose they've renamed those, too."

"Nope," I said. "They're still the same—unless Marc-Paul's doing a GNVQ or something, Karen?"

"No. He is taking A levels in Art, Drama, and English."

All the subjects you take when you don't know what else to do. I know, 'cos I did them too.

"I understand you have a background in these subjects?"

I nodded warily. "Bad A level grades in all of them."

"Excellent." She flashed me a rare smile. "If you play your cards right, you might be able to retake them."

I was starting to feel slightly sick. "I might what?"

"Of course, you hopefully won't be there that long."

"Won't be *where* that long?"

"Longford Grammar. Of course, it's not a grammar school any more, it just keeps the name... Sophie?" She got out a penlight and aimed it at my eyes. "Are you sure you're not concussed?"

I felt physically sick. As she checked my pupils, Karen told me all the details—I'd be a student in Marc-Paul's registration class, we'd take the same subjects, I'd shadow him as closely as I could, become his friend...

I had to go back to school.

Out in the bright, clean air of the morning I felt like I'd woken from a really horrible dream. I was always having nightmares about going back to school. They'd come and get me and tell me that the break was over, I'd had my fun playing at being a grown-up, and now it was time to *go back*. It *wasn't over*.

I'd wake up in a cold sweat, terrified it was real.

Well, here it was no nightmare. Term started tomorrow. I was Sophie Green: Teenager once more.

"Oh God," I said to Luke as he half-carried me out to the car. "Oh God, oh God."

"You'll be fine," he said, but he was grinning too hard to make it plausibly reassuring.

"Fine? Luke, do you remember being at school?"

"Sure. When I was a prefect, I got to wear my own waistcoat."

"Oh, fuck off," I snarled half-heartedly. Luke's parents, who died when he was small, had been very rich and sent him to Eton. From there he joined the RAF, then the SAS, and then SO17.

I went to a bog-standard local high school, principally because Chalker was there and my friends were going there—I really do have absolutely no direction of my own—for seven years and by the end I really couldn't bear it. People who say your school years are the best of your life should beware they're upping the teenage suicide rate.

Luke had eagerly asked Karen if I had to wear a uniform, because he thought that as my colleague he ought to help me buy it and make sure I was wearing it right, but we both shot him filthy looks (even in shock, I can control my sarcasm) and

107

Karen explained that sixth formers at Longford didn't have to wear uniform. The dress code stipulated "office wear" with no leather or denim or training shoes; heels of less than two inches and a single pair of earrings could be worn. Ooh, how grown-up.

Luke had looked disappointed. I was mildly relieved. Even if I'd have to take out some earrings.

"But why do I have to do it?" I'd begged. "Can't one of the others do it?"

They both stared at me.

"Sophie," Luke said, "Maria and I are both the wrong side of thirty. And Macbeth—"

He broke off. He didn't need to say that Macbeth had never been a teenager.

By this point I was breathing heavily and Luke took me outside for some air. He had in his hand a sheaf of paper—letter of induction (Longford obviously thought it was more important than it was), timetable (I'd never get the hang of it), dress code (at least there weren't makeup guidelines like Ace had, but otherwise it wasn't far short of the mark) maps (eek!) and a whole load of other crap. He sat me down in the car and bobbed down between my knees on the pavement.

"You okay?"

I shook my head. "I hated school."

"Why? I loved it."

"Because you were posh and you probably actually learned stuff. At my school if you learned something that meant you were brighter than the teachers. So they hated you."

"Can't have been that bad."

I closed my eyes in recollection, and an image of my seventeen-year-old self swam before my eyes. I'd been a skinny little girl, but in my teens I somehow acquired puppy fat. And spots. And my lovely wispy blonde hair darkened into a sludgy, lifeless non-colour that hung fine and shapeless around my round cheeks. I was sarcastic and bored and a little too clever, and I knew it. I was never really unpopular, but I sure as hell wasn't popular, either. My school was small—a hundred or so kids in my year—so everyone knew everyone, and everyone knew who was cool.

I was most avowedly not cool.

When I opened my eyes I was looking at Luke, and I just knew that at seventeen he'd been having the time of his life—gorgeous, athletic, smart and rich—well, who wouldn't?

"Trust me," I said, "it was that bad."

Luke took me back to my place, where I took a grateful shower and fed Tammy, who was very disgruntled with me. She has one of those automated feeders for when I forget to come home, but I never remember to fill it.

Sitting on the sofa with my head in a towel, wrapping up my feet (which had been bare at the office, for lack of time) with plasters, I watched Luke look through my school photo box. It was a bit unnerving—that box was my life. Or at least, my life from the age of eleven to eighteen. I had all the family photos in my flat. They were in shoeboxes on top of my wardrobe, and Luke had laughed to see them all neatly labelled, I guess because they're the only thing in my house that falls into any kind of order.

"Wow," he said, coming up with a picture of me giving the camera the finger, a typically charming pose. I'd always really wanted to be one of those *Princess Diary* girls who just has to pluck her eyebrows and cut her hair and she's gorgeous. But it took years of acne medication and bothersome dieting and expensive highlights to make me look this good.

And honey, sometimes I look really good.

Right now, wrapping tape around my feet to hold the plasters onto the ugly red and white weals all over my feet, I was less attractive. Not as bad as manky Sophie in the pictures—I mean at least my skin was okay and I wasn't wearing chunky loafers—but I could have looked better.

"What's this?" Luke held up a picture of me covered in plaster of Paris, sculpting a hideous wobbly statue.

"Expressive Arts."

"Which is...?"

"One of those cop-out GCSEs. They were always asking for back-up work, which I never did, so I just got Evie to take pictures of me aiming Modroc at stuff."

"...okay." He pulled out another picture. "Is this them?"

I looked at it and grimaced. Ella and Evie were my friends from about sixth form onwards, when we discovered we had things in common by virtue of being deeply uncool. Also because we didn't really have too many other friends. Evie was bullied mercilessly because of the backbrace she wore to stop her spine from curving, and Ella was a manic-depressive who brought alcohol into school when her parents split up. Although they're pretty cute now, they matched me in the attractiveness stakes at school.

"Yep," I said.

Luke looked at the picture a while longer. "You must really have hated school," he said thoughtfully.

The insight of man.

I made him come shopping with me for new clothes (he wasn't to know I still had a lot of the stuff I wore at school. I'm not *stupid*) and things for school. A new bag, obviously. A pencil case and ring binder and paper. (Luke was amazed that the school didn't give us exercise books, until I reminded him that it was a state school, and therefore penniless.) I fretted a while about art stuff. I mean, presumably the school had some art equipment, but if it was anything like the stuff they'd had at my school, it wouldn't have taxed a four-year-old.

And then I remembered that I had a whole load of stuff at my parents' house, decaying gently in the damp garage. All my old artwork, which doubtless the school would want to see. And when Luke heard about it, he wanted to see it too.

"I bet it's really good," he wheedled.

"If you bet that you'd be really poor."

"Come on, Soph. I know you're creative," he said suggestively, and I blushed. "Wow, that really clashes with that top."

I scowled at him. "Other than my skin tone, is it okay? Do I look seventeen?"

He shrugged. "You look hot. No one will care how old you are."

Very sweet of him, but I needed something more useful. "What about this?" I grabbed a micro mini. "Tell me truthfully, will my bum look big in this?"

The truth was that my bum would hardly have been covered by the thin strip of material, but Luke covered up diplomatically by saying, "It'll show up that bruise on your leg. And you don't want to have to explain that."

I sagged. "Bollocks. So I'll have to wear trousers. And long skirts."

"Make up for it with low-cut tops," Luke suggested eagerly.

"Are you trying to get me chucked out of school? For all I know Marc-Paul could be a total...*greebo* who only likes girls with dreadlocks."

Kate Johnson

Greebo? I hadn't even thought that in years. Dear God, I was regressing already.

Luke was looking at me critically. "I don't think you'd look good with dreads."

Good grief.

It was late when we left the mall, the only place I could think of that was open on Sundays and had more than one shop available, and on the way home I called my mum, who doesn't understand text messaging or how to work her voice mail, and asked her if she knew the whereabouts of my old artwork.

"In the garage, I think."

Since the storage space in their garage is roughly equal to the living space in the house, this wasn't much help.

"I just thought I'd get it out. Keep it at my place."

"Oh, good idea. Your dad and I have been meaning to clean up the garage for a while."

"Is it okay if Luke and I come over to look for it?"

There was a pause while I imagined my mother smiling fondly at the idea of her daughter finally pairing off with someone. More likely she was getting misty-eyed over the someone himself. She's incorrigible, my mother.

"Why don't you come for tea? We thought we might have a barbecue. Make the most of the nice weather."

Uh-oh. Two nights of the parentals in a row? This might kill Luke.

Ah well. He's strong. And my mum makes really good potato salad. And I needed some comfort after the horror of the Going Back To School bombshell.

"Sure," I said. "We'll be there in an hour."

I dumped all of my new shopping on my bed for Tammy to make a nest out of, shoved some food in her bowl and looked in my cupboards for something to take up to my parents'. But the cupboards were bare. Old Mother Hubbard would have to take herself off to Tesco.

Luke backed out of supermarket shopping with me, which was a relief as I didn't really want him to see me piling in the pore strips and packets of Oreos which were an essential but hidden part of my life.

I got home and changed into jeans with trainers and thick socks, a T-shirt and sweater and my fleece, just in case. My dad has a thing about sitting outside to eat during the summer, despite that it's almost never warm enough to do it properly in England. Consequently whenever Mum announces that tea is ready in the summer, we all rush to get sweaters and shoes so we won't freeze to death while we eat. Today had been warm, but not very warm, and there would be no heat left in the evening.

I picked Luke up and drove him the couple of miles to my parents' house on the edge of the village. It wasn't the house where I grew up, that was a Sixties Lego brick in the middle of the village. My parents moved here not long before I moved out, first to go to university, which I hated and only stuck at for a couple of months, and then into my flat, which used to be my grandmother's and is now owned by my mother. I go back there a lot, because my mother can be bothered to cook properly, and because the place is full of comforting things, and because I actually quite like my parents.

My God, I'm a freak.

Both their cars were outside, clean and dripping from a recent wash. The grass had been recently mown and the smell of barbecue hung in the air, a last clinging memory of summer.

"Looks like they've already started," Luke said, and I laughed and shook my head.

"What, are you kidding? Dad won't start the barbie until about an hour after everyone's stopped saying they're hungry. That'll be the neighbours, eating at a normal time."

Sensibly, Luke said nothing, but followed me through the open front door.

"Hola!" I called.

Nothing.

"Hello, burglars? Come to nick your telly!" I looked up at Luke. "Well, might as well get the hi-fi while I'm at it. It has surround sound."

Norma Jean, Chalker's beautifully stupid blonde dog, padded in and made a noise at us that sounded like a car revving.

"Some guard dog," Luke said as I bent down to her and she licked my arm.

Someone called my name from the back garden, and I snapped my fingers. "Damn, foiled." We walked through to the back garden, which was looking damp from a recent watering, thriving and green and lovely. I was always teasing my parents that gardening was a really middle-aged thing to do, but I had to agree it looked good.

Mum was sitting at the garden table with a glass of wine and the Sunday papers. She grinned and ran her gaze over Luke, who was looking lush in a blue shirt that matched his eyes. I'd teased him about being a tart and doing it on purpose, but he'd kissed me until all my lipgloss came off and I had to admit, tart or not, he looked damn good.

"Sophie, there's some white in the fridge," Mum began.

I waved Ted's keys at her. "I have to drive."

"Oh. Well, there's some water there too. Luke, what do you want to drink?"

"Whatever you have," he said politely.

Mum and I looked at each other. "Wine?" She gestured to her bottle of red. "There's white in the fridge, too."

"Any beer?"

"Lager or bitter? I'm not sure if there's some Guinness, too."

"Or you could have a vod and tonic," I said.

"It's in the freezer," Mum said. "With the gin."

"Or just a Coke," I finished. "Or maybe some Orangina?"

Luke looked mildly stunned.

"Dad works for a brewery," I explained.

"And he keeps the entire stock here?"

"No, we're happy little alcoholics."

"Ah. What's the bitter?"

"Directors."

"Sounds good."

He followed me into the kitchen, which I'd bullied my parents into letting me help them design, and I opened the fridge. I found the water, but no cans of anything.

"It's in the garage," Mum called through.

I poured my water—not as prison ration as it sounds, for Mum to think about getting bottled water in for me shows thoughtfulness on her part since she knows I can't stand the local limescaley tap water—and led Luke through the house to the garage. The thump of a bass beat came from the corner where Chalker had his little studio, full of band crap and girlie posters and CDs. I listened for a while.

"So he got the 'Phonics CD too?"

"How can you tell?"

"When you grow up with Chalker you get to recognise anything by its bass line. Or drum beat. Or sometimes a chord change."

"I'm impressed." Luke watched me cross to one of the old display fridges that helped to fill the garage, and sort through it until I found his beer.

"Want a glass?"

"No, I'm good." He looked around. "Seriously, is this all your parents' stuff?"

"Well, mine and Chalker's, too."

"You're not secretly running a storage business?"

"Nope. You should see the loft."

"God."

While we were there, we figured we might as well start going through things for my art stuff. From what I remembered of my own A levels, I'd spent the entire first year drawing fruit and bits of draped cloth, then painting them, then enlarging sections of the paintings and painting them, then making Modroc sculptures of the enlarged bits, then drawing them, then painting and enlarging them until I was so bored I would sit there and cry. I hoped Longford would be slightly better.

"What exactly are we looking for?" Luke asked, brushing cobwebs off a cupboard door.

"Um." I tried to remember. "Probably some of it's still in my 'folio. A2 size. And there was a 3D thing with a sort of face and a sword...I did some stuff on Stonehenge that was sort of psychedelic... Um, I had some printed cloth that was—wait, what's this?"

My obsession with all things Dark Ages had manifested itself in sketches of druid stones and tableaux of Arthurian myths. I'd wanted to illustrate a book, but apparently that wasn't artistic enough. It didn't represent anything. What enlarged sections of fruit were supposed to represent I had no idea, but I'd figured out early in my school career that you didn't get anywhere unless you sucked up to the teacher, big time.

I pulled out a sort of odd twirly hat made of wire and gold papier maché, tangled up in a printed veil.

"What's that?" Luke asked cautiously.

"I think it was something to do with Isolda."

"Who?"

Heathen. "I'll lend you the book." I went on searching through the shadows—the electrics in the house have never been good and in the garage half of the lights don't work at all. There was ivy growing in under the eaves and it kept tickling me, making me jump.

And then something else tickled me and made me jump.

"Luke, cut that out."

"I can see right down your top from here."

"Excellent. Could you use that twenty-twenty vision to look for artwork instead, please?"

By the time Dad came in to get the barbecue, we were dusty and grubby and still hadn't found anything. Dad greeted Luke as politely as Luke had greeted him the night before and asked what we were looking for.

"Oh," he said, when I'd told him. "I put that up in the loft ages ago."

I ground my teeth and fetched the ladders and carried them through the house. On our way through the sitting room, Luke stopped and stared at the wall.

"Did you do this?"

I glanced at the purple flowers on the wall. "Yeah. They never let me crayon on the wall when I was little, so..."

He looked impressed. "It's really good."

Actually, it wasn't, but a mural always seems to impress people. My mother hadn't been able to find a print to go on the sitting room wall that pleased her layman's taste ("I don't like people and I hate all that modern stuff. I want to be able to see what the picture's of,") *and* matched the carpet. So, annoyed with her, I said she could mix up some paints at the DIY shop and I'd splash them on the wall for her.

She took me seriously.

"Yeah, well," I said to Luke, "I can hardly take the wall into school with me, can I?"

He got out his phone and snapped a photo of the wall.

"Sure you can."

Smartarse.

We found my stuff in the hot, low, dusty loft and when we were done were so scruffy that Luke suggested taking a communal shower, and I'd have agreed if my parents weren't right there in the house.

"Okay," he said as we washed our hands, "but when we get home, I don't care if you're dead on your feet—"

"I get it," I said. "You, me, bed, shag."

"Succinct. I can see my best lines will be wasted on you."

"Luke, you got me. I'm sleeping with you. It's a bit late for lines." Let alone any kind of persuasion. He'd say my name, and I'd take my clothes off.

When we went downstairs Dad had started the barbecue, Mum had finished her bottle and Chalker was pulling at the strings of his guitar, looking anguished.

"Sophie," he said, "what is that bloody song? I've had a bit of it in my head all sodding day and I can't think what it is."

Mum started singing something and he glared at her. "Not helpful." He played a few chords, a beautiful change, and I thought about it.

"Play it again."

He did, and I started smiling.

"You know this," I said to Luke.

"Do I?"

"Tara sings it to Willow on the bridge. It's from *Buffy*," I told Chalker, who looked really pissed off. He disapproves of my *Buffy* obsession, but he still has a poster of Sarah Michelle Gellar in his studio.

"Luke," Mum asked, "do you eat meat?" He nodded. "Chicken?" Another nod. "Not like Sophie, then."

"But she eats fish," Dad said, putting a bit of chargrilled tuna on my plate, looking slightly anxious in case I'd changed my mind.

"I don't eat things with legs or shells," I clarified.

"Why?"

"Because things with legs are cute, and things with shells are gross." There are other reasons, but I didn't feel up to a detailed discussion of the merits of vegetarianism.

Luke shrugged, like this made perfect sense. "Okay."

I always get completely stuffed with barbecue food, but sitting at a table with both Chalker and Luke was an education. They both started by piling their plates high with food—Luke added some salad but Chalker didn't fill up unnecessary space with leaves. Then, by the time I'd eaten my first (veggie) sausage, Chalker had got through two burgers and Luke two hotdogs and half a chicken leg.

119

"God bless your belly," Mum said, and he looked slightly taken aback until I explained that she was from Yorkshire.

"So where are you from, Luke?" Dad asked.

I looked at him interestedly. He'd been born in London, according to his file, but I didn't think he'd lived there.

"All over," he said. "My dad was in the air force. We moved around a lot."

"Is he still with them now?"

"No." I checked his face. There was no sign of pain. "My parents died when I was six."

There was a silence around the table.

"Car accident, right?" I said, kicking myself for not being able to think of anything more sensitive to say.

He nodded and picked up the mustard.

"It's okay," he said to my momentarily silent family. (God, they must be shocked.) "It happened twenty-five years ago. I'm over it. This potato salad's really good. Is it homemade?"

Somehow we got past it and conversation started flowing again. Luke asked Chalker about the band, and Chalker replied in his usual laconic style, letting my mother rabbit on about it so he could correct her in the important bits and still say relatively little. He's a man of few words, my brother, especially when it comes to talking about himself.

"Oh, hey," he said to me in a lull, "I meant to tell you. Guess what I saw the other day."

I considered this. "John Lennon's ghost? No, I know. Anna Kournikova doing a strip-tease in the middle of Cambridge Road?"

He gave me a "very funny" look.

"A Vanquish. Dark blue. Damn, that's a pretty car."

I bit my lip and couldn't look at Luke. A couple of months ago I'd driven an Aston Martin Vanquish. I wasn't supposed to—it belonged to a...well, a friend, who at the time I suspected of trying to kill me and... Let's just say I *borrowed* his car, mine being unsuitable for the purpose and him being unsuitable for driving. Being that I'd shot him.

"Hot," Luke said, looking right at me, and I knew what he meant. "Sophie saw one a while back. A really hot car."

I squirmed. It had been even hotter when it had got blown up. The injustice of it!

"Have you seen the new one?" Luke was asking now. "The— what is it, Soph? The baby Aston."

Chalker and I both said, "V8 Vantage," at the same time. Luke and my parents stared at us.

"Spooky," my dad said.

"She's such a petrolhead," Luke said fondly, nudging me.

I think that was a compliment.

Eventually, Mum having got more wine and finally gone to bed, Dad having watered down the barbecue with a teapot and Chalker having self-consciously played a few more songs on his guitar, we left, me with a Tupperware box of barbecued veggie sausages for me and a load of chicken that had fallen on the floor for Tammy. We shoved all my art stuff in the back and took off.

"Yours or mine?" Luke asked.

"Mine. I have to go to school tomorrow," I said glumly. "Luke, what am I going to wear? What if the kid is a total goth?"

"He wouldn't be allowed in a hotel on Park Avenue," Luke said calmly.

"What if they figure me out?"

"What if the other kids don't like me?" Luke mimicked. "You'll be fine. Just wear something short—"

"Bruise," I reminded him.

"Well, something low-cut, then. Smile a lot and flip your hair. Works for me."

"You're not one for subtlety, are you?"

He grinned at me.

We pulled up in the little car park outside my flat and I stood looking at the clutter in the back.

"Leave it there," Luke advised, tugging at my hand, "sort it out tomorrow."

"Is someone desperate for a shag?"

"Someone is. Where are your keys?"

We got in, I dumped the food on the counter and Luke pulled off my sweater.

"Did you miss me?" I asked pertly.

"Yes," he said, going after my T-shirt too. "Very much. Why are you wearing so many layers?"

"It's cold outside."

"But it's hot in here."

"'So take off all your clothes...'" I sang, looking up at him. (I was going to say through my lashes, but that's impossible and anyway, it makes you look really stupid. See, now you're trying it.)

"Well, if you really want me to," Luke said, obeying orders and kicking off his shoes as he threw his shirt across the room.

"Slow down," I laughed, pulling off my trainers and trying not to wince as I peeled back the socks over my blisters.

"Can't. Been waiting a week and a half already." He pulled me to him and kissed me again, and I shivered happily against his hard, warm chest. He really is so beautiful. Sometimes I think I'm dreaming.

My jeans joined the pile of clothes on the floor, and my bra soon followed it.

"No fair," I said, "you're still wearing your jeans." Blood was pounding in my ears as I watched him unfasten the fly and—

No, wait. That wasn't in my ears. That was outside my ears. That was someone pounding on the door.

Luke's eyes narrowed. "Ignore it."

The phone started ringing.

"God dammit." He stalked over to the phone, lifted and replaced the receiver, none too gently, and the knocking on the door started up again.

"I am trying to fuck my fucking girlfriend," Luke yelled at the door. "Fuck off!"

I know I should have been offended, but really, you should see Luke half-naked. "If that's my mother I will laugh so hard." I giggled as Luke fastened up his jeans again and stomped over to the door, bare feet pounding the crap out of my wooden floor, and yanked open the door.

"What?" he snarled.

And then there was silence for a few seconds.

I picked up Luke's blue shirt and slipped it on and padded over to the door, where I fell silent, too.

Chapter Seven

Eventually I found my voice. "Xander? What the hell are you doing here?"

He looked frozen, and really miserable, hugging a holdall to his chest. His gaze was rooted to Luke's torso. I couldn't blame him. Straighter men than he had stared.

I waved my hand in front of Xander's face. Luke sighed, looking pissed off, and leaned against the door frame, arms folded.

"Go away," he said, in a patience-tested voice.

"I don't have anywhere to go," Xander said pitifully.

"Well, you're not staying here. Your brother lives just up the road—"

"I went there," Xander said. "They're not in. There's no car or anything."

I frowned, and remembered Angel mentioning some date with Harvey.

"They won't be back 'til late," I said, pulling Luke out of the way. "Come in."

"*Sophie*," Luke said, and I ignored him.

"How do you know where I live?" I asked Xander as he shuffled inside and looked around, still clutching his bag.

"Phone book," he said.

"I thought you were going to go ex-directory," Luke said, still standing in the little lobby.

"Yeah, tell the phone company that. Xander, what happened to you?" I said, looking him over. He looked like he'd been sleeping rough.

He looked gratefully at my sofa and fell onto it, still holding his bag. "You mean today? Or since you hauled ass and left me there on my own?"

"Hey, I had reasons for leaving," I said, a touch guiltily.

"What happened to your leg?"

"That would be one of them. Luke, for God's sake stop glaring at me and put some clothes on."

"You're wearing my shirt."

I looked down. So I was. I went into the bedroom and pulled on a dressing gown, handing the shirt back to Luke at the doorway.

"He's not staying," he said stonily.

"Well, where else is he going to go?" I hissed. "Look at him, he's a wreck. Angel and Harvey are out and he doesn't know anyone else."

"So you're just going to take him in?"

"Do you have a better idea?"

We glared at each other for a bit.

"He can go to a hotel," Luke said.

"Who'd let him in, looking like that?"

Luke ground his teeth. "He is not—"

"He *is*, Luke, and if you think having a shag is more important than looking after a friend, who is a witness in this case," I added for good measure, "then you can fuck off. Go on, go."

I pushed past him and collected up his shoes and socks and threw them at him. "I have to be up early tomorrow," I said. "I don't need any of this."

"Sophie, you're being unreasonable," Luke began, and I turned murderous eyes on him.

"And I have a gun in my room," I said. "Two, actually. So even if one misses I might hit you with the other one. Are you going to be sensible about this or are you going to leave?"

He glared at me, then glared extra hard at Xander.

"I'll see you tomorrow," he muttered, and stomped out to walk home.

I locked the door behind him, feeling almost like crying, hoping he'd come back and tell me all was forgiven, of course Xander could stay, we'd work something out.

But there was nothing.

Xander was still huddled on the sofa, looking more miserable than he had before.

"Did I interrupt you guys?"

I nodded.

"I am so, so sorry. But I didn't know where else to go."

I forced a smile onto my face. "That's okay."

"Really?"

"No." I slouched over to the kitchen. "Drink?"

I found some vodka and Xander drank it neat.

"So what did happen to you?" I asked. "I came back and you were gone."

"I went for some ice," he said. "I remembered the key and everything, but when I came back there was someone waiting outside the room..."

"Someone familiar? With a gun, maybe?"

126

"The guy from the lobby. The second one."

"Yeah. I saw him too."

"Did he get you?"

I paused. "You tell me yours first."

He sighed. "Well, I ran. I got on the subway and went back to my apartment for some stuff," he patted the bag, "but when I got there they were waiting for me."

Must have gone straight there from hitting me. Vicious bastards.

"So I ran some more," he said. "I got a taxi to the airport. God knows what'll happen when they cash the cheque."

I frowned. "What flight were you on?"

"Delta, six-thirty."

So he missed me by an hour and a half. Ha!

"But—that means you've been in England since yesterday! Where have you been?"

He looked miserable. "I didn't have Harvey's number and I don't understand your phones—" probably because they weren't vandalised, "—so I couldn't get him to pick me up. I got a map, and you live really far from the airport. I thought you worked there?"

"I work at Stansted," I said. "You flew into Heathrow."

"Oh," he said. "That might explain it. But anyway, I found where you live and I had to hitch a ride. Well, several rides. I slept at the airport. It's taken me all day to get here."

"If you found me in the phone book, why didn't you call me?"

Xander pointed and I looked over at my answerphone. It was flashing madly.

"Oh." I collected myself. "What about your luggage?"

He gave a little smile. "Bought it at the airport. Thank God I had my chequebook, huh? By the time they bounce no one will be able to find me."

"Is there anything in it?" I asked wearily.

"Sketchbook. Pencils. Cool sneakers I found on sale..." He was shaking.

"Xander," I said, "I think you need some sleep. And a bath."

He looked like an abused puppy who'd finally stopped getting kicked.

"I have to—" I couldn't say "go to school". I just couldn't. "I have to work tomorrow, but I'll take you up to Harvey's first thing, okay?"

He nodded gratefully, stood up suddenly and hugged me.

"Sophie, you're the greatest."

Funny, I didn't feel that fab.

I was woken hideously early by what sounded like a burglar in my kitchen.

Sighing, I rolled over and tried to go back to sleep. But the noises went on. I squinted at the clock. Bleurgh.

Swinging grumpily out of bed, recalling how late I'd gone to bed and then how even later I'd finally fallen asleep, I took the key for my gun cabinet out of my goodie drawer. Then I got out my lovely SIG Sauer P-239, loaded it, and pushed open the bedroom door.

Then I stared at the intruder, so surprised I nearly pulled the trigger by mistake.

"Xander?" I yawned, watching him turn my cupboards inside out. "What are you doing?"

"Looking for coffee."

"It's right there by the kettle!"

He looked at it with disgust. "Real coffee."

"What's that? Scotch mist? This isn't Starbucks. That's the only coffee I have."

"Don't you got anything with a filter?"

American grammar.

I had some filter coffee, but it was older than my flat. I'd last seen it when I used the filters to make hats for Tammy at Christmas.

"No," I said shortly. "I don't."

His face softened when he saw my expression. "I'm sorry, Sophie. You've been really good. This is fine. You want some?"

I nodded. "I'm going to take a shower."

When I came out, finally free of the faint smell of smoke that had been clinging to me since the gig, I spent a while deciding on what to wear. Eventually I decided on a pair of black trousers and a tight blue top with a loose draped neckline, and my faithful old black boots. I was just packaging up my feet when Xander knocked on the door and came in, bearing coffee.

I sipped it. "You're forgiven."

"What happened to your arm?"

I sighed and recounted the story as I did my makeup. Xander was amazed and immediately apologised for being so snarky about me leaving him. Not that he'd realised I wasn't coming back.

I glanced at the clock. It had just gone eight. I had enough time to throw all my school things into my bag, lock up my gun again (part of me longed to take it with me and the other part, the part that remembered Dunblane, very much wished that the first part of me didn't exist) feed Tammy, who Xander was in love with, and take him off up to Angel's.

"What's all this stuff in the back?" Xander was leaning over to look through my warped cardboard folders.

"Just some old school work of mine."

"It's good."

"Really?" I couldn't help being pleased. Xander was an actual artist.

"Well, it's okay."

Oh. Cheers.

Angel lived about five miles away in a pretty village named Ugley. Yeah, I know. Apparently it's Saxon or something. Her house was a converted medieval church, complete with spire and creepy crypt, and she lived there quite happily with Harvey, the Perfect Boyfriend.

He answered the door, and his jaw dropped. It was like a weird mirror.

"Xander? What the fuck are you doing here?"

Xander gave a wave. He'd taken a shower and shaved with Luke's razor and I'd thrown his clothes in the washing machine overnight, so he looked a hell of a lot better, but there was still a rough edge to him, a pallid tone to his skin and shadows around his eyes.

"Long story," Xander said, looking at me ruefully. "You reckon I could stay here, big bro?"

Harvey nodded, then he paused and turned to Angel, who was hidden behind him. She looked ridiculously perky for someone who didn't have to get up so early. "Can he?"

"Of course! Xander, it's nice to meet you. I'm Angel…"

I stepped back. "Okay. I have work to do."

Harvey followed me a few steps out of the porch. "Sophie? What's going on?"

I explained about Xander coming to me because they'd been out. "I think he's had a rough couple of days," I said. "Be nice to him."

"Did you hear about Shapiro?"

I nodded. "Floating in the Hudson. Xander is probably going to be a suspect."

"Why? Does anyone know the body was at his apartment? You didn't tell anyone..."

"No, I didn't, and Luke won't have either, but it won't be hard for them to find out Shapiro owed Xander money. And that Xander—who is vastly overdrawn, by the way—has now left the country."

"Great." Harvey rubbed his face. "Okay. Looks like I have work to do today too. Thanks for looking after him."

"No problem."

Harvey smiled at me, and that was reward enough.

I got back in Ted and pointed him north, towards Longford, on the road to Cambridge. The village was long and old and pretty, with a river running under the main road (boy, they really didn't have to think so hard about that village name, did they?) and the high school at the far end. It reminded me a lot of my old school. From the road, across the lawn, I could see cars parked outside what I assumed was the main hall, so I turned up the lane that ran through the middle of the school, and swung Ted neatly into a parking space.

And then I got out, and a stern-looking woman with "History Teacher" written all over her tapped me on the shoulder and asked if I was a student.

"Of course," I said, laughing a little nervously. I'd passed the first hurdle. "Why else would I be here?"

"This is staff parking," she said. "You'll have to put *that*," Ted was given a disparaging wave, "somewhere else."

"But—where?" I fought to keep from scowling at her treatment of my beloved car.

"There's a car park outside D Block for students," she said, and swept off.

Great. Where the fuck was D Block?

I got back in and rummaged for my school map. No map. Great.

So I got back out—by now people were starting to watch me—and grabbed a kid in uniform and said, "Do you know where D Block is?"

He nodded.

"Do you know how to get to the car park?"

He nodded again.

"I'll give you a fiver if you show me."

Eagerly, he hopped in, looking around my car in amazement, and I remembered what a small economy kids operate on. Five quid was probably a week's lunch money. And I had a car—when I was at school hardly anyone had their own car. The ones that did drove beat-up Novas older than themselves and thought they were the business.

He directed me left onto the lane, past a clutch of ugly low-rise buildings, and up a steep drive on the other side of the road. I found a space behind the gym and paid the kid off.

"What's your name?"

"Rob," he said, looking at me like I was a goddess. "8F."

I assumed that was his class.

"Thanks, Rob. Now, er, run along."

And he did. Bless.

I went back down the slope and round the front of D Block to the newer building Rob had said was the sixth form block. According to my letter of induction I was to go to my form room for a twenty minute registration period, before my first class at eight fifty-five. I was five minutes early. Go me!

I walked into the S Block lobby (there being six buildings, A-E Blocks, plus the new, bewilderingly named S Block for the Sixth Form. And they wonder why kids today are so confused) and everybody turned to look at me.

I'd checked myself over in the rear-view mirror before leaving the car and I knew I looked pretty good. The difference between a schoolgirl and a grown woman, I guess. Not that I feel like a grown woman most of the time—I feel like that geeky teenager. Still, I know I look better. Hell, I couldn't look worse. I'd like to think it's something in my manner that indicates I've grown up, but I'm fairly sure I act like a daft teenager most of the time.

Better hair and a more experienced hand with makeup had, however, given me the edge, and certainly I'd grown up in terms of clothing since the last time I walked into a school building. I'd given up trying to dress like a skinny clotheshorse a long time ago, and instead decided to embrace my curves, in the hope that maybe someone else might want to embrace them, too.

By the looks of it, a few of them did.

I preened.

"Excuse me," I asked a girl on her own, "where's S3?"

She pointed to a locked door. "You in Devvo's form, then?"

I blinked. My form tutor was supposed to be a Mr. Devely. "I guess," I said uncertainly. "Are you?"

She shook her head. "Hemlock."

"Ah."

I *hoped* this was another nickname.

For something to do, I got out my phones and pretended to check for messages. There were none. Apparently Karen had finally found something she trusted me with and Luke still wasn't talking to me. Great.

Then, aware I probably looked like a prat with two phones, I hastily put them away, just as the door to what I assumed was an office opened and a tall man and the History teacher came out. She gave me a tight-lipped glare as she swept past and opened the door to one of the classrooms. The girl who had said she was in Hemlock's class filed in after her. Good nickname, I thought, watching the iron back disappear into the classroom.

The tall man—Devvo, I presumed—nodded amiably at a few students and opened up S3, switching on lights which flickered and hummed, sitting down at his messy desk and taking out a folder. He looked around the class, ticking off names on the register, and I was impressed at his casual control.

Then his eyes flickered over me, and I looked away instinctively. I learnt to avoid eye contact a long time ago in History lessons when I didn't want to get asked anything.

"Right," he said loudly in a Geordie accent, "shut up, you lot, I know it's your first day back but we've got some notices to get through. Sit down…"

The class found seats on swivelly chairs and the edges of tables. I perched nervously by a computer. Computers and swivel chairs! In my day it was hard plastic chairs and there were only half enough computers in the whole school for one class at a time.

My God, now I felt old.

"Okay. Firstly, anyone here does Art...?"

I meekly raised my hand. So did one of the girls and a boy I hadn't noticed before, a very pretty boy with black hair and long lashes. I ached to see what colour his eyes were, but they were cast down at the floor.

"Okay. You have no class today, 'cos the new teacher hasn't arrived yet."

There was a chorus of "typical" from the class, which Devvo gamely ignored.

"Don't forget to sign in and out when you go down the village for your lunch and don't forget that's the only time you're allowed to go," he read off a note, and his expression matched that of his class—not bloody likely.

"Auditions will be held in the Music Suite for a new saxophone group... All right, sod this, no one cares. How was everyone's summer?"

People shrugged and muttered "All right," and generally turned to each other to chat.

"And before I forget," Devvo raised his voice again, "we've got two new students. Marc Shapiro and Sophie Green. Would you like to come forward."

It wasn't a question.

I found myself liking this man—it was better not to think of him as a teacher—and his lazy, dry manner. Why hadn't I had a form tutor like him? Why was mine the floopiest, most risible flake ever to get a teaching degree?

The pretty boy and I shambled to the front of the class to be presented.

"Would you like to tell us something about yourselves?" Devvo went on, and I revised my opinion of him. He was a sadist.

Marc—not Marc-Paul, I noticed—glanced at me, and I sucked in my breath. He had the most dazzling, sapphire blue eyes I have ever seen. Wow. I could live in those eyes.

Aware I was staring, and the class was sniggering, I wrenched myself away and looked back at the dozen or so bored faces before me. Marc was making no effort to speak, so I cleared my throat.

"Hi. I'm Sophie." I gave a little wave, which was parodied at the back of the class. "But I guess you know that, since I don't look like a Marc." B'dum chh.

Nothing. I tried again.

"I, um, I just moved here. From...Yorkshire." Well, I did move here from Yorkshire. When I was two. "I'm taking Art and English and Drama." *In which I already have A levels, so this should be a cinch.* "I, er, hope we all get on..."

Okay, that was the worst introduction speech ever. I looked up at the ceiling as Marc straightened.

"I'm Marc," he said, and there was a very slight hint of an American accent there. "I used to come here, for, like, a year, then I moved. I got thrown out of my old school for setting someone on fire. My parents are divorced, I live with my mom in Green Roding and I'm doing the same subjects as her."

He jerked his thumb at me, then, without making eye contact with anyone, sloped back off to the back of the class, leaving me there on my own, feeling completely uncool.

Green Roding, I thought, to try and distract myself as I went back to my seat. I knew whereabouts Leaden Roding and Margaret Roding were. I guessed Green Roding was nearby.

The bell rang, and I had to try and remember what lesson I had first period.

Marc was gathering his bag and moving towards the door. I caught up with him, wincing as my own record bag (thankfully, apparently still cool) bashed into my bruised thigh. I took it off and swung it to my other side, accidentally catching him.

"Oh, sorry." I tried a smile, which he didn't return. He was moody behind his black hair and long eyelashes, with a pretty mouth and cheekbones almost as good as Luke's.

Almost. Not quite.

"Hey, erm, do we have a lesson now? You know, doing the same subjects. How weird is that?!"

He shrugged. "English."

"We have English now? Great." No, not great, what was I talking about? "Where is it? I, er, lost my map."

He looked at me like I'd just announced I liked Elton John (which I do, but would never admit to a seventeen-year-old).

"E Block," he said, and walked out.

I made a face and started following.

E Block was up a flight of outdoor steps—they sure made you get your exercise at Longford—and was a single story, depressed-looking building of grey cement with aluminium-framed windows. I followed Marc in and made a right. He went into a classroom and slouched at a table on the far side of the room. I decided that to sit beside him would be pushing my luck, so I took a seat at the next table.

The room quickly filled up and I found myself on what was plainly the loser table—all the people no one else wanted to sit with. Girls flocked to Marc's table, and loads of boys came up to say hi. No one seemed to know anything about his father being found dead yesterday. I wondered if Marc even knew.

The teacher, a bored, frazzled-looking woman who probably had kids my age, came in and asked the class to get out their copies of *Tess of the d'Urbervilles*. Eek. No one had told me what we were supposed to be reading.

I put my hand up.

"Yes?" Ms. Williams asked wearily. "Who are you?"

"Sophie Green. I'm new—"

"And you don't have a book." She sighed. "This is what set lists are for. Okay. Go next door and see if they have one. And be quick."

I got up, aware everyone was watching me, and went and knocked on the door next to my classroom. It was full of first years, looking mildly terrified as they were interrogated by someone who was clearly the head of department. Big, grey-haired, a hard expression on his face.

I was less scared. *I've done all this*, I told myself, *I'm a hell of a lot better than them.*

"I need a copy of *Tess*," I said. "Ms. Williams said you might have one."

I was looked up and down briskly. To him I was just another student.

"You might ask more politely."

I put on a big fake smile. I wasn't making any friends here. "Please may I have a copy of *Tess of the d'Urbervilles* by Thomas Hardy?"

"Where's your own?"

"I don't have one. It's my first day."

"Well, I don't have any either."

I gave another fake smile. "Thank you," I said, and walked out, leaving the door open.

When I went back in it was clear the class had overheard it all. I glanced at Ms. Williams. "He didn't have any," I said.

"Well, you'll have to do without. I presume this means you won't have read it over the summer?"

I paused. I did this for GCSE. "I've read it," I said. "I did it at my old school."

"Then you'll be able to tell me one of the main themes of the book."

I was back in my seat now, and everyone was looking at me.

"Guilt," I said easily. "Self pity. Martyrdom."

She looked surprised. "Martyrdom?"

Well, in for a penny and all that. "Tess is a born martyr. She does everything for other people, but she does it so they know how much she's suffering. She even gives herself up at the end. She pushes Angel away from her—"

"What makes you think that?"

"Well," I said, settling back in my seat, "he tells her his secret and she confesses hers is just the same, and then she sits there and feeds him everything he needs to leave her. All this 'Am I too wicked?' stuff. She gave him an easy way out and he took it."

"Typical bloke," said one of the girls from my form group, and the class sniggered.

"You don't think Tess got the short straw?" Ms. Williams asked me.

"No. Well—maybe. She got some tough choices. But she made herself what she was—she made herself a victim. Hardy has all this sympathy for her and it drove me mad. She should have stood up for herself."

I was amazed to see a couple of people nodding. How cool was this?

Ms. Williams was nodding too. "Right," she said. "Books out, and I want you to make notes on victimisation. See if there is any depth to Sophia's claim."

"It's Soph*ie*," I said, but I said it under my breath. No need to annoy her. I might have made an ally here.

I shared a book with the girl next to me and made notes on why I thoroughly despise Tess Durbeyfield. I've never come across a wetter heroine in my life. I wanted to shake her. Bloody Victorian melodrama.

The lesson—a double, two hour episode—ended and the bell rang for break. You have no freaking idea how weird it was being back in a classroom, making notes on the same book I had when I was sixteen. I was more than a little weirded out, I can tell you.

I went back to Ted, who was harbouring a Mars Bar and some normality for me, and as I got back out saw someone watching me.

Marc.

"Your car?"

I nodded.

"What a hunk of junk."

The *Grease* quote didn't go unnoticed. "He—it's a great car," I said.

"It belongs on a farm."

"It belongs on the Cool Wall," I said without thinking.

A flicker of interest. "You watch *Top Gear*?"

Teenage boys, and a motoring programme. Go figure.

"I subscribe to *Top Gear*," I told him.

He nodded. "Need to get that fender fixed," he said, and walked off.

I wasn't sure if that meeting had gone well or not.

I followed him, subtly, down to the corner where the Drama Studio dwelt. A black box with lino floors and baffles on the walls, it might have been a good space on paper. But the ceilings were too high, the seating rows inadequate, and there was no ventilation. This I knew because it was exactly the same studio as the one I'd done my A levels in. Put more than five people in there and it'd become an oven.

Apparently we had a Drama class next, and apparently it was pretty much the same class as English. I could see why—half of the set texts were the same.

We were put into groups to talk about how we'd stage a scene of *A Doll's House* (oh good, more cheerful Victorian melodrama). I wasn't grouped with Marc, but he was within eyesight.

"God, he's fit," sighed one of the girls from my form group. She had a stripe of orange eyeshadow and thickly lashed eyelashes, and every time she blinked it was like spiders mating.

"Good job growing up," her mate agreed.

"He used to come here, right?" I said.

"First year. Then he left 'cos his dad sent him to some mega expensive boarding school."

"Like Longford wasn't good enough for him."

The first girl—I think her name was Amber, which fitted, with the eyeshadow and all—snorted. "S'not bloody good enough for anyone," she said. "I can't wait to get out of here and off to uni."

"God, me too," said the other girl. "All those blokes. All that booze."

"All that work," I reminded them, and they gave me dirty looks.

"Anyway, what was that about in English?" Amber asked. "You got a degree in Hardy, or something?"

"Oh, I did it at my old school," I said. "Hated it. I hate Hardy."

"Can't tell the sodding difference," Amber's mate moaned. What was her damn name?

"At least it's not that one who fancied his mother," Amber said.

"Lawrence?" I groaned. "Don't tell me we've got him."

"You did D.H. Lawrence at your old school?"

"I feel like I did bloody everything," I said, and at that moment my phone started shrieking in my bag.

Every head turned in my direction so fast there was a whoosh of air. I turned crimson and delved in my bag for my phone, which had suddenly become utterly tiny and slippery and elusive, and finally found it and switched it off.

In the silence, I could feel the eyes of the trendy jeans-wearing teacher on the back of my neck.

"Sorry," I said in a little voice.

"All phones off," he said wearily. "Or at least on Silent."

I nodded meekly. A minute later the phone buzzed in my bag with a voice mail.

"Okay," I said. "Nora and Torvald. Where are we?"

At the end of that lesson I had a free period, and then it was supposed to be lunch. This I had gleaned from Mr. Jones, or Uncle Todd as the class called him, I think with some kind of post-modern irony. Very impressive for seventeen-year-olds.

After lunch should have been Art, but it was called off because of teacher absence. I thought this was a crappy show. After all, I'd turned up on my first day and it wasn't as if I was getting paid for this...

Oh no, I was.

There was apparently a common room somewhere hidden in the maze of older buildings, but Marc followed his very new-found cronies down to the props room behind the stage, where someone put a stereo on and someone else opened some crisps and people sat around talking to each other and ignoring me.

For something to do, I picked up my voice mail.

"Hey," it said, in Luke's voice, and I was surprised. "Call me back, I have something to tell you."

That was it. No greeting. No apology. Oh, Jesus, was he breaking up with me?

Again?

Making a face, I stabbed the button to call him and listened to the ring tone, looking moodily around the dark little room, scented fetchingly with cheese and onion crisps and cigarette smoke. Eventually he answered.

"Nice of you to pick up."

"I was in a class," I said. "What do you need to tell me?"

"You know those lovely chaps who tried so hard to kill you in New York?"

"Uh-huh," I said, a bad feeling in my stomach.

"They're not in New York any more."

"Why does that not surprise me?"

"They're in—is that Atomic Kitten?"

"What?" Oh, yeah, the stereo. "I'm behind the stage."

"What?"

"Never mind. Where are they?"

"Well, currently they're mid-Atlantic. But very soon they'll be at Heathrow. After that, it's anybody's guess."

"Mine isn't too hard to fathom."

"Mine neither. Did you take Xander up to Angel's?"

"Yep."

"Was anyone there?"

"Yep."

"Are there people listening in?"

"Yep."

"Okay. Look, just be on your guard, all right? They'll be landing at seven, which at least gives us some grace. They won't be here before eight or nine, depending on traffic."

Great. So I had eight hours to live.

"Okay," I said. "I have to go. I don't suppose you feel like being charitable, do you?"

"Depends on the cause," Luke said cautiously.

"I have about a million books I need. I have some of them at home—can you get the others for me? I'll text you the list."

"Read them out. It's got to be quicker."

I got out the lists I'd been given and reeled off names and titles I'd hoped I'd never hear again.

"I have some of those," Luke said. "I'll see you later, yeah?"

And before I could ask whether that meant I was forgiven—or did I need to forgive him?—he was gone.

I ended the call and looked around. Amber and Lucy were reading a magazine together, a skinny boy I think was called

Laurence was reading the paper, and Marc was engaged in conversation with an earnest girl whose name I didn't know. I think she was in my form group, one of the Amber/Lucy crowd.

I sat and looked at them all for a while. All three were watching Marc, and trying to look like they weren't. All three were skinny, and all three were pretty, but in different ways. Amber was quite tall and was clearly in love with herself. Her hair was short but she tossed it constantly for all it was worth. The girl sitting with her—Lucy?—was smaller and very sweetly formed. She looked vaguely familiar—I might have done ballet with her sister when I was tiny.

Well, as tiny as I ever was.

The third girl—the one who'd moaned about D.H. Lawrence—was different. She had her hair in pigtails and she wore glasses and bizarrely coloured clothes. She wasn't unattractive, but neither was she conventional. I got the feeling that if she wore contacts and stopped plastering makeup on, if she sorted out her hair and wore normal coloured clothes (who ever, *ever* thought fluorescent pink, orange and yellow would look good layered together? She looked like a fruit salad on acid), she would be gorgeous.

Marc didn't look very interested in them. His body language was all wrong. He wore a dark shirt and trousers, his hair was slightly spiky, his shoes clean. I wondered if the blackness was in response to his father. How the hell did you bring something like that up in conversation?

Eventually, just as I was trying to think of a way of insinuating myself into the group, Amber looked up and said to the pigtail girl, "Clara, you still on for bowling tonight?"

Clara? What was this, 1903?

"Yeah, sure," Clara said, and immediately flicked her attention back to Marc. "You want to come? There's a bunch of us going. We always do something on our first night back."

Since when? I wondered. I bet probably none of them had cars, or could even drive.

Marc shrugged. "Where?"

"The place next to the cinema in town. You know it?" He shook his head. "It's quite new. Do you know..." And she launched into a complicated set of instructions that would have been a hell of a lot simpler if she'd just said that it was opposite the station.

Eventually Marc shrugged again and said he'd see them at eight.

"Hey," I broke in, "I love bowling." Liar.

But it didn't matter, no one paid any attention.

"And that new place is really nice. They have pool tables too." Or is it snooker? Hell, like I can play either of them.

Still, no one was biting.

"Do you have to book?" I asked.

"No," Laurence said, taking pity, "I think you just turn up. But you have to have at least two people for a lane."

So not pity, then.

By the time I got home, after Clara had got a lift and taken Marc with her ("Oh! You live right near me!" Fancy that), I was feeling pretty uncool. I was feeling like I used to feel when people would hand out invites for a party where I wasn't welcome right in front of me, and never even pretend about it.

Luke called while I was trying to decide between chocolate and crisps, or maybe both. "You feel like coming and cheering me up?" I asked in a small voice.

"Why, what's wrong?"

"I hate school. It sucks. I thought I was free of it all. I'll have nightmares for years now."

"Explosions and gunfights don't trouble your conscience, but going back to school gives you nightmares?"

"Blegh," I said.

He laughed. "What sort of cheering up were you thinking?"

"Whatever kind you like."

He was at my door in five minutes.

"Okay," he said. "Phone off?"

I switched off my work mobile and my private mobile, went over and checked the answer machine was on. I even silenced the ringer.

"Door locked?" I asked, and Luke turned all the catches.

"Where's Tammy?"

"Out."

"Lock the cat flap," he said. "No distractions. I don't care if the building falls down—"

"It never stopped you before," I said, remembering, and Luke took advantage of my nostalgia to pull me close against him and kiss me silly.

And then he took off my blue top. And then he led me into the bedroom. And then he—

Mmm.

Later, lying there feeling much, much better (if only I'd had a Luke when I was at school, eh?) I told him about my day.

"School hard?"

"Yeah, school hard," I sulked. "Although I kicked ass in English."

"Do you know you have Elizabeth Jennings on your set list?"

I made a face. "I know. I hate Elizabeth Jennings. If you're depressed you take Prozac, you don't write poems to torture schoolkids."

"I don't think that was her intention. Or Shakespeare's, before you start on him."

"Shakespeare I can cope with. Shakespeare I quite like."

"Mmm." Luke stroked my shoulder. "So apart from the horrors of the English language, how was your first day at school?"

I got the feeling he was strongly resisting calling me "pumpkin" or something else stupid.

"Crappy. The cool kids don't like me."

"Probably because you argued with the teacher about Hardy. Which, by the way, I find incredibly sexy."

"You do?"

He bit my shoulder. "I do. What about Shapiro's kid?"

"Shouldn't he just be Shapiro now? After all, it's not like there's a daddy."

"Did the cool kids like him?" Luke persisted, sensibly ignoring my ramblings.

"Yeah. They invited him bowling. They didn't invite me bowling," I said moodily. "Now I need a drink."

He laughed as I got out of bed. "It's four in the afternoon."

"So?"

"You alkie."

I pulled a face at him and padded out into the kitchen. "You want anything?"

"Any beer?"

I cracked open one each and was about to take them back in when I heard Tammy scratching at her cat flap and went over to unlock it for her. But the lock was stuck, so I checked the peephole and opened the door instead.

And then I nearly died.

Chapter Eight

Standing there looking at me with an indefinable expression was someone I hadn't seen since I accused him of trying to kill me, shot him twice and threw him in a cell, then stole his car and got it blown up.

"Hi," I said, in a rather strangled tone of voice. "I'm not wearing anything, am I?"

He shook his head. I felt my whole body blush.

"I—I'm going to go and put something on..."

I scuttled back into the bedroom, where Luke was frowning. "What's going on? No one's allowed to see you naked but me."

"Docherty," I said, feeling faint. "I opened the door for Tammy and he was there."

"You didn't see him? He doesn't look much like Tammy."

Indeed he didn't. Docherty looked like God, in a sulk. "He must have been lurking."

"Ah, yes, I know how he likes to lurk." Luke got out of bed and pulled some clothes on. "Are you going to get dressed? Or is this an Emperor's New Clothes thing?"

I snatched up my kimono and pulled it on, following Luke out into the sitting room. Docherty was sitting on my sofa, looking like a Bond villain, stroking Tammy who was doing her best to look fat and white and malevolent. She failed on the first two counts, but was making up for it with the third.

"Hey," Luke said, and Docherty looked up, amusement flickering across his fine-featured face (do I know how to alliterate, or what?).

"No need to ask what you two have been doing."

"No," Luke agreed. "No need." He picked up the beer I'd left on the counter and took a swig in a rather proprietary manner. "What are you doing here?"

Luke and Docherty go way back. Apparently. Although neither speaks much of the other—actually, Docherty hardly speaks at all, unless spoken to—they're both very well thought of in what you might call our business. Docherty is more freelance, and a couple of months ago we hired him to look after Angel, who was in some danger. And then Harvey came along, and I jumped to certain slightly erroneous conclusions about Docherty, and, well, a lot more stuff happened.

Tall and dark and Irish and very good-looking, Docherty's one of those people about whom you're desperately curious, but never ask any questions. Not if you want to keep various body parts. The last time I saw him he was driving an Aston Martin Vanquish (yes, *that* Vanquish). I wanted to know what he was driving now, but all I could see through my window was Ted, and Luke's Vectra.

"Thought I'd pop by. See how my favourite sharpshooter's doing," he raised an eyebrow at me, and I blushed.

"She's doing fine," Luke said, and added pointedly, "Nice of you to drop by."

Docherty looked between us.

"Did you want to see my new car?" he asked me idly, probably remembering how flustered I'd got over the Vanquish.

"What is it?"

He gave a very elusive smile. "Come and see."

And, like a little girl going to the devil, I followed him, Luke trotting behind me to keep me out of trouble.

It was sitting in the middle of the small car park, looking magnificent. Long and low and powerful, like Luke doing push-ups. It was black and shiny and had a weird central cockpit. Damn, Docherty actually is Batman.

I checked surreptitiously for a badge, but didn't recognise it.

I glanced at Luke, but he was frowning too.

"It's familiar," he said, "but I..."

Docherty was grinning—well, the closest he'd ever get to grinning. Which is to say, not very. But he was amused.

"You want to know?"

"Yes!"

"Koenigsegg."

I searched my petrolhead memory and came up with a Swedish supercar that nearly killed the Top Gear driver. Fast, dangerous, and utterly unpredictable, just like Docherty.

We stared some more. Then Luke shook his head. "Damn," he said. "I'm impressed. Stay the hell away from my Vectra."

Even Ted looked nervous. Poor Ted.

"Is that all you came for?" I asked, and Docherty shrugged.

"There was one other thing."

"What?"

He beckoned me closer. I stepped towards him, and he leaned down and said very quietly in my ear, "You owe me an apology."

I shivered, and it wasn't because I was wearing a satin kimono and nothing else in September. I knew precisely what kind of apology he was after. And I wasn't sure how I'd feel about giving it to him, even if it wasn't for Luke.

Docherty got in the beautiful car and it made a beautiful noise before gliding beautifully away.

"What did he say to you?" Luke wanted to know.

"I—nothing."

"Sophie..."

"He says I owe him an apology."

Luke glowered at the driveway where the Koenigsegg had been. "He's not getting one."

"No. He's not. Anyway. I need more than just a beer now. Did we finish that vodka?"

"You can't drink vodka."

"Why not? I'm a grown up."

"No, you're not, you're seventeen." Luke grinned as he pushed the door open. "And anyway, you have to go bowling tonight."

I gave him a death look. "No, I don't. Were you not listening back there?"

"So they didn't invite you. Turn up at the next lane and have a better time than them."

"All by myself? I'm enough of a Norma No Mates as it is."

"Not by yourself," Luke said patiently as I picked up Tammy's bowl and started searching for cat food. "With your cool SO17 friends."

I put down the can I was holding. "I don't mean to burst your bubble," I said, "but you three are not really the sort of people a seventeen-year-old girl should be hanging around with."

"Ask your other mates then. Eva and..."

"Evie and Ella. Yeah, 'cos they're not ripe for ridicule. They were as uncool as me at school." Besides, then I'd have to explain to them how I knew all these teenagers in the next lane.

"But you're cooler now," Luke said, looking exasperated. "Angel, then. She's very cool."

He was right. Angel's mother had been a gorgeous sixties diva. Angel was baby-faced—she might get away with seventeen, even though she was ten years older. And she was undeniably cool.

"Okay," I said, "so that's Angel and me..."

"And me," Luke said. "What, you think I'll leave you all on your own when there are men like Docherty around?"

"I can handle Docherty," I said as haughtily as is possible when forking out Whiskas.

Luke shook his head. "That's what I'm afraid of."

I dressed for the occasion. Bowling in my mind has always been a Fifties thing, *Grease* and teenagers and rock'n'roll. I love Fifties style—its a curvy girl thing. I wriggled into a circle skirt and a little wrap top, put my hair into a ponytail and watched it fall out. Well, hell, I was trying to look younger, so I fastened it into pigtails instead.

Luke, who'd gone home to change, came by to pick me up, dressed in jeans and a faded T-shirt. His pale blue eyes were hidden behind dark contact lenses and his hair had been darkened a shade and ruffled into spikes.

"What's this in aid of?" I asked, running my fingers through them as we settled in Luke's car.

"Disguise. Do I look like a seventeen-year-old?"

I looked at the muscles filling out his T-shirt, the fine lines around his eyes and the chiselled shape of his beautiful face.

Damn if I ever knew a seventeen-year-old like that.

"You'll do," I said.

"Are we meeting Angel there?"

I nodded. "She said she'd bring someone but I don't know who. I think Harvey's still working—trying to get something on these guys who are," I looked at my watch, "somewhere over London as we speak."

"So long as he shares it with us." He glanced at me. "You look hot."

"Thank you."

"You want to be a little bit late?"

Jesus, start him off and he never stopped. "You've had me once tonight," I reminded him.

"Can't I get you again?"

"We have a job to do."

He made a face. "Sodding job."

I knew how he felt.

We parked up and sat outside MacDonalds to wait for Angel. I was slightly nervous about who she was bringing, and when I saw her tripping up to us in massive heels and tatty jeans, I looked behind her to see someone with peroxided-blond-and-green hair, a nose ring and massive, massive jeans, slouching along, looking pissed off. He looked like the sort of kid mothers have nightmares about their daughters bringing home.

"Oh, Jesus," I muttered to Luke, who looked horrified.

"I know. Does she have a cousin or something we don't know about?"

"Her parents were only children," I replied, and then Angel and her friend got closer, and Luke suddenly started laughing.

"What?"

And then the nightmare looked at me and grinned, and I nearly fell off my chair.

"Harvey?"

"Close enough."

"*Xander?*" Of course, he still had the cut on his face. "What—but you look—your *hair!*"

"I know," he said ruefully, touching it. "She made me," he said pointing to Angel, who rolled her eyes.

"You're supposed to be in disguise," she said. "There are people after you, you know."

"So how come when there were people after you, you didn't dye your hair green?" Luke wanted to know.

"And what about Harvey?" I asked.

"Oh, partly we did it so I could tell the difference," Angel said.

"No, I mean, what if someone thinks Harvey is Xander and..." I mimed taking a potshot.

"Harvey can look after himself," Angel said, but without absolute conviction. "Shall we go in?"

We'd timed it so we were there well ahead of Marc and the cool gang. Luke gave everyone ludicrously fake names on the scoreboard, even me. Taking his cues from *Buffy*, he christened us Randy and Joan, then looked speculatively at Angel for a while before adding her as Darla, and started to type in Xander's real name before thinking better of it and adding him as Oz.

156

"After all, you have the hair," he pointed out, and Xander scowled.

"The green will wash out by tomorrow," Angel whispered to me, "but he doesn't know that."

I always start off really well at bowling—well, sort of well, anyway—and go rapidly downhill. I got two spares and two eights, and then three gutterballs. By the time the school gang had turned up, I was clutching at Luke and wailing, "I'll never score anything ever again!"

"Well, you can score with me later," he said, playing with my pigtails, "if it'll make you feel any better."

I nodded. "Much."

"In fact, why don't we slope off now—joke," he added, seeing me open my mouth.

"They've just come in," I said, nodding over my shoulder.

Luke looked at them for a while. They were getting bowling shoes, the girls giggling, Marc silent. Laurence was with them, and another guy who was getting very tactile with Amber, whose mascara was so spiky I was amazed she could see. He wasn't up to much, but he had "boyfriend" written all over him.

"Your turn, Randy," Angel said, but Luke ignored her.

"He's the one in the black shirt, right?"

"Right." I frowned. "He hasn't changed."

"Maybe he's in mourning."

"He never mentioned it, that's the thing." I blinked. "Ready, Randy?"

"Ready, Joan."

Luke bowled a strike, his fifth of the evening. "Can I switch my name with yours?" I pleaded, and he shook his head, grinning at me.

"You can get me a drink, though."

I made a face and picked up my bag, a very kitsch little thing shaped like a corset, with ribbons and padded breasts. I called it my booby bag. Xander adored it.

"What are we drinking?"

I went up to the bar with the order in my head, and while I was waiting, Marc came up and stood beside me.

"Small world," he said, verbose as ever.

"Sure is."

"Like your bag."

"Thanks. Me too."

The barman came over, and I ordered pints for Luke and Xander and soft drinks for me and Angel, who were both driving.

The barman looked at me, and Marc, and the girls twittering over their shoes, and asked me for ID.

I was mildly insulted. I've never been seriously ID'd in my life. And then I remembered that I was trying to be seventeen, so I reached in my wallet and pulled out my driving licence.

"Okay." He handed it back. "That was two pints of IPA and two diet Cokes?"

I nodded, and as he moved away, Marc asked, "Was that real? Or did you go back a year?"

I deliberated. "I have a cousin at the DVLA," I said. "He fixed it for me."

"It's fake?"

I put my finger to my lips. "Just the birth date. How do you think I drove to school?"

I got my drinks, paid and carried them back to our lane.

"He thinks my ID is fake," I told Angel. "This is great."

I bowled my next turn and hit two pins, then another three.

"Maybe going to the bar has done you some good," Luke said, flicking my pigtails. "You can get every round in."

I saw Marc sloping back to his lane with a round of Cokes, and had to hide a smile.

By the end of the evening, Luke was winning by about a million points. Xander was doing pretty well, Angel not too badly, and I had about thirty points, most of them flukes.

"Can we go now?" I said grumpily.

"Wait until they've gone," Luke said. He was on his third pint and reasonably happy.

"But it's half past ten! Don't they have school tomorrow?"

"Don't you?" Angel said, and Xander laughed really hard. Jesus, American beer must be really weak if he was that pissed.

Finally the kids played their last game. Nothing interesting had happened. Marc was a good bowler, Laurence okay and the three girls and Amber's boyfriend were as bad as me. But I'd caught all of them looking over at our happy little group. I think Marc fancied Angel. But then, everyone fancies Angel. I'd think he was abnormal if he didn't.

"So," I said to Luke as we watched them troop outside to wait for various lifts, "am I cooler now?"

"Oh, you're subzero," Angel assured me as Luke played with my hair some more.

"They loved you," Xander agreed. "Can we go now? My arms are aching. I haven't bowled in, like, years."

"Since you left Ohio?" Luke asked, slightly nastily. He always said Harvey was from a backwater. I kept reminding Luke that he lived in a village with a population around the six thousand mark.

"Yeah, since I left," Xander said, not noticing the undertone, or at least brushing it off. "Jesus, I was younger than these kids."

"You left home at sixteen?"

"Yeah." He shrugged. "Had a bust-up. Don't need to tell you what about."

"Is that when you went to New York?"

He nodded. "It was so rough back then. I wanted to live in Manhattan but I ended up in this revolting place in Queens...took me years to work my way out of there. I cried every night."

"Poor baby. Hey, Xander," I thought of something, "is it true all Manhattan apartments are shoeboxes?"

He shrugged, tugging on the laces of his (or probably, Harvey's) trainers. "Pretty much. Why?"

"Your apartment," Luke said, realising.

"It's really big. And nice."

"That's because it's not really an apartment," Xander winked. "It's a warehouse. And I get a discounted rate anyway."

"How come?"

He smirked. "The guy who owns it is—what's that phrase, Angel?"

"Bent as a nine bob note."

"Yeah. But he doesn't want people to know."

"So he lets you live there really cheap?"

"Not just cheap," Luke said. "Illegal, too, if it's supposed to be warehouse space."

Xander shrugged again, his smile fading. "Doesn't matter now," he said. "I guess it's gone."

I tried to think what I'd feel like if I had to leave my home and everything in it, with no notice. Like being a refugee. It'd kill me.

We went outside, Luke with his arm around me, and I forgot about school and started to feel pretty good. Sharing body heat with a sexy man will do that.

We walked past Marc, Clara and Lucy. Clara looked pissed off that she had to share Marc, but I had a feeling it was Lucy providing the lift home.

How did I ever manage without Ted?

"Are they looking?" I asked Luke quietly. "Are they watching, am I cool?"

Luke suddenly stopped and swung me into his arms and kissed me with cinematic intensity. Randy and Joan never had moments like this.

When he let me go, I was dizzy.

"Wow," I mumbled, and he grinned.

"Now they're watching. Now you're cool."

Is this man the best, or what?

"Exhibitionists," Angel called as she walked off, backwards, after Xander.

"Jealous," Luke called back.

"Of you? Never."

Luke stuck a finger up at her and then used it to stroke the hair from my face.

"Now then, cool girl," he said, "wanna go back to my place?"

I nodded, incapable of speech.

It was the hair that did it.

I tried to slip into the back of the art class as quietly as I could, but everyone turned and looked at me, and I knew they could tell. I was wearing yesterday's clothes, but only Marc and Lucy would be able to tell that. I was wearing minimal makeup—applied in the car—but so were a few of the other girls.

It was my hair—tousled, unbrushed, wiggly from being left in plaits all night, and almost still bearing the imprints of Luke's fingers—and the scent of his deodorant that did it.

I'd have brushed my hair, but all I had was the booby bag which contained my purse, phones and a lipgloss. Besides, those pigtails had done a damn good job on it last night, not to mention Luke's added tousling. No three-second brushing would have made it look tame.

It was pretty clear that I'd spent the night at Luke's place, and pretty clear we hadn't been playing Scrabble.

Lucy was giggling. Marc looked at me with his cool blue eyes, and I couldn't tell what he was thinking.

"Boy, he's going to be mad at you," Lucy whispered, and I looked around for the new teacher as I slunk to an empty bench. I was fifteen minutes late for the lesson and I had no artwork at all. It was all in the back of Ted, who was still sitting in my car park at home. I didn't even have a pencil.

This morning I'd woken in Luke's soft bed, tangled up with him in a hot, gorgeous mess. I stretched out, feeling pretty damn good, and wondered what I had to do today.

And then I remembered.

And then I looked at the clock, and screamed.

Luke's eyes slammed open and he reached for the gun by his bed.

"What?"

"I was supposed to be at school ten minutes ago!" I leapt out of bed, tripping over Luke's leg and landing painfully on my knee. "Ow! Bollocks, shit..."

He dropped the gun on his beside table and looked at me lazily.

"Blow it off," he said.

"Are you nuts? Luke, this is the first time I've been given something like surveillance all by myself. I am not going to screw it up. Now where the *hell* is my underwear?"

I sat there and tried to look composed. This is a look I've been practising my entire life, and I still haven't managed to pull it off. God knows how I got my Drama A level.

"What's he like?" I asked Lucy now in an undertone. She, like everyone else, had her entire portfolio out on the desk and I remembered my induction letter telling me to bring everything to the first lesson for assessment. Which was why I had put it in my car. But Luke had dropped me off this morning and I'd hardly had time to put my knickers on. My feet were killing me because they hadn't been parcelled up properly, and my pretty shoes were grating on the raw patches.

"The new guy?" She shrugged. "He's really cute. And he's really pissed off you weren't here."

Oh God.

I looked up to the little office at the top of the room. So much for me trying to charm him into lending me a pencil and some paper. Not that I felt up to drawing much as it was.

"I'm only fifteen minutes late."

"He's calling Devvo now to see if you've come in. Did you sign the late book?"

I looked at her blankly.

"In the office."

163

"What office?"

"The main one. In A Block."

"I don't even know where A Block is!"

"Down by the Drama Studio..."

"Wouldn't that just make me later?"

She shrugged, grinning. "Like it's supposed to make sense."

The office door opened and a voice said, "No, she's still not—Sophie?"

I stared. I think my mouth fell open.

Lucy nudged me. "Told ya."

Oh, he was cute. He was very cute. But he was also living with my best friend.

The compulsion to yell "Harvey, you wanker, what are you doing here?" overwhelmed me, but somehow I managed to control myself.

"I'm really sorry I'm late," I said, "I overslept..."

"This is only your second day," he said, looking stern.

And it's only your first. "I'm sorry," I began again, and he crooked a finger. Lucy sighed.

"Can you come into my office?"

I got up, and every single eyeball in the large room watched me walk slowly, on sore feet with aching legs (ahem) up to the door at the top of the room. Harvey closed it behind us, then turned to face me.

"Surprise!"

I bashed his arm. "You nearly gave me a heart attack!"

"Likewise." He fingered my tousled hair. "Luke?"

"Is it that obvious?"

He nodded, grinning. "You even smell of him."

"In a good way?"

"I guess."

Cheers. "Didn't you know I was going to be here?"

He nodded. "That's why I was worried. Shapiro's men got in last night—Doyle and Maretti—and they haven't been seen since. When you didn't turn up I panicked... I was about to try your cell."

"I'd have been in a hell of a lot quicker if Luke hadn't hidden my underwear," I said grumpily.

Harvey laughed. "More than I needed to know."

Something occurred to me. "Angel knows about this?" He nodded. "And Xander?" Another nod. "That's why he was laughing. Does Karen know?"

"Yes. She's not too happy. She wanted you to do this on your own."

"Am I right in thinking this is a more direct order?"

"From right across the pond. They think Doyle and Maretti could be after Marc." He glanced out of the little door window at Marc, who was bent over a sketch pad, silent. "What do you think of him?"

I shrugged. "Hard to tell. He's in black again."

"So he knows."

"Or he's just a miserable bastard." I yawned.

"Am I keeping you up?"

I nodded. "Yes. I want to go back to bed."

"Didn't sleep?" Harvey asked, hazel eyes dancing.

"No. Not at all. Bloody Luke."

"I'll remember that next time you two slope off somewhere. Right. Where's your portfolio?"

I bit my lip.

165

"In the back of my car."

"Where is your car?" Harvey asked patiently.

"At the back of my flat."

"You know, I could mark you down for this."

"You're not really a teacher," I reminded him. "And I'm not really a pupil either."

"Yeah, but isn't this fun?"

Was he insane?

"Maybe for you," I said.

"I'd love to go back to high school."

He *was* insane. "We could swap?" I said hopefully.

"Bit late now."

Story of my life.

I borrowed a pencil from Lucy and got some paper from the pile and sat there trying to sketch Marc. But he was elusive, and I always need to warm up, sort of get in practice, before I can make a sketch look anything like its subject. I was relieved when the bell went and I followed him, as subtly as I could, back down to the room below the stage. It was dark in here, the bare bulbs shaded with lighting gels and even one stolen gobo that made the far wall look like a church window. The radio was playing something quiet—unusual, that, because even uncool teenagers like me always played the radio at full volume, no matter who was in the room and what they wanted to say.

Clara was there, and her face lit up at the sight of Marc. She didn't look so pleased to see me, however, and spent the next hour trying her best to ignore me.

Lucy went straight over to Amber and they giggled together for a while, before looking up at me.

"Hey, Sophia," Amber said.

"It's Sophie," I replied.

"Whatever. Weren't you wearing that last night?"

Clara and Marc both looked up at me, as did Laurence, who I'd thought was dozing on one of the ugly props sofas.

"Erm, maybe," I swallowed.

"What—don't you have a washing machine or something?"

"No, I—" Shit, what did I say? In any other company I would say I'd spent the night at my boyfriend's house, why not, I was allowed to. And even though, theoretically speaking, a seventeen-year-old was allowed to too, it would just never happen. Not with parents around. Not on a school night.

"Or didn't you go home?" Marc asked, his piercing eyes on mine. For a second he reminded me of Karen, the same uncompromising stare that made you feel about three inches tall.

Amber pounced on this. "That guy you were with. Luce, didn't you say—"

"You were snogging him outside Maccy D's," Lucy said.

"I saw that too," Clara piped up.

I felt my face get hot. Dammit, why did I have to be a blusher?

"Well, really *he* was snogging *me*," I attempted.

"And then later, was he shagging you, too?" Marc enquired, still cool and impassive, and the sudden thought flashed through me—I don't like you.

"Is that any of your business?" I asked.

"Ooh." Amber made clawing motions with her fingers. "Anyway, I saw him drop you off this morning. In his dad's car."

His dad's car. Luke'd love that.

"It's his car," I said. "He's thirt—" I broke off, wincing, because I should probably have played that down a little more.

They all stared at me, even Marc.

"Dirty old man," Lucy exclaimed.

He's not, I wanted to say, that's only a few years older than me, but "a few" sounded like I was covering up for "a lot". And anyway, to them it was more than a decade. Which *was* kind of a lot.

"What does he do?" Amber asked, fascinated.

"He's, er, he's a PSA," I said, then had to explain. "Passenger Services Agent. At the airport. He's on check in." Well, he used to be. While he was undercover.

"I thought you had to be gay to do that," Laurence said.

"You'd know," Amber flashed back. "Does he get to fly?"

"No. That's cabin crew." And most of them *are* gay.

"How long have you been going out?"

Wow, I was interesting. They wanted to know about me. And suddenly I remembered that when I was at school, the girls with boyfriends in their class were slightly cool, the ones with boyfriends outside school were cooler, and the ones with boyfriends who didn't go to school were subzero.

Like me.

I'm *cool!*

I was enjoying the attention so much I almost didn't want to leave for English. Actually, scrub that, I didn't want to leave at all. But at least the three girls and Marc were going too. Laurence, from what I could tell, didn't go to any classes at all, but spent his whole time sleeping behind the stage.

They commandeered the big table in the centre of the room and I, spying an empty chair and recalling with ferocious effort that it had also been empty yesterday, casually took it. Amber even shared her *Sons & Lovers* with me as we looked up Oedipal quotes.

"So," she said in a low voice, "was it him who called you yesterday? In Drama?"

I hesitated. I'd been telling them mostly the truth, that being much easier to recall than a tangled web of lies, but with certain glaring omissions. Like that I wasn't a seventeen-year-old A level student, for instance. Little things like that.

"Yeah," I said. "He wanted to know if I was going out. He's big on bowling."

"I saw," she said. "He got loads of strikes. I'm not too good."

"Me neither."

"I saw him teasing you. He's really cute," she blurted, and I preened happily.

"Yeah, he is."

At the end of the lesson, we walked out together, and the girls asked each other what they were doing now.

"History," Clara said, looking depressed.

"Free now, but Business Studies fifth," Amber said, and Lucy gave a dispirited nod.

"Marc?" Clara asked.

"I'm done," he said. "I'm off home."

"You drive?" I asked, and he nodded. "What?"

"Corsa," he said, a touch defensively, but I didn't react. A Corsa was a perfectly good car for a seventeen-year-old.

"Where do you live?" I asked hopefully, even though I knew.

"Miles away, past the airport."

My eyes must have lit up, because Amber started laughing.

"Someone wants a lift," she sang.

"Well, I didn't bring my car this morning." I smiled hopefully at Marc. "I live right on the main road..."

Clara was glaring at me but I ignored her.

"And why didn't you bring your car?" Marc asked.

"I, er, didn't go home last night."

"I knew it," Amber breathed.

"Can I please have a lift?" I begged, and Marc shrugged.

"Your boyfriend won't mind?"

"He'll be at work," I said. "And besides," I added belatedly, "he doesn't live at my house, so he won't know, will he?"

Marc took a set of keys out of his pocket. "Come on, then."

His car was behind the gym, where mine had been yesterday. An unremarkable ten-year-old Corsa in an unremarkable shade of blue. I wondered why, if his parents were so damn rich, he was driving a car like this.

Marc was silent as we got in the car, reversed out and waited at the crossing for the kids changing lessons to stream across the road. It couldn't be good, I thought, to have a road like that in the middle of the school. Someone could get hurt.

I frowned. If Shapiro's men turned up, someone probably would.

"So," I said, as we eventually turned onto the main road, "how come you left Longford in the first year?"

"Second year," he said. "My parents split up."

"Oh, I'm sorry," I said. "Do you live with your mum or your dad?"

"Used to be my dad," he said. "I went to boarding school and then over to his place in France in the holidays." France, eh? I'd have to remember that.

"So why'd you come back here?"

"Got chucked out," he said shortly.

"You really set someone on fire?"

A tiny smile tugged at his mouth. "You know that thing where you flick a match on the box and set it on fire midair?" I nodded. I could hardly ever do it right, though. "Well, the match landed on someone."

"Ah."

"A teacher."

"Oops."

"And then I dropped my cigarette on him too..."

"Say no more." *How to put this? So did you move back here because your dad was found floating in the Hudson, or was this a decision made before that?*

I guess Harvey would find that out, but would he share?

But I left it too long, and Marc unexpectedly filled the gap with, "Why did you come here?"

"What? Oh. Closest sixth form to where I live, I suppose..."

"No, why'd you leave your old school?"

Shit, what was my reason?

"Company move," I said. "Dad got relocated." Phew.

"D'you miss your old school?"

I shrugged. "Miss my friends."

"You seemed to have a few last night."

Double shit!

"They're Luke's," I said hastily. "His friends."

"Right," Marc said slowly. "And you met him...when?"

He was testing me, I realised. Dammit. People are always playing me at my own game. What did he suspect? Or was he just bored?

"At the airport," I improvised wildly. "We were flying out to—Antigua, and the flight was horribly delayed. And he was the poor sod who had to hand out LRVs," I said, warming to my subject. This was a job I despised.

"LRVs?" Marc asked.

"Light Refreshment Vouchers." Oops. "For the delay. And people were being really horrible about only getting a voucher, and you could see he was totally out of his depth, it was like his second week or something—he says only newbies get that job—so I said I felt sorry for him, and we got chatting, and...when we came home he was meeting the plane and he remembered me, and we went back to Baggage together and he asked for my phone number..."

Damn, I should be a romantic novelist. It was certainly a hell of a lot better than the way we'd really met. At the airport, yes, but Luke had been undercover as an Italian called Luca and got me into all sorts of trouble before I found out who he really was, got first hired, then seduced by him.

"Like a movie," Marc commented.

"Yeah, it was," I said, thinking "movie" was an American word.

We were in Stansted now, and he slowed down a little. Not too much though. He *was* seventeen.

"Whereabouts are you?" he asked, and I thought, I can't let him see I live in a flat by myself.

"Just pull into the pub car park," I said, pointing. "You can't park outside my house." Besides which, I wasn't sure I wanted him to know I lived there. There was something about Marc that freaked me out.

He let me out and I walked down the hill to my building. I wasn't lying when I said you can't park outside it—well, not really. Docherty once left the Vanquish there, but the traffic flowed around it like people around a beautiful sculpture. The car park is down a narrow lane at the back of the building, and my flat opens onto a little courtyard off this lane. It's nice. I have my own outside door, and in summer I guess I could sunbathe out there, if there were ever any sun. Or have barbecues, if indeed I owned such a piece of equipment.

Tammy was sunning herself in the three-by-five patch of light by the door. She squeaked eagerly at me, obviously hoping I'd feed her. Must be nice being a cat. Eat, sleep, be adored. Don't worry about money or relationships or sex—and if someone starts neglecting you, run off and find someone else.

Actually, that part's not true. Tammy's feeding pattern is somewhat erratic—she wasn't fed this morning, for instance—but she still comes back. Because I tell her how beautiful she is and cuddle her. And then give her tuna and a big bowl of milk.

When I got in there was a note from Luke stuck to the mirror by the door (first and last place I check. Cheeky bugger). *Tammy fed 9.30. How did you get home? L x*

Wow, I merited a kiss.

I hauled out my phone and called him.

"Haven't I been a clever girl?" I said.

"I don't know, have you? More literary discussions?"

"Not quite. I got to sit with the cool kids, though."

"Well done! How?"

By being cool, I almost said, but had to admit, "By turning up fifteen minutes late in yesterday's clothes, smelling of you."

He laughed. "Excellent. Damn, I wish you'd been at my school."

"Would they let a girl within fifty paces of Eton?"

"Not to my recollection. Are you at home?"

"Yes. Marc gave me a lift on his way home."

"Nice one. You talk to him?"

"Yeah, a little bit." I was curious about where he lived, though. "Luke, you fancy going out tonight?"

"More teen thrills?"

"No, just a quiet drink."

I could tell he was suspicious, but he agreed to come with me.

I needed to take a shower—which quickly became a long bath—and eat something, since my insides were hollow, so I arranged to meet him at his place and go out for a drink in Green Roding, which, coincidentally, was where Marc lived.

I drove to the Rodings, of which there are about half a dozen. They're all small hamlets about twenty minutes' drive from me down tiny twisty lanes. These sort of lanes make me sick as a parrot when I'm a passenger, but I'm better in the driving seat, so Luke didn't ask me too many questions. Of course, investigating Marc's house was not an unreasonable thing to want to do, but I couldn't quite think of an explanation as to why I wanted to do it.

The Spotted Dog in Green Roding was the sort of old, low, dark pub that could be smoke free for generations and still be perfumed with Eau de Marlboro. I actually love the smell of old pubs, the smoke and the beer. It reminds me of my childhood, which probably says something about me.

"So how was your day?" Luke asked me cutely as he paid for the drinks.

I shrugged. "The cool kids like me. Well, actually," honesty forced me to admit, "they like you."

He grinned. "Excellent. Always nice to know I'm useful."

We took a table in a far corner. I didn't expect to see anyone I knew here, but then again, anyone at all could be listening in.

"Any news about Doyle and Maretti?"

Luke narrowed his eyes. "How do you know their names?"

"I've been clever again. Is there any news?"

He sipped his Guinness and put it down with a shrug. "None whatsoever. No bodies, no shootings, no attempted hit'n'runs... How's your leg, by the way?"

I shrugged. "No better, no worse. An interesting mixture of shades."

He smirked. "I remember."

"Yes, and did you have to keep squeezing it?" Seeing him grin and lean back in his chair, I lowered my voice. "I was in pain this morning."

"I'll kiss it better later. How did you know about Doyle and Maretti?"

I took my time having a drink. When I put my glass down, I said obliquely, "I met my new art teacher today."

Luke blinked. "That's nice."

"Yes. So is he." I took another sip.

"Sophie..." Luke said warningly.

"He's so nice I was thinking of setting him up with someone. Say, Angel, maybe?"

Luke was quicker on the uptake than I'd ever be.

"You have got to be kidding me," he said, bouncing forwards in his chair.

I shook my head.

"The son of a bitch! I'll bloody skin him."

"Direct orders," I said. "Higher powers."

Luke got out his phone and tapped out a furious text. Then he glared at me.

"This bloody place has no signal."

As if it was my fault.

"That's because it's in a time warp. Luke, don't take it out on Harvey."

"I was texting Karen. You're supposed to be doing this on your own—"

"Yes, and if it wasn't for—" I glanced around "—Harvey's boss, then I would be. He said she's really mad."

"Insane, I should think." Luke thumped his phone down and sat back, fuming.

"Well, look at it this way. Harvey has four classes a week with him. I have twelve. Plus Registrations. Study periods—"

"When you do so much studying," Luke said sarcastically.

"No, I do work, Luke. I already got a lift with him. I asked him about his parents."

"And?"

"Unforthcoming."

"That's not even a word."

"It is in my dictionary. Why are you so bad moody?"

"Pissed off with Harvey. What if someone makes the link between him and Xander?"

"They won't. It'll be okay."

He didn't look convinced.

"I looked up Marc's address," I told him as a distraction. "It's just down the road from here."

"Ah. I did wonder why the change of venue."

"It's called Mont House. I looked it up on Google Earth, it looks pretty big." I frowned.

"And...?"

"Well. Marc was driving a ten-year-old Corsa. Why is he doing that if he lives in a huge house?"

"Maybe it's a huge house that's been subdivided. Maybe he just lives in a normal flat or something."

I shrugged and picked up my drink. "Well, maybe."

Luke cocked his head. "You're not convinced."

"I'm just curious," I protested.

"It's just a car, Sophie."

"Just a car?" I said, voice rising slightly. "Just a car? Luke Sharpe, you know better than to say that to me."

"Sorry," he said, smiling a little.

"Cars are important."

"Of course they are."

"To your identity. Your car says something about you."

"Of course it does." He sipped his drink. "You're not going to get into another Vectra rant, are you?"

I scowled. Just because I understood why Luke was driving such an invisible car, didn't mean I approved of it.

I stabbed the straw into my drink a few times, and Luke watched.

"Sophie."

"Luke."

"Why are we here?"

"I want to go and see why he's driving a Corsa."

Luke paused. Then he said, "What?"

"I mean, he's got to have a better car hiding away somewhere. I want to go and stake out his house."

"Why?"

"Just...humour me."

"Sophie," Luke saluted me with his drink, "I always do."

I'm not sure that's particularly complimentary.

Mont House was set back from the road, up a steep drive it shared with a couple of other expensive residences. Mont was the oldest of them, a lot of the land having been sold off some time in the last half of the last century, leaving the big house with a drastically smaller garden.

It was in this garden that we crouched, half-hidden in the shrubbery, cold and wet from a recent watering by the sprinkler system.

"So why are we here?" Luke whispered, and I shh'd him loudly.

"I want to see his other car."

"What makes you think he'll have another car?"

"He will," I said, and rolled up my sleeves and took off through the shrubbery towards the garage at the back of the house.

It was locked.

"Damn," I said. "Damn and bugger."

"Maybe next time," Luke said, slinging an arm around my waist.

I frowned. "There must be a window or something."

"Yes, because cars flourish in the natural light. Sophie. Someone could see us."

"No, they won't."

"Yes, they will." He pulled me back to him and the sensation was not unpleasant.

"Why are you here if you're not going to spy this out with me?"

"Why?" He nuzzled my neck. "Can't argue with spending some quality time in the bushes..."

I shrugged him off. "Later," I said. "I want to see at least what kind of car his mother's got."

I found a window at the back of the garage, hidden by the fence holding in the rubbish bins. I peeked in and it took my eyes a while to adjust to the gloom inside.

"I can't see anything."

Luke joined me. "Well, that's the Corsa," he pointed to a familiar headlight cluster.

"What's that? Old Beemer?"

We both squinted. "That," Luke said, "is an old 7-Series. And that," he pointed, "is a dead body."

Chapter Nine

We both stared at it for a while.

"This is not good," I said, suddenly feeling rather cold. The more my eyes got used to it, the more I could see, clearly, that it was a man in a suit, lying on his side. I wasn't sure, but I thought there might have been a big dark bloodstain on his back.

"This is really not good," Luke said.

"What do we do?"

He looked at the body again.

"Go," he said.

"What? Why?"

"Because I've just seen a light come on in the house. Go."

I scurried away, towards the bushes, and skirted my way around the garden to the drive, my heart pounding. Where was Luke? He wasn't following me!

God, what if he got caught!

I knew the police couldn't do too much to us, but it surely couldn't be a good thing for us to be caught snooping round someone's garden late at night, especially when there was a body involved.

I made it down to the road and leaned against the wall by the drive, panting, worried, adrenaline pumping through me. I waited one minute, two, my active imagination inventing all sorts of awful things to have happened to Luke.

When he eventually came sauntering down the drive, I launched myself at him.

"Where were you? I was so worried…"

He put his arms around me, sounding puzzled. "I was right where you left me. Mrs. Shapiro came to put some bottles out. Boy, is she a faded glory."

I pulled back and looked at him. "You saw her?"

"Yeah. Pickled. Satin robe, airborne hair, three wine bottles."

"Maybe she had company."

"No lights on. Drinking alone and in the dark."

You had to feel sorry for Marc. Dead gangster father and alcoholic mother.

"Jesus."

"He won't help you." Luke put a hand on my thumping heart which was, conveniently for him, right under my left boob. "But I could think of a way to pass the evening…"

I woke up in the middle of the night, parched, and stumbled to the kitchen for a glass and lots of water. When I came back, I stood in the doorway and looked at Luke for a while, lying there looking unutterably beautiful in the slight light from the street light outside. Still a little bit drunk, I started to wonder why on earth he was in my bed, why he'd chosen me out of all the sleek, sexy girls out there. Why funny old me? Or young, as the case may be—surely I was too young, too curvy, too silly, too useless for a man like Luke?

What did he see in me?

Sighing, feeling sorry for myself without quite knowing why, I crawled back into bed and let Luke enfold me in his arms again. He didn't wake up, just held me.

If I wasn't a spy, would he be with me? Did he love me? *Could* he love me? When we'd first got involved, Maria had warned me the only thing Luke had ever formed an emotional attachment to was his SIG. I'd figured all we'd ever have together would be sex. And yet here he was, cuddling me as he slept, meeting my parents and being nice to my friends.

I guess that made me lucky. I closed my eyes, and tried not to think of it.

Next time I woke up it was to the tuneless twitter of my alarm clock, grabbing me out of sleep at what felt like an unearthly hour.

I looked at the clock. Seven-thirty.

Completely unearthly.

Sighing, I pulled myself upright. At least I was in my own bed this morning. And I had loads of time.

Luke, lying on his stomach beside me, reached out with one hand and slammed the top of the alarm clock with his fist until it shut up.

"Good morning to you too," I said.

"Are you going to school again?"

"Yep. Apparently I didn't learn enough before."

He didn't seem to think this was funny.

Rolling onto his back, he squinted up at me and said, "Soph? Did I dream it or did we find a dead body last night?"

I pulled a face. "God. I'd forgotten."

He rubbed his eyes. "I'm going to have to go and sort that out, aren't I?"

"What do you mean? We just left it there last night." Something occurred to me. "Marc or his mother are going to find it, aren't they?"

"In all probability. Unless one of them put it there."

I stared at him. "You think one of them killed him?"

"It's a possibility."

"He's seventeen!"

"And you were never murderous at seventeen?"

"I never killed anyone. Well, not when I was seventeen," I amended guiltily. I didn't like to think about the shots I'd fired since I joined SO17. I considered them a form of pest control and tried to leave it at that.

Luke swung out of bed, and for a few seconds I was stopped by the beauty of him. Then I shook myself. I should have got over that by now.

"Got any spare bullets?" he asked, pulling clothes on.

"Why? Who are you going to shoot?"

"No one." He chucked me under the chin. "Just protection is all. Whoever got the guy in the garage could still be out there."

This was not a comforting thought, and I almost threw myself at his legs and begged him to stay as he downed some coffee and left. Instead I sipped my own black nectar and silently wished the angels on his side, then told myself off for being so sentimental. Luke was good at what he did. He rarely got shot at.

Generally, that was my job.

I got showered and dressed and fed Tammy, who was always grumpy with me whenever Luke had stayed over, because she wasn't allowed in my room. Well, I didn't want to corrupt her. Then I checked I had everything—billions of books and folders and crap, God knows how I was supposed to carry it all without getting a hernia. Did I have this much to carry when I was at school? Or did I just never bother with most of it?

I just never bothered with most of it.

Harvey had obtained for me a proper copy of my timetable and his extension number in the art department, should I need him. I was due to see him fourth lesson today, after English first and Drama second.

I drove up to school, desperately telling myself that Luke would be okay, he knew what he was doing—even if I didn't—that there was probably a perfectly ordinary explanation for there being a body in the garage of the son of the person who'd been found dead in the apartment of my friend five days ago. My friend, whose identical twin was doing the same job as me. Probably doing surveillance on me. I was never sure whether I could professionally trust Harvey. And as M said, knowing who to trust *is* everything in this business.

How the hell had I survived? I barely even trusted myself.

I walked into Registration and was greeted with a smile from Amber and Lucy. Clara was ignoring me. Marc wasn't there.

Uh-oh.

"Hi," I said, going over.

"Wow, new clothes," Amber teased. "Wet hair...you stayed at home last night, huh?"

"Yes," I said, unable to resist (and wanting an alibi besides), "but not alone."

Their eyes widened. "Don't your parents mind?"

Shit, crap. I forgot I'm supposed to be living with them.

"Oh, it's a big house," I said. "We're at opposite ends." Of the *village*.

Evidently they were impressed, although Devvo wasn't, when he called me over and asked where I'd been yesterday morning.

"Your Art teacher wasn't impressed," he said.

"I overslept," I said. "It won't happen again."

"Next time sign the late book," he said. "Three signatures and you get a warning. Two warnings and you get a detention."

I stared. Not much of an incentive to sign the book then, eh? "You can still put me in detention?"

He nodded.

Jesus. I've faced people with guns who've wanted to kill me or at least maim me, I've been shot at and nearly blown up and threatened with much more violent things, but the thought of detention still scares the shit out of me.

The bell rang and I looked down at the register. "Is Marc not in?"

He shook his head. "If you see him—"

"I'll tell him to sign the—late book." I nearly said "bloody late book", but swiftly judged that it wouldn't be a particularly wise thing to do.

I followed the girls up to English, hanging back and texting Luke that Marc wasn't there. We passed D Block and the Art department, and I so nearly rushed in there to tell Harvey everything. But I contented myself with a text to him, just to tell him Marc wasn't there, and to call Luke if he dared.

Apparently he did dare, because partway through the lesson, with no appreciation for how hard it was to write an essay on Elizabeth Jennings with absolutely no preparation (i.e., reading any of her poems in the last four years), my phone

185

started buzzing in my bag. Pink-faced, I reached in and cancelled the call, but not before I saw that it was Harvey.

Ten minutes later, Luke tried. I cancelled that, too.

I tried to listen to my voice mail on the way down to Drama (helpfully right at the other end of the school, over the road), but I saw the stern-faced head of English coming my way, and swiftly stowed my mobile in my bag. It would *not* do for him to confiscate my phone.

Ha! Although wouldn't I love to see his face when he found out the numbers I had in there!

I itched my way through Drama, desperate to know what Harvey and Luke knew, and when the bell finally rang for break, I raced down behind the stage and hid in the grotty loos until I'd listened to my messages.

"You have...two...new messages." God, could she speak any slower? "Message...One." Before I get old. "Sent...today at Oh. Nine. Hundred. Hours. Twenty. Three. Minutes."

I'd bitten all my nails off now, and was starting on my hand.

"Sophie, it's Harvey. I got your message—what do you know about Marc? Or more to the point, what does Luke know? I'm gonna wait until you call me back before I call him. He never tells me anything anyway. Oh, shit, you're probably in a lesson. Sorry. I'll smooth it over later. Bye."

Smooth it over? How? *Sorry to interrupt, Ms. Wilson, but I had to call one of your students on a private matter.* Yeah, like that wouldn't get the both of us chucked out.

"Message...Two. Sent...today at Oh. Nine. Hundred. Hours. Thirty. Five. Minutes. Soph? You're not going to like this. The body's gone, and so is Marc's car. I called the house phone and no one answered—I couldn't see anyone. You're definitely sure you saw that body too, right? I'm starting to think they're all hallucinations. Anyway. I'm going up to the office. Call me."

I did, straight away.

"What about her car? Was that gone?"

"Yeah."

"'Cos she'd have to have driven over the—" I lowered my voice "—*it* to get it out."

"Which means either she left after it was removed..."

"Or she removed it. Shit."

"Yep. You can't even do decent surveillance outside that house. There's nowhere to park."

"Did you try the pub car park?"

"Yeah. Can't see the road over the wall. Look, I'm going to go back and check in a bit—keep calling them up and stuff. Let me know the second Marc walks in, right?"

"If he walks in," I said gloomily. "Okay, speak to you later."

I emerged, and I must have looked pretty pissed off, because Amber made a gesture of mock fear.

"Boyfriend," I said, and she nodded.

"Yeah. They can be right bastards. Was it him who rang you in English?"

I nodded.

"Twice?"

"He's persistent."

"Yeah."

"I wouldn't mind him being persistent around me," Lucy said wistfully, and I laughed at that, breaking the tension a little.

She walked up to Art with me when the bell rang. "Have you seen Marc today?" I asked.

She shook her head. "Maybe he's ill. You can never tell with him, he's so quiet."

I nodded. "Did you know him? Before—when he was here in the first year?"

She shrugged. "I knew of him. He was Clara's friend. Like they came from the same primary school. I was in a different class. Didn't see much of him. He grew up well though, huh?"

I nodded. "Yep. Great job."

She came with me to fetch my portfolio—now slightly more organised than before—from Ted.

"This your car?"

"Uh-huh."

"It's kinda...kinda big."

"Yeah. Well. So am I."

"How do you park it?"

"Sort of aim for the space between the lines."

Lucy seemed to think this was really funny. "I can't park at all. It's what I'm worst at. Well that and reversing around a corner."

"You're still learning?"

"Yeah. For about seven months."

"Don't worry. It took me a year. And I failed twice."

She was frowning, not the usual hilarious response I get to this. "A year? When's your birthday?"

Shit, this truth stuff is a bad habit. "Right at the beginning of September," I said. "I passed a couple of weeks ago." Shit shit shit.

"Wow. Did you already have the car?"

"Yeah. Been driving my parents around for ages. Well, driving them up the wall, anyway. Hey, look at that, five minutes late already."

We went inside the block and I carried the heavy folder up the stairs.

"I meant to ask you," Lucy said, "what did he want to speak to you about yesterday? Mr. Harvard. He looked well pissed off."

It took me a second to realise what she meant. Harvey. Right. Must remember to *not* call him that.

"I, er, well, that I was late," I said. "And had no work. Hence all this."

"What's your personal study?" Lucy asked, apparently satisfied with this explanation (which was slightly true, anyway).

"Erm." Might as well use what I had. "It's sort of a Dark Ages thing. Haven't really narrowed it down yet." Should I have? I really couldn't remember that far back.

What was wrong with my brain? Was it the Guinness? I kept forgetting stuff. Maybe it was Luke, wiping out some brain cells with every orgasm. Maybe it was stress. Maybe I was getting too blonde.

I heaved my 'folio onto a work bench and plonked myself down on a stool, which was nearly as high as the bench itself and guaranteed to give me backache. Oh well. Backache could take a number. Today and for the last three days I'd been wearing tops with sleeves long enough to cover the massive graze on my arm, which stung constantly in the background. I didn't want to answer questions about it, and I really didn't want anyone, like Doyle or Maretti, to see it and realise who I was.

Speaking of Doyle and Maretti... I tried to catch Harvey's eye but he was talking to a girl about some sculpture work she

189

wanted to do. Maybe he was boning up on art facts from his brother. My phone buzzed in my bag and I thought, if he yells at me for reading a text I'll— Well, I don't know what I'll do, I'll do something to him.

I pulled the phone out. As so often, it was my fancy work Nokia, not my ageing personal Siemens. The text was from Luke and said simply *Call me. NOW.*

Frowning, wondering what could be so important, I picked up my bag, slid from my seat and approached Harvey.

"Sir?"

He looked surprised, then a flicker of amusement crossed his handsome face.

"Can I go to the toilet?"

He looked puzzled as to why I was asking, but he nodded and waved me off to the door. Men never ask questions about girls and toilets, because they don't want to get involved in any nasty women's problems debate.

I found the girls loos around the corner—graffiti'd and smelling of many things, of which cigarette smoke was about the most pleasant. Ah, schooldays. I checked under the doors of all the cubicles, then called Luke.

"What's so urgent? I'm in the middle of an art class."

"I'm sure Harvey won't mind."

"Yes, but my sketching is suffering. What's happening?"

"You know the police radio I have?" Stupidly, I nodded. "Well. I heard something very interesting ten minutes ago. A body has been found. In the woods outside Green Roding. Not a very long way from Marc's house."

"Eep."

"Er, yes. And it's a male body, in a suit, dead for at least a day."

190

"Uh-oh."

"And what I'm thinking is, we go out there and have a look."

"They'll let us in?"

"Do you have your ID?"

"Of course."

"Then they'll let us in." He told me where the body was and told me to get there ASAP.

I signed off, trying to think of a way to get out of this. No. I had to go and see the body. I had a rather nasty suspicion I might know whose the body was.

Which left me with trying to think of an excuse to get out of class. Thank God it was Harvey, and not a real teacher.

I drummed my fingers on the edge of a sink, then looked at the sink and washed my hands. There was nothing to dry them on—at least, nothing that wouldn't merit a second bathing in, say, bleach—so I stood there with wet hands for a bit.

Then someone came in, and I darted into one of the cubicles.

"Sophie?"

Christ, it was Lucy.

"I, uh—" Perfect excuse. "I'm really not feeling too well. I think I ought to go home."

"Oh." She sounded surprised. "You looked okay..."

"Well, it's sort of come on suddenly. I think if I go back in there I might be sick. Could you—could you go back there and tell Harv—Mr. Harvard I really feel bad. I think I should go home."

"Can you drive?"

I ground my teeth. "I'll be fine. I don't live far."

I waited in silence for her reply.

"Well, okay then." She sounded reluctant. "Hope you feel better."

As soon as she was gone, I dashed out and in the opposite direction, out of the building and round to Ted. I jumped in and off we went, making it to Green Roding in far less time than was legally possible.

The great advantage of a car like Ted is that if you have to rumble off over a field to look at a body or whatnot, he takes to it perfectly happily. No worrying about scratching paint work or anything. It's already pretty scratched.

I pulled up on the edge of the little wood, where a couple of police four-by-fours were parked up, and a young copper was stringing stripy tape around the trees. I could see Luke leaning against one of the cars, talking to a guy in a white coat.

The young copper tapped on my window. "I'm afraid you'll have to move on, miss," he said. "This is a crime scene."

"Duh," I said, opening the door. "That's why I'm here." I showed him my ID (I love doing that) and went over to Luke.

"Took your time," he said.

"Had to get out of class. So," I looked at the copper in the white coat, "what's going on?"

"Who are you?"

"She's with me," Luke said, and I couldn't help a smug little smile.

"Woman with her dog found him," the copper said. "About half an hour ago. Doesn't look like he was killed here—there's no blood around and he's not lying right. Must have been left somewhere else while he stiffened up."

And I know where, I thought. "Do you have an ID on him yet?"

He shook his head. "No wallet or anything."

"Can I see?"

"Be my guest."

"Sophie—" Luke caught my shoulder as I made my way over to the steep bank, at the bottom of which was a cluster of people and a police photographer taking pictures.

"What?"

"Do you remember last time you saw a body?"

How could I forget?

"You nearly passed out."

"That's because it was on my sofa. Besides, I think I have an idea of who it is."

"Who?"

I shook my head and made my way down the steep slope. The body was now on its back, one arm broken at a grotesque angle, and the shiny suit was muddy and torn. My guess was it had been rolled down the bank, quite some time after death as the pathologist had suggested, and although I couldn't be sure that the arm hadn't been broken in the garage, I was pretty certain it wasn't normal for people to die with their arms stuck up in the air.

"...must have been on his side for quite a while," one of the policemen was saying. "Look at that arm."

Ha! One step ahead.

"And what's that stuff on his side?" asked another. "Petrol?"

I made a mental note to check Marc's car for petrol leaks.

As I got closer, I felt a shudder run through me, and it wasn't just because this body was dead. It was because last time I'd seen it, it had been pointing a gun at me and firing.

Chapter Ten

"Frank Doyle," Karen said, slapping a grainy file photo down on the desk.

"That's him."

"Well, well. Made it here and got a knife in his back."

"What kind of knife?"

"Don't know, haven't got the path lab reports back yet. We'll know tomorrow. You haven't seen anything of this character, have you?" She put another photo on the desk.

I looked at him. "Is this Maretti? I saw him in New York. I think he was driving the car that hit me."

Karen nodded and sat back down at her desk. "Chances are he's dead too. Luke, keep monitoring those channels."

Luke, leaning against the wall with his arms folded, nodded.

"In the meantime, we need to find where our friend Marc has got to."

"We checked his house on the way back," I said. "No one there."

"Maybe they ran away," Luke said idly.

"I've checked with the office in Dunmow where Shirley Shapiro works," Karen said. "She's there."

"Did you ask her about Marc?"

"How could I, without alarming her? Oh, and Sophie, what was the car that hit you?"

I stared at her, nonplussed. "Big. American. Hard. Why?"

"I've been checking Manhattan police records. When they found Shapiro's body they also found a Crown Victoria, registered to Mario Maretti."

"In the water?"

She nodded. "It had a rather fetching Sophie-shaped dent in the front bumper."

Luke laughed. I made a face. "Could have been made when it went in the river," I said.

"Not if it was Sophie-shaped," Luke said. "Mmm. Bet it was curvy."

"Shut up," I said. "I don't suppose there'll be any skin traces on it or anything?"

"No. Not any more. But trying to prosecute Maretti for a hit and run would be hard enough if he was in the country. Don Shapiro's men are a set apart from the police."

"Plus, he's probably both out of the country—" I began.

"And dead," Luke finished.

"We can only hope."

Luke stayed to look up some contacts for Maria, who was still in Spain, and I drove home alone. My phone started ringing when I was halfway there. Ignoring safety protocol, I answered it, driving with one hand.

"Harvey?"

"Are you okay? Lucy came in and said you were going home... All your stuff's still here."

"It's only artwork. And barely that. I'm okay, I just got a call from Luke, there was something I had to do."

"Are you gonna tell me what?"

There was a note of concern in his voice, and I forgot that I was professionally mad with him. "Yeah. Remember Shapiro's friends? Doyle and Maretti?"

"Uh-huh."

"Well, it seems all we have to worry about is Maretti."

There was a pause. "This cannot be good," Harvey said.

"Nope."

But when I got home there was more bad news waiting for me. Docherty was leaning against my front door, looking like sin, catching the rays of the sun on his high cheekbones. Well, fancy that. He doesn't combust in sunlight.

"What are you doing here?" I said, rummaging in my bag for my keys.

"Got news for you."

"Oh, goody. But I meant out here. Usually you just let yourself in."

"Felt like being polite."

That must be a new sensation.

I found my keys and Docherty followed me into the chaos of my little flat. It's not that I'm untidy, it's just that... Okay, I'm untidy. There's always stuff everywhere, usually covered with a fine patina of dust and cat hair. I flipped some laundry (clean) off the sofa and gestured for Docherty to sit down.

"Tell," I said.

"Firstly, did I hear that one of your pursuers has been found?"

"You mean Doyle? Yeah. Just goes to show, if you work for the mob you'll get stabbed in the back."

"Shapiro wasn't a mobster," Docherty said, calmly ignoring my bad joke. "He wanted to be, but he'd never have made it. Really he only had those two to call his mob."

"So I don't have to worry about a dozen irate Americans trying to kill me," I said, rolling my shoulders to try and get rid of the art room backache, not to mention the tension Docherty induced in me. "That's always nice to know." I frowned. "I'm still not very sure on why they were trying to kill me."

"Possibly it's something to do with you seeing the body," Docherty said dryly, and I wondered, not for the first time, where he got his information from. "It's that I wanted to talk to you about."

"Are you my counsellor now?"

Why was I being so scratchy? The body? Or was it Docherty? At the back of my mind I remembered his threat about the apology. I thought I had a good idea of what he wanted, but with Docherty you could never be sure.

Besides, that's a hundred and fifty grand car I'm paying off. Whatever terms he's working on, I can't afford them.

"Be nice, or I won't tell you," Docherty said. "I found out what killed Shapiro."

"I was going to go with the slit in his throat. But maybe that's too obvious."

"Yeah," Docherty said, "too obvious."

He held my gaze for a while. Eventually I said, "Okay, so what did kill him?"

"It was probably the knife that did it," Docherty conceded, "but there was also the matter of the bullet in his back."

I blinked. "Xander didn't mention that."

"Ah, yes. Xander. Your American friend. In whose apartment the body was found?"

"Well, so he says." I started pacing. "It had gone when I got there. Are you saying he was shot before his throat was slit?"

"Either before or after. It's impossible to tell."

"Wait—how do you know this?"

He smiled. "I have contacts."

Of course he did. Everyone had bloody contacts.

"But that's not the best part," Docherty said. "The best part is, they found the gun that shot him. Right there in Xander's apartment, under a pile of canvasses."

"Good. Do they know whose it is?"

He gave me a steady look. "Yes. Xander's."

Docherty didn't stay long after he'd dropped his bombshell. I wondered if Xander knew. Or Harvey. Or anyone else.

I wondered why Docherty had told me.

I sat around for a while, feeling scratchy. It was still only early afternoon—school wouldn't be out yet.

I made a decision and put some books in my bag, then put my bag in the car. I got in too, to keep the bag company, and together we set off for Mont House.

I was feeling icky about Marc. A body turned up in his garage, then vanished, and was found later just down the road. And Marc hadn't been seen all day.

Just like in New York.

I pulled up his steep drive and parked outside the house. It looked dull, no movement behind the windows. No TV. I rang the doorbell and waited.

And waited.

A is for Apple

I rang a couple more times, my alibi in my bag. Still nothing.

Oh well. Nothing ventured, nothing gained.

Ted and I motored back the way we'd come and further, up towards Ugley and Angel's church. I didn't know if she'd be in, but I was pretty sure Xander would be there.

Outside her door a gargoyle peered at me, and something inside its gaping mouth whirred and clicked. The door opened, and Xander looked out at me nervously, his hair still shocking, although it had faded to an ugly khaki now.

"Hey."

"Hey," I said brightly. "Can I come in?"

He pulled the door back. "Sure. Are you on your own?"

"Yep. Luke's working."

"Oh." He went over to one of the sofas in the nave and collapsed, looking boneless.

Well, that's not exactly true. He didn't look boneless so much as bony. Skinny.

"Have you lost weight?"

He shrugged and lit up a cigarette. "I guess. Kind of. Maybe." He looked up at me. "Not on purpose. Angel's always cooking but I..."

"Not hungry?"

He nodded. "Yeah."

Bastard. Whenever I was shocked or depressed I made a beeline for the fattiest, sugariest food there was, and hoovered up the calories.

"Does Angel mind you smoking here?" I asked.

He shrugged again. "She has air fresheners all over."

That wasn't really an answer.

"Xander," I began, about to tell him about the gun, but right at that exact moment Angel walked in, looking beautiful, carrying some shopping bags.

"Sophie! What are you doing here?"

"Came to see Xander. When's Harvey coming home?"

"I think three-thirty." She checked her watch. "Not long now." She sorted through her bags and chucked a couple at Xander, who looked inside, then up at her with an expression of joy.

"These are really French Connection?"

"Of course. Although over here we have FCUK. Far funnier."

Xander pulled out a couple of slogan T-shirts. "Cool as FCUK" and "I'm not perfect...But there are parts of me that are FCUKing excellent."

"Oh, I love this," he held up "FCUK, feel the swell".

"Very cute." I had a couple of Franglais T-shirts from there myself.

"This is excellent. They had some in Bloomies, but not like this. And jeans! Angel, you're an—well—"

"I know," she said, resigned to the joke. "I'm a seraph. Anyway. Sophie—how's school?"

I made a face. "School's hard."

"Is Harvey behaving himself?"

"He's very convincing."

"I've been tutoring him," Xander said proudly.

"Xander," I broke in, hating to interrupt his admiration of his new clothes. "Did you hear about the body?"

His face fell. "What body? My apartment body?"

"Yes—well, actually..."

I told him about Shapiro being found on Sunday, which he already knew, and then about Doyle, which he didn't. Angel messed around in the background, putting away her new clothes, coming out and showing us some shoes, making up some cake mixture. I wanted to live with Angel. She was such a good *wife*. And she took the whole SO17 thing completely in her little stride. You didn't have to pretend with her.

"Does Harvey know?" she asked as I told Xander about Doyle.

"Yes. Well, sort of. Not in detail. Not with, you know, visuals."

"Maybe he could paint it," Xander said.

"And there was one more thing. Until we get this sorted out you're going to have to keep a very low profile," I said.

"Why?"

"Because they found a bullet in Shapiro. And it came from your gun. Which has bits of his blood on it."

Angel put down her wooden spoon and stared. I knew how she felt.

"But—I didn't—I never used the gun—in fact, I kept it in a drawer by my bed," Xander stammered.

"So why was it under the sofa? In Shapiro's blood?"

He did a dramatic palms-up. "I don't know! I was really stoned that night."

I sighed. Angel sighed.

"Maybe you should keep off the grass while you're here," she said.

"Like I could get any."

There was silence for a bit, broken by my phone ringing. It was my Siemens, and the number on it was my parents' house.

"Hola?"

"Hello, love." My mother. "Listen, I'm just off to Tesco's, is there anything you'd like me to get?"

I thought about this for a while. "You do know I don't live with you any more, right?"

"But you're coming for tea."

"Am I?"

"Didn't you get Charlie's message?"

"Apparently not. What are you having?"

"Tuna steak. And those little Celavita potaoes..."

Oh. So that was it. "Mum, do you want me to cook the tuna?"

There was a pause. "Well, you know you always do it better than me..."

This was true. I am, by and large, not the world's greatest cook, but I do damn good tuna.

"See if Luke wants to come," she offered eagerly.

"I think he might be working."

"Oh." She sounded disappointed. "Well, ask him anyway. Do you want to come over about seven?"

Luke still hadn't called. I suspected that whatever Maria needed from him was going to take a while.

"Okay," I said. "I'll call you if there's any change."

I ended the call and looked at Angel and Xander.

"Hours to kill," I said.

"Where's Luke?"

Honestly, was I not a separate entity any more?

"He's got some stuff to do," I said. "Do you want me to go?"

I gave Angel my puppy eyes. The scent of chocolate cake was gorgeous, and her sofa was really comfy, and her TV was really big, and look, there were all these *Buffy* DVDs just piled up next to it.

"Which series?" she asked, and I beamed.

I sent Luke a couple of texts, which he replied to halfheartedly. One appeared to be in Russian. I had a feeling he wasn't going to be up for tea with my parents.

At six forty-five, I picked myself up and stretched. "Bye bye, Spike." I waved to him on screen, and he gave me a smouldering look. "Mmm. See you guys later," I addressed the real occupants of the room, who waved goodbye as I got in Ted and drove back to Stansted and through to my parents' house.

"Isn't Luke coming?" Mum asked as I went in, and I started to feel a bit annoyed.

"No. He's working. He has his own life. Working. We don't go everywhere together."

She looked slightly taken aback. "Okay, all right. I just wondered."

"Why are you so desperate to see him?"

"He's nice. He likes you."

I should hope so, he was sleeping with me.

I cooked the tuna, incinerating Mum's and leaving mine slightly rare, as always, and we ate outside. Chalker was out with whatever girl he was currently seeing, so the three of us sat and bickered pleasantly about airport expansion (my family is one of those where, even when we all agree on a subject, we can still argue about it for hours) until it got cold and dark and Mum went to bed. Dad and I sat out for a while, listening to music coming from the neighbours. There was a bottle of wine on the table and I really fancied a glass, but I had to drive home some time and I'd rather do it now than in the morning. Besides, I'd got rat-arsed last night after we'd found the body.

"Okay," Dad said after a while. "I'm going to bed. Are you stopping out here?"

"I think I might," I said. "If that's okay."

He smiled, looking surprised. "Of course it is. Just lock the doors when you go, and drive safely. Unless you want to stay...?"

I shook my head, although the prospect was tempting. "Got overtime tomorrow," I lied, wondering how long I could go on bullshitting my parents, who could always see through whatever imaginative excuses I came up with as a child.

After Dad had gone I sat for a while, enjoying the silence that followed the neighbours' retreat to their beds. The house backed onto farmland and the air was very still and quiet. I shivered into the jumper Mum had lent me and wondered how long I'd stay out here, in the dark, looking at the net of fairy lights I'd put up years ago over the patio, now shining like little golden stars against the dark sky.

Don Shapiro was dead, and so was Frank Doyle, one of his henchmen. I fully expected Mario Maretti's body to turn up soon, and I wouldn't be at all surprised if it turned up somewhere near me.

Oh well. At least with those two out of the picture I might be a little safer. Although whoever was killing them might want me, too.

It's an odd thing, to know that someone wants you dead. All at the same time it's horribly, horribly scary, yet you know with the same conviction that the sun will rise, that you'll be okay.

I don't know what time it was that I heard the car pull up outside the house. Assuming it was Chalker, I stayed where I was and poured out more water, looking out at the dark, dappled oak tree that stood at the edge of the garden and wondering if I might ever be as stable and magnificent.

No. Probably not.

And then I heard a voice calling out my name, and I looked up, frowning. "Luke?"

He came to the back door and stood there, looking beat. "Hey. You're still here."

"Looks like it."

He came over and pulled me to my feet to kiss me, long and slow, before falling onto the bench under the lights and taking me with him. I think it was supposed to be romantic, but I didn't want to squash him so I reeled back and let myself hit the bench in a different spot.

Luke pulled me closer. Oh, well, I couldn't really complain.

"I went to your house," he said. "Thought I'd wait a while for you."

"I did tell you I'd be here."

"Yeah. I remembered eventually."

I was touched he'd come up here to see me.

"Long day?"

He nodded. "Doyle seems like yesterday."

"What did Maria want?"

He pulled a face. "First a contact with the Russian embassy. And then a translator... I don't know *what* she's pulling out there."

"She's still in Spain?"

"I assume so. Did Karen tell you the happy news?"

"On which subject?"

"Xander's gun shot Shapiro."

"Oh. Yes. I know." I wasn't going to tell him how I knew. Somehow it didn't seem right. "I saw him this afternoon."

"And?"

"And he says he never left the gun under the sofa."

"He said he was really out of it. He could have shot Shapiro without remembering."

"And slit his throat? Then called Harvey and not remember any of it? I don't think anyone could be that stoned."

"You ever try it?" Luke asked.

"I'm a good girl, me."

"Hmm."

He had his arm around me, slouched down on the bench, and I could feel exhaustion leaking from him. He didn't look like he could stand up, let alone drive home.

"Luke?" I said.

"Mmm?"

"Do you want me to drive back?"

"What about my car?"

"I could drive that."

Mild horror burnt through his weariness. "You hate my car."

"You're too tired to drive. Look at you. Your eyes are closed."

"Resting them."

"You need to sleep. How long were you talking Russian?"

He shrugged and yawned an "I dunno." He pulled me closer, like I was a giant teddy bear, and rested his head on mine. And while I knew we couldn't stay out there all night, I didn't want to wake him.

It must have been the cold that eventually did it. I think I was dozing, stiff and chilly, but Luke suddenly jolted awake, pulling me with him.

"What the—" he looked at his watch. "It's half past one!"

Wow. I didn't think we'd been there that long.

"Home," he said, pushing me away and getting to his feet. I looked up at him, and the sudden thought flashed through my mind—I am home.

"We could stay here," I said.

"At your parents' house?"

"Yeah. They won't mind. Besides, half the school thinks you stay here all the time anyway."

"You still have to go in tomorrow."

"I only have double Drama tomorrow, and it's third and fourth. I could go in late."

"Missing Marc, if he's there..."

"Okay, all right." I stood up. "We'll go home and not sleep all night."

Luke was looking at me oddly.

"What?"

"You looked just like your mother then," he said, and I narrowed my eyes. "And again."

"Okay, you're driving yourself to your place and I'm going home to mine—"

"Soph," Luke laughed, "I like your mother. We could stay here. It'd be cool."

In theory I wanted to protest. In practice I was really tired. So I led him in and locked all the doors, told him he'd have to use my toothbrush or go without, and fell into bed in my underwear. Again.

In the morning my phone alarm woke me, and I was confused for a while—parents' house, single bed, and Luke—until I remembered what was going on.

"Come on." I nudged him. "We have to go. Or at least I do."

"Mmm," he said sleepily.

"Are you going to stay here?"

"Maybe I will."

I got up and pulled on my clothes, figuring I'd go home and take a shower there. Luke remained where he was, facedown, watching me through a half-closed eye.

"You're really staying?"

"Would they mind?"

I thought about it. "So long as you put some clothes on, probably not. Be nice and don't drink all the coffee."

"I wouldn't. Soph." He caught my hand with a lightning reflex that was far too fast for someone so sleepy.

"What?"

"I like your family."

I blinked at him. My own reflexes, physical or mental, weren't so sharp.

"Me too."

"Good." He let go of me and closed his eye again. "Later."

What a strange man.

I gave my mother a surprise when I met her in the kitchen, foraging for quick coffee to make sure I didn't fall asleep on the short drive home.

"Oh," I added when I was on my way out, "and Luke's upstairs."

I didn't stay to hear her reaction.

I went home and made myself presentable, fed Tammy and checked my bag. Then I set off for school, desperately tempted to go down the road and see if Marc was there. Or if there were any more dead bodies hanging around.

I like your family. Was this his way of telling me he'd be sticking around? Was this why my stomach felt unsettled? Because something I'd never really expected to come to pass was actually happening?

Or was it just the prospect of finding Mario Maretti?

In Registration the girls and Laurence were talking about the body. Marc, to my relief, was there, hardly contributing to the conversation while everyone talked over his pretty little head.

"Hey." I waved. "I heard."

"You and the rest of the country."

"Well. National press and all that. Did you see it?"

He shook his head.

It could be that this really was totally innocent. That he had no idea there'd been a dead body in his garage. It could be that Mrs. Shapiro was the one in charge of that. Or maybe neither of them knew.

The bell rang for first period and people peeled off. Marc headed down in the direction of the Drama Studio, but turned off and went into the library instead. I was impressed. This place was big and old, with massive oak tables and shelves of impressive books that the students probably weren't allowed to look at.

"Hey," he turned to me at the door, "are you following me?"

What an astute boy he was.

"I—well, no, I wanted to get some books out. For English." I tried to sound casual. "We're supposed to be reading other works by Hardy, by the way. I don't know if anyone gave you the work from yesterday..."

He nodded. "Clara called me."

Of course she did.

"Where were you?"

"Ill."

"Was it that stomach bug that's been going around? My brother had that." Maybe I had it. No wait, I'd just invented it. Damn.

"Yeah. Something like it. I'm okay now."

It was like talking to a brick wall. He was giving me nothing.

"Okay." I browsed for a while, watching as he got his *Tess of the d'Urbervilles* out and started to make notes from it. I wasn't going to get anything from him today.

But there might be something I could get from his mother.

I went out, sneaked up to my car, and miraculously drove off without anyone noticing. No wonder so many kids play truant. It wasn't exactly hard.

The garage at Mont House was open and Mrs. Shapiro's ageing Beemer was parked within, badly. I went up to the door and tried my hardest to look seventeen. Or, I guess, eighteen, now I'd told Lucy I was older.

The woman who answered the door was, as Luke had said, a faded glory. Fag in hand, bright childlike makeup seeping into the crinkles of her face, which looked like the After picture in a feature on cosmetic surgery gone wrong. Her mouth was lopsided, puckered with smoking wrinkles, her skin was thin and crêpey and her eyes drooped. Her hair was like straw.

I tried not to shudder.

"Hi," I gave her my best I'm-not-a-threat smile, "is Marc in?"

She frowned. "Marc's at school."

"Oh. Right. It's just he wasn't in yesterday and I thought I'd come by and see if he wanted any of the catch-up work."

She eyed me with suspicion. "Who are you?"

"Oh! Silly me. I'm Sophie. I'm in some of Marc's classes."

"The one who follows him everywhere."

So she'd heard of me, then.

"Yeah. Well. We have a lot in common. So he's back at school today, then?"

She nodded. "Twenty-four hour bug."

And why aren't you at work? I wanted to ask. *Why are you at home?*

"It's just," I was repeating myself here, "I heard about the, you know, the body, and I wondered if he was okay. It was pretty close to here, wasn't it?"

I was being ridiculously perky, and she knew it.

"Down the road," she said. "It traumatised me. I've had to take the day off."

"Ah. I see. Is that your car?" I pointed to where it wasn't visible from the house. Dammit. "It's great. I love BMWs."

"Yeah. Bought when times were better."

So she'd come out of the divorce badly.

"I heard about Marc's dad," I said. "I'm really—"

"How did you hear?" Mrs. Shapiro asked sharply.

"It was on the news." Seventeen-year-olds don't watch news. "My boyfriend watches the news all the time."

"Your boyfriend, huh?" She slouched against the doorframe. "Is he cute?"

As cute as a lion. Luke was many things, but cute wasn't one of them. "Yeah. Yeah, he is."

"Is he rich?"

"I—" I'd never thought about it. He owned his own home. "He's okay," I said. And his family must have been rich, to send him to Eton like that.

"Well, you won't get a penny out of him," Mrs. Shapiro said with satisfaction. "He'll string you along while you're still pretty—" ooh, preen, preen, "—but when the surgery he wanted you to have goes wrong and you're not a doll any more, then he'll drop you and get his lawyers in and take everything you've got. Even your son."

There was so much bitterness in that I took a step back.

"I'll bear that in mind," I said faintly.

"I tell you what," she said fiercely, "I'm bloody glad they found him in the river. Someone had the guts to get rid of him."

"Who do you think it was?"

"Someone braver than me," she said, and slammed the door on me.

Blimey.

I got back in Ted and sat there for a while, thinking. So Don Shapiro had married Shirley when she was young and pretty, got her tarted up, and dumped her when the surgery went wrong. As so often. She came out of the divorce with nothing, not even Marc, who by then had been packaged off to boarding school and, by his own admission, spent most of his free time with his dad. He hardly saw his mum.

And now, with Don dead, she was saddled with him. A teenager about whom she probably knew nothing. She didn't have much money, no looks to speak of, and now this kid. And even if she'd wanted him back then—I couldn't tell—it still must have been a shock to her.

But Marc was set to enroll at Longford before Shapiro's body was found. So this must have been an arrangement made before she knew he was dead.

Unless she'd killed him, and it was possible. Certainly the motive was there. It was just that I couldn't really see Shirley Shapiro doing anything more violent than opening a bottle of wine. She seemed to have sunk down into her troubles.

Either way, I found myself putting the car in gear and going up to the office, where I booted up the computer and started checking airline records for Shirley's name.

But she hadn't been to New York in the last three months. One flight to Alicante with Ace Airlines—low cost, cheap sun—in July. With a large group that had Singles Holiday written all over it.

I checked Don Shapiro's name too, just for the hell of it. No. He'd been in New York since April. They hadn't been near each other.

It was possible she'd hired someone to kill him, but not very possible.

Karen came out of her office and looked surprised to see me.

"Aren't you supposed to be at school?"

I checked my watch. "I don't have a lesson for half an hour."

"You sound like my children. You're supposed to be watching Marc Shapiro."

"I watched him make notes for twenty minutes. He thinks I'm following him. I went to see his mother."

"And?"

"Zip. Zilch. Nada. She's far too sorry for herself to have done something like kill her ex husband."

Karen sat down on the edge of my desk. "Do you have any idea who it might be?"

I shrugged. "Could have been Maretti or Doyle. But then Doyle is gone too, so I guess it could be Maretti. They came to England for a reason, and I guess..."

"What?"

"Well, they could be here to kill Marc. Or to stop him."

"You think it's Marc? He's seventeen."

"Hey, I don't know about you, but I was a vicious little bugger when I was seventeen." I sighed. "I don't think it's Marc."

"Why not?"

"He's just too..." I waved my hand, looking for the word and coming up with, "...laconic. Apathetic. That's the one I wanted."

"You think he doesn't care? Have you talked to him?"

"Tried. He's not a big talker."

Karen nodded slowly, her eyes serious. "Sophie, did it occur to you that the police might have the right idea?"

I snorted. "Never."

"About Xander? He could have killed Shapiro."

"And then Doyle, too? No. He's been at Angel's the whole time."

"Even when she and Harvey are out?" She shook her head. "You said he imagined Shapiro's body in his apartment because he was stoned. Could he have been stoned enough to have killed Shapiro and not realised?"

"Have you been talking to Luke?"

She smiled. "I know Luke doesn't like that family much. It's just a thought."

"Yeah. But I don't think Xander did that."

"Why? Gay men aren't killers?"

"Not this one. It'd mess up his commission," I joked.

"Shapiro still owed him money?"

I sighed. "About three thousand, English." I was proud of myself for working this out.

"Well, that's a motive."

"Another person with a motive. I'd lay money it wasn't Xander."

Karen stood up and gave me one of her trademark piercing looks. "Because of a personal feeling?"

I nodded.

"Sophie." She sighed suddenly, and I had a bad feeling about what was coming next. "I know your personal feelings have sometimes been a bonus, hunches often are, but do you remember Docherty? He still bears scars from your last hunch."

I didn't need reminding.

"You mustn't let personal feelings cloud your judgment," she said, looking straight at me. "Or get in your way."

Idly I wondered if she was warning me off personal relationships while I was working. Then I straightened. I was *in* a personal relationship. "Are you talking about Luke?"

"Which is more important to you, Sophie? Your job, or your boyfriend?"

I knew what the professional answer should be. But, hideously, I found myself agreeing with it. "My job," I said, and I must have sounded surprised, because she broke eye contact and laughed.

215

"Well done. Luke didn't sound so convincing last night."

"He didn't?" He thought I was more important? But Luke loved his job.

Uh-oh.

Chapter Eleven

I got back in time for Drama, and didn't seem to have been missed. The two hour lesson kicked off with some daft games for "warm-up" (trans: no lesson plan) and then we worked through scenes from *A Doll's House*. This was mildly amusing, since between the fifteen people in the class there were about five different translations of the text, so that a reading went something like:

Helmer. And what's in that parcel?

Nora: No.

Helmer. Tell me, my little spendthrift, what do you want for Christmas?

Nora: You know, Torvald, you don't have to buy me anything for Christmas.

Helmer. Oh, yes, you do. Now tell me, what would you really like?

Nora. It's not a problem.

Amber was reading Nora, and she read her well—sweet and girlish and petulant and, to my mind, bloody annoying. I fully believed that she could twist her husband into giving her whatever she wanted, and Dr. Rank too, and she'd do it so prettily no one would ever suspect they'd been had.

Frequently there were patches where someone would say, "What do you think, Christine?" And Clara, reading Christine (now spelt Kristin) would look blank and say, "It's Rank's line."

So the first hour passed reasonably quickly, while I wondered if Ibsen made any more sense when it was properly translated. I suspected not.

The unintentional hilarity helped keep my mind off what Karen had said. And off the squirly feeling in my stomach. And off the looming sense of dread that I somehow didn't think was remotely connected with the case.

When exactly did I start ranking my job above my love life? And when did Luke stop?

The bell went for fourth period and we all stayed where we were, sprawled in a ragged circle on the Drama Studio's black floor. Uncle Todd (it was catching) went off to get some photocopies done and the class stretched out and started talking amongst themselves. Lucy, Amber and Clara were huddled together like three witches, occasionally shooting terribly unsubtle glances in my direction. Occasionally Clara would put her hand up and whisper behind it while looking right at me. Five-year-old behaviour.

No, that was unfair. More like four-year-old.

I turned to Laurence, who was looking through his book, a bored expression on his skinny face. He wore narrow-framed glasses and he was very thin. If you put him in contacts and white Lycra he'd be a dead ringer for Freddie Mercury.

"Not very subtle, are they?"

"Three witches? Nah. Not very."

Pleased he'd thought of the same analogy as me, I pressed on. "Were you in a class with them? Before sixth form?"

He nodded. "With Clara. And Marc, in the first year."

"Were you friends then?"

"Not really. He was a bit of a rich kid, you know? Hung out with his own crowd. I guess I filled his place."

"But he was friends with Clara?"

Laurence looked at me sharply.

"Lucy said. And you can tell she has the hots for him."

"What, you mean Lucy?"

"Clara."

"Oh. Yeah." He relaxed. Someone fancies Lucy, I thought. "They hung out loads. They knew each other from primary school. And then last year he came back from boarding school early and met up with Amber in town and they all got friendly."

"With Amber? She was friends with him before?"

"No—well, sort of. Clara and Luce and Amber have always been in a sort of clique. They live near each other, or used to, anyway..."

I was really confused now. "But they met up with Marc last year?"

"Yeah. Well, last school year. After he got chucked out. Amber probably wasn't that bothered, but then he said his dad was living in New York and we could all go out there and see him... I didn't think anything would come of it, but the girls got really excited and got some last minute cheap flights and all went out there."

Woah.

"When was this?" I asked, as casually as I could, and got another sharp look. "It's just, I was in New York this summer. With my dad. On business."

"Wish my dad took me on business trips with him," Laurence said bitterly. "It was August, I think."

"Oh. I wasn't there then. Did you go?"

He shook his head. "Even a cheap flight's expensive."

Uncle Todd came back in the room then, so I turned away from Laurence and pretended to be reading the play.

Clara and Marc used to be friends, way back. Now Clara fancied Marc, but he wasn't interested. Maybe he was interested in Amber, seeing as how he met up with her in the summer...and then he invited them all out to New York. That wasn't something you do for someone you hardly know.

What was going on here?

I hardly paid any attention during the rest of the lesson, and when the bell went I automatically went after Marc, but Amber called me back.

"Clara saw your car yesterday," she said.

"That's nice." I tried to keep my eye on Marc, but he was already gone.

"At the murder scene."

That got my attention. "What?"

"I was on my way past," Clara explained, "and I'm sure I saw your car."

Past where, I wondered. Green Roding wasn't on the way to *anywhere*.

"Unless it was one like it," she went on. "But I'm good with number plates." And she reeled mine off.

Shit, shit shit.

Bollocks.

"I—have a friend who lives round there," I said carefully.

"Did you see the body?"

"No. They wouldn't let me near."

"Isn't that an old folks' home, up that road?" Amber said.

Double bollocks.

"It's—well, yeah, she was visiting her granny. Got Alzheimer's. Very sad." I started walking. They fell back, apparently having run out of things to say, and I rushed up to the car park. Marc's Corsa wasn't there.

Annoyed, I got in Ted and pointed him homewards. I drove too fast, and eventually spotted the Corsa in the distance ahead of me. I followed it to Green Roding, watched it turn into Mont House, then did a sloppy three-pointer in the pub car park and went home.

I opened my gate, wondering how it had got closed, since the wood swelled and I usually left it open for Tammy, and then I saw the heap of black plastic by my door, and realised.

I kept my eyes on it while I got out my phone and speed-dialed Luke.

"Where are you?"

"Angel's. Why?"

"I need you to come over. Now."

"Why, what's up? Another spider?"

Okay, so maybe once or twice I've got him to kill spiders for me. But they were really big ones. And I always rewarded him.

"No," I said, "not a spider. Not unless we have six foot spiders in this country. Wrapped up in black plastic. Smelling like dead bodies."

That did it. The phone went dead and Luke's car tore into the car park four minutes later. I was impressed. I didn't think Vectras handled that well.

He came into the courtyard and almost walked into me. We stood for a while, looking at the lump of black plastic.

"Have you touched it?"

"No."

Luke got out his phone and snapped a picture of the body—for I was pretty sure by now that it was a body. And I didn't have to make my little blonde brain work too hard to figure out whose it was.

Luke leaned over the body and fitted his key into my front door. He went in, and came back with two pairs of rubber gloves, which I knew I'd have to destroy later. I get through so many gloves this way.

We peeled back the black plastic, and there it was. Gangster Number Two. His face matched that of Maretti's file photo, and I was pretty sure he'd been the guy driving when Doyle tried to shoot me.

"Okay," I said. "So I guess we know the killer's not Mario Maretti. Unless it was a suicide attack."

I was trembling. You'd think I'd have got used to seeing dead bodies by now, but I hadn't. I didn't think I ever would. Maybe if they were all clinical and set out in clean morgues…maybe not, but definitely not right outside my home. Not bloody and smelly and wrapped in sordid black plastic.

Luke put his arms around me and I rested my head on his shoulder. Thank God I had him.

"I'm okay," I said. "It's just—why do they keep turning up at my house?"

"You're a magnet," Luke said.

"Whoever it is knows I live here."

"You've got to get yourself unlisted."

"Yep." I pulled back. "I'll call Karen."

Karen, aside from being our boss and a qualified doctor, also doubled as a useful pathologist. She came to collect the body, borrowing my car to drive it up to the lab under the office.

Luke followed in her car (I was not to be trusted with a Saab), and came back twenty minutes later with Ted.

"Remind me to clean him out again," I said.

Luke stood and looked at me. I'd got in the shower and got changed and my clothes were swishing around in the washing machine. I'd even taken off my nail polish.

"You sure you're okay?"

I nodded.

"Are you sufficiently disinfected yet?"

I shook my head.

"Want to share a shower?"

I nodded, and Luke pulled me into the bathroom. Job, boyfriend. Sometimes one was useful for the other.

Later, curled together on the sofa watching Buffy kick demon ass, I said to Luke, "Karen thinks it's Xander."

Luke didn't take his eyes off the screen, where Willow and Tara were kissing. "Xander couldn't kill a spider. He's more of a girl than you."

"But she still thinks it's him."

"What do you think?"

I sighed. "I was hoping we could pin it on Maretti."

"Well, you can keep on hoping, but I'm going to have to put you in therapy."

We were both silent for a while as Buffy got off with Riley.

"He looks like Harvey," I said.

"You don't like Americans, right?"

"I like Harvey. And Xander."

"Wrong answer."

I grinned. Winding Luke up is one of my favourite past times.

And then I remembered what Karen had said about Luke favouring me above his job, and my smile faded. How did I feel about that?

Uncertain. And that couldn't be good.

"We need to check out Marc's car," I said dispiritedly.

"Why?"

"To see if Maretti was in it. We need to get him away from the car so Karen can, uh, swab it for DNA or something."

"Did you take Science at school?"

"I have a B in Biology," I replied, affronted. "I can tell you all about osmosis."

"Oh, please do."

"See, if you have a text book full of knowledge, and you stare at it with an empty head, then the knowledge osmosises into your brain. It goes from a large concentration, to a small."

Luke stared at me.

"How did you pass," he said, "knowing only the principle of osmosis? And not even knowing that properly."

"I stared at my text book a lot."

He rolled his eyes. "You think it was Marc?"

"I can't get him out of my head. I think, who could have killed Shapiro and Doyle and Maretti, and his name appears. He was there for all three. Doyle's body was in his garage, for God's sake."

"But he has no motive."

"So? Who cares about motive?"

"Sophie, he's a seventeen-year-old boy."

"Your point being?"

224

"I don't think he killed anyone."

I wasn't in the mood to argue, so I let it drop. But in the back of my mind I thought, I wasn't watching Marc this morning. I wasn't at my flat. Who would know where, in a school of seven hundred people, one sixth former was? He was so apathetic, but maybe it was a mask. Maybe he really was a vicious, psychotic killer.

How the hell am I supposed to know?

Next morning I scanned his face carefully for any hint that he might have put a dead body outside my door, but he was as impassive as ever. The girls were talking about going clubbing tonight in Chelmsford, and I was astonished to be invited. I wasn't sure how to ask if Marc was going without sounding like—well, like Clara, so I agreed to go anyway. If I found out Marc was staying home, then I would, too. I gave Amber my mobile number and promised to use Ted for lift purposes.

Was this the only reason they were inviting me? Big car?

The day passed uneventfully. Harvey, who had heard about Maretti from Karen, tried to catch my eye several times in Art, but I looked away. Harvey reminded me of Xander, and I knew Xander had no alibi for Shapiro's killing.

I tried to get an angle on Marc's artwork. After all, it was pretty personal stuff, right? But he was working on a personal study about native American cave art, in which I couldn't find any useful allegories.

Although it would give him a useful excuse to make trips to America.

At the end of the lesson, I went up to Harvey on the pretence of asking about lino printing, and when I'd got him to myself, after the bell had rung and before the next class filtered in, I said in a low voice, "Where was Xander yesterday?"

He frowned. "Why?"

I sighed. "Because—" Some kids came in and I stamped my foot. "I'll text you," I mouthed. He looked dissatisfied, but nodded me away.

It was the end of the school day, so I dragged my stuff out to my car and put it in gear. I couldn't think of anything else to do, so I went up to the office to see how Karen was getting along with Maretti's body. I found her in her office, as always (didn't she ever go home? I mean, *ever*?), looking unruffled.

"Four," she greeted me (no "Sophie" today). "Any news?"

I shrugged. "I'm going clubbing tonight."

"This had better be a professional assignment."

I threw myself at a chair. "I don't know if he's going or not. I've hardly seen him today. I think he's avoiding me. Karen, he's getting suspicious. I think I should lay off."

"He could be our killer."

"He could also be a kid whose father is dead and who has had to readjust his whole life."

She looked at me calmly. "What do you think?"

"I don't know! My head is too full of Elizabeth Jennings to think about anything important."

She smiled. "At least you're learning something."

"Yeah—I hate Elizabeth Jennings. Did you autopsy Maretti?"

She nodded. "Not a lot to tell. He was hit on the head, then his throat was slit. He was probably killed some time yesterday morning."

While I wasn't watching Marc. Shit.

My phone rang and I looked at the display. My parents' house. "Do you mind if I answer this?"

She gestured to the door and I went into the outer office to take the call.

"Hey, Mum."

"Hello, love. You were off early yesterday."

It didn't take a genius to see where this was going. It had probably taken a whole day for her to work out how to approach the subject.

"Yeah. Like I said. I was doing overtime."

"Well, so long as they're paying. Luke's a nice lad, isn't he?"

Nice lad? He'd probably shudder if he heard that.

"Er, yeah," I said. "He's great. Look, I hope you don't mind that—"

"Of course not!" My mother, who prides herself on being very liberal, wouldn't have got married if my parents hadn't made me, free to do whatever you like, etc., laughed. "He's nice."

Again with the nice. "He wasn't too much trouble, was he? It's just he'd been working really late and he came to see me and he was too tired to drive home and..."

"Well, he was very polite. I've washed your bedding."

That wasn't what I needed to hear.

"Thanks," I said uncertainly.

"And I've got some strawberry jam in."

What planet was she on?

"That's nice."

"Because he likes it. The two of you can stay whenever you like," my mother explained.

"Oh. Right. Thanks." That would be never, then.

"Are you coming for tea tonight?"

What was it with my mother? I didn't see her for weeks and then it was "Come over" every night. Because I had a boyfriend now. And she could hardly believe it.

Come to think of it, neither could I.

"I'm going out. Work thing." Not strictly a lie.

"Tomorrow?"

"Erm. No. I have to work." Well, I might.

"You spend too much time at that airport."

If only she knew.

"Bye, Mum."

I had hardly finished putting that phone away when my Nokia rang. God, what was this?

"Piccadilly Circus," I snapped.

"Sophie?" Luke sounded confused.

"Sorry. What's up?"

"Got an invite for you."

Now it was my turn to be confused.

"Come again?"

"On Saturday. Mrs. Shapiro and her son have been invited to a garden party."

"How lovely. Can't you go?"

"Well, that's the thing." Luke sounded like he was half laughing, half exasperated. "I'm invited too."

This time I was at a total loss. "What?"

"My great aunt is holding the party. Some charity thing. I've been trying to get out of it for years."

"Well, that's great. You can go and I'll recover."

"What?"

See, that's what it's like to be in on only half of the conversation. "I'll tell you later. Where are you?"

"Home. Want to come over?"

Karen released me and I drove on back to Luke's. The air was very still and thick, like there was going to be a storm or something. Ted's version of air-conditioning is driving with the windows down, which wasn't much help to me.

Inside, Luke was sitting with all the windows open, drinking water that was mostly ice, sticking to the leather of his sofa.

"Hey." I greeted him with a kiss then went through to the bathroom.

"Hello to you too." He sounded bemused.

I peeled off my tights (I'd forgotten how lovely it was to not have to wear synthetic fibres on hot days), splashed cold water on my wrists, and went back out. Almost as soon as I hit the living room, my phone rang. Again.

"What?" I snapped.

It was Harvey. "Are you okay?"

"I'm okay. It's just people keep phoning me up and making no sense."

"Ah. Well, in this case it's me who's confused. Why did you want to know where Xander was yesterday?"

"Because Luke and Karen think he killed Maretti."

Luke handed me some cold water, frowning and mouthing, "No I don't."

"That's insane," Harvey said.

"Well, I think so too. It's just…"

"*What?*"

"Well, what they said about the gun that killed Shapiro. And Doyle and Maretti were both killed by ordinary kitchen knives."

"It could have been anyone."

"Yes—look, Harvey, I don't think Xander did it. He couldn't kill a bug."

"He could. Just because he's gay doesn't mean he's a wuss—"

"Okay, all right!" God, men. "All I'm saying is you better talk to him. Get an alibi."

"I'm pretty sure he's been at home the whole time," Harvey said, sounding calmer.

"Okay. I just need to *know* all this. Tell Karen. I'm just warning you."

"All right. Thanks. Sophie, I heard about Maretti. Are you okay?"

I sighed. "Wouldn't be the first time I've come home to a dead body."

"Let's hope it's the last."

"Yeah." Somehow, I thought dispiritedly, I doubt it.

"I don't think Xander did it," Luke said when I put the phone down.

"Yes, you do." I looked at my water and tried to decide whether to drink it or chuck it over my head. When had it got so hot? Bloody English weather. One day it chucks it down, the next the air is like soup. Whatever happened to those fine English summer days people used to write poems about?

"No, I don't. Don't you get the feeling he'd scream at the sight of blood?"

I downed the water and opened the fridge for more. Aahh, cold air. Damn Luke for having such a small fridge. I wanted to live in it.

One of my phones chirruped and I stuck them both in the fridge until they calmed down. When I stood up Luke was regarding me with amusement.

"You okay?"

"I'm hot."

"I second that."

"I mean—you know what I mean. And I have to go clubbing tonight. I hate clubbing."

"Is Marc going?"

I did a palms-up. "Who knows? He never speaks a damn word to anyone."

"Are you coming to the garden party tomorrow?"

I gave him a wary look. "I thought you were going."

"Yeah, but you could come too. Professional assignment." He drained his water and came over for some more. "And you could meet my great aunt."

Yeah. I thought that bit might come up.

"Luke, do you like this great aunt?"

He shrugged. "I don't really like any of my family."

"Oh, that's nice. So you're taking me as an offensive weapon."

"Well, you have to admit you can be pretty offensive." He took my cold phone out of the fridge. "You have a message."

Still annoyed with him for the offensive thing, I snatched the phone up. The message was from Amber's number and said, *Hi!!! :-) Stil on 4 2nite? Can u pik us up from clas house at 8 pls? Also pik up marc b4 u cum. U no where he livs rite? Amber xxx.*

Clas? Oh. Clara's. I texted Amber back for Clara's address and leaned against the counter.

"Luke," I said thoughtfully, and he looked up nervously.

"What?"

"If I was hurt and you had to do a work thing, would you do it?"

He gave me a look like I'd just got off a spaceship.

"What kind of hurt?" he asked carefully. "And what kind of work thing?"

"Something, I don't know, urgent. On both counts."

"You're asking me whether I'd choose between you or work?"

I nodded. I must be crazy.

He blew out a sigh. "That's not fair."

"Isn't it?"

"No, it bloody isn't." He looked angry as he sloshed some more water into his glass and stomped back over to the chesterfield. He slammed at the remote control until he found some Spanish football and stared determinedly at the screen.

I think I touched a nerve.

"I won't be offended," I said gently, and Luke all but snarled, "Can we not talk about this?"

"Fine." I put up my hands. "I have to go home anyway. I have homework to do."

I drained my water, retrieved my Nokia from the fridge and made to go. Luke caught me at the door, barring my way.

"Are you mad at me?"

I blinked. "Why would I be mad?" If anything, I was reassured that Luke hadn't had a total personality transplant and suddenly decided that his job *wasn't* the most important thing in the world. As jobs went, it was a pretty important one.

It was a little...well, upsetting, I guess, but only what I expected.

"I don't know," Luke said. "It's just the sort of thing girls get mad about."

Now *that* annoyed me. "What, you not telling me if you value your job more than me? Yeah. I guess *girls* might get annoyed by that."

Luke looked frustrated. "I don't—look, you know I—it's just I—"

"I understand," I said. "You're emotionally incompetent. It's okay. It's a guy thing."

He narrowed his eyes. "I am as emotionally competent as you."

"Oh, yeah? Let me tell you something, Mr. Cool Hand Luke, right now, at any given moment, there are millions of emotions running right through me. So many I don't even know the names for some of them. Some of them don't even have names. How many emotions that are not to do with sports do you get through in one day?"

"That's not fair," he said again.

"No. It's not. Why do we get all the turmoil and you go through life completely calm? It's not fair."

"Do I look bloody calm to you?" Luke said, and I had to admit, he did look frightening. "I have emotions. I have lots of emotions. And most of them are centred on you."

I was a little taken aback by that. But not as taken aback as I was when Luke grabbed me and kissed me, hard, with passion.

"See?" he said, a little triumphantly.

"That wasn't emotion," I said, breathless. "That was a primitive reaction."

"Oh, for God's sake," Luke said, and kissed me again, getting his hands involved in the action too.

"That's still—" another kiss, I was arching into him now, "a primitive—" and another, getting sweeter, "reaction—God, Luke, fuck me."

He grinned. "And that's not primitive?"

"You bastard."

"Yep." He began to relieve me of my clothes. "I'm just an emotionless bastard. That's me. Don't give a damn about anything."

"That's right."

He took me by the hand and led me over to the kitchen where he opened the fridge and took out the bottle of cold water.

"No," I begged, "don't waste it, I'll die without that..."

He grinned evilly and opened the freezer instead, going for the ice tray. "Whatever you say..."

Makes a change.

Chapter Twelve

"Okay," I said, "but now I really have to go."

It was getting late, and I was lying on the floor wearing nothing but some melting ice.

"Where?" Luke said, looking pouty. "Can't you stay here?"

"I have to go clubbing," I said, sitting up. "Marc's going to be there."

"You spend more time with him than you do with me."

"He's my job. There's a slim chance he might be a serial killer."

"You don't really believe that?"

My heart said I didn't, but my head said it was looking sinister.

I stood up. "Where are my clothes?"

"I threw them out." Luke stretched out on the floor, like a big sinewy cat. "You won't need them."

"It's not that sort of club." I hoped.

"Can I come with you?"

"No."

"Why not?"

"You'll distract me."

Luke caught my ankle and started kissing it. I nearly fainted.

"Okay, stop that," I panted.

He didn't stop.

"Luke, I really have to go. I have to go home and shower and change into something slutty—"

"*Please* can I come?"

"No." I shook my foot free, nearly kicking him in the nose. "Be told."

I don't know what was wrong with him. Usually he was much more...I don't know, maybe more professional. Still as horny as a rhino, but not as clingy. What was up with him today?

I eventually made it home and chucked myself in the shower. At least Luke had helped me burn off some calories. My clubbing outfit might fit.

I have one clubbing outfit. I go so rarely that it wasn't likely to be remembered by anyone. I pulled it on—a minuscule black skirt with pink ribbons at the sides and a very tiny pink top that just about covered my bra, and not much else. I'm the sort of girl who can't so much as stand up without some sort of architecture to stop me bouncing, so even with this backless top I had to put on a clear-strap bra. I jumped up and down a few times experimentally. Okay. Didn't seem as if I was going to blind myself.

My feet were not as torturously painful as they had been, but I knew my shoes would put an end to the bliss. I put plasters on the vulnerable bits of my tootsies, then strapped on my favourite shoes: bright pink with heels that make me as tall as my brother and little pink flowers on the toes. Excellent.

I checked myself out in the mirror, and my face fell. There was the massive yellow bruise on my thigh, and the graze on my shoulder.

Dammit. Damn and bugger it to hell.

If I put on something that covered me up more, I might run the risk of melting in the heat. And I was so hot already—the sky was rumbling—that I couldn't even bear to have my hair loose. I scrunched it up on the back of my head and started on my makeup. Nothing too scary, my outfit wouldn't allow it. I smeared some concealer on the bruise and it looked okay. The graze would have to stay though.

I downed some popcorn by way of nourishment, fed Tammy (she looked like she wanted popcorn but she got Whiskas. I'm good to my baby) and clattered out of the house. Five minutes I was back for some trainers to drive in. And a shirt, in case it got cold later.

I picked up Marc, who was impassive about my outfit. He was still dressed in black, I noticed.

"You don't mind not drinking?" he asked.

"No. I'm okay. Need a night off every now and then."

And that was it. That was our conversation for the ten miles to the suburbs of Chelmsford. I tried to rouse him by pointing out that we were passing the village of Shellow Bowells, and got no response.

Luke finds place names funny. So does Harvey.

I didn't like Marc.

I found Clara's house in a maze of identikit brand new streets, and opened up the back of the car for the three girls to climb in, trailing clouds of strong teen perfume, faces made up like strippers, flashing their knickers to the world as they scrambled up into Ted. Clara, I noticed, was wearing her hair in streaky dreadlocks finished off with clacking beads. Her outfit was a million colours and her shoes were four inch stacks of plastic.

Subtle, she was not.

"Wow, it's like being on a farm," Amber breathed (good for her—I was suffocating from lack of unperfumed air).

"Don't be rude," Lucy scolded. "Can we put the radio on?"

"He doesn't have a radio," I said, and there was silence so intense I half expected to see a dustball wheeling across the road.

"*No radio?*" Clara said in tones of utter denial.

"Yeah. He—it's a basic spec. Secondhand."

"Can't you put one in?"

"Well, yeah, but I don't really have much cash at the mo." I turned the key and Ted started up with a diesel rumble. "Ready to go?"

"We're picking up Laurence too, right?" Clara said.

I looked back at them. "Are we?"

"Yeah. Did I forget to tell you that?" Amber said, giving me a look that would have worked a hell of a lot better if she'd been blonde.

"Yes," I said. "Where does he live?"

In a hamlet twenty miles from anywhere, was the answer. I got lost several times, because the girls weren't sure where they were going, and Marc forbore to comment on anything. When we arrived outside Laurence's pretty little cottage, I got out and opened up the back for him wordlessly.

"Cool car," he said.

"Yeah. Icy."

I got back in and tried to figure out my way into Chelmsford. No wonder, I thought, turning round for the fourth time, girls have such a bad rep as navigators. These three were hopeless. Not that Laurence and Marc were helping much, either.

My phone rang when we halfway there. I half expected it to be Luke, announcing he was in my rear view mirror and was going to drag me off into the bushes to take advantage of my tiny little skirt, but in the few seconds before I answered it I saw that it wasn't his number showing.

"Hello?" I held it to my ear. I have a hands free kit, but who ever remembers to plug that in when they get in the car?

"Are you driving?"

Deep and Irish. Docherty. "How can you tell?"

"Car noise. People noise." He paused. "Sounds like a lot of teenagers."

"There's a reason for that."

"Shouldn't you be on hands free?"

"Piss off."

"Now, that's not a very nice way to treat someone who has important information for you, is it?"

I scowled at the road and switched the phone to my right hand so I could change gear. Beside me, Marc winced as I took my hand off the wheel.

"And what might that be?" I asked, trying to be as un-suspicious as I could.

"Are there people listening?"

"Yep."

"The kids from school? Great, well, this BEEP BEEP BEEP so listen up."

I frowned. "Docherty? I'm getting pips."

"You're *what?*"

"My phone's bleeping, it's BEEP BEEP BEEP...running out of battery," I finished, eventually.

"You want me to BEEP BEEP BEEP."

"No, I—shit." I looked at the display "It's pretty much BEEP BEEP BEEP."

The phone gave one little flash, and died. I pressed the power button over and over, and nothing happened.

"Fucking phone," I cursed, banging it on the steering wheel. Bad signal, empty battery. This shit never happens to James Bond.

"Who was that?" Amber asked nosily.

"Uh, boyfriend."

"Someone called Docherty," Clara said loudly.

"Thought your blokey was called Luke?" Lucy giggled. I glanced at her in the rear view. She'd been at the alcopops before she left the house.

"Um, yeah. Luke Docherty."

"You call him by his last name?"

"Sometimes. In a Scully and Mulder sort of way. You know."

"Oh my God, I love Mulder!" Clara wailed. "Why did they ever cancel the *X Files?*"

"Because it had been running for a decade and they'd run out of freaks to show," Laurence said.

A hand touched my shoulder and I jumped, nearly running into the middle of the road.

"What happened to your arm?" Marc asked, his voice low behind the chatter of the girls in the back.

"Oh! I, er..." Shit, you'd think I could have come up with an excuse by now. "I fell over. On holiday."

"In America?"

"No!" This time I nearly hit a tree. "How do you know I went to America?"

In my head, I crashed the car good and proper for being so bloody stupid. I should have asked what made him think I'd been to America. Stupid, stupid Sophie.

"Laurence said. Last month, right?"

"Yeah. With my dad."

"You went to New York?"

If I said I'd been to Boston or Florida or LA, doubtless he'd call my bluff.

"Yeah. Just for a few days."

"It's cool. But you can't drink there."

Wanna bet?

"You can't drink here," I said. "Officially."

"Oh, yeah," Amber piped up. "Sophie, do you mind getting in all our drinks? Marc said you have a fake ID."

"I thought you were eighteen," Lucy said, sounding confused.

Dammit, I should be a better liar than this by now.

"Well, yeah," I said, "but only just. I haven't got my full licence through yet."

This seemed to satisfy them and we drove the rest of the way in comparative peace. Every now and then the girls would break into a bad rendition of an even worse pop song, and Laurence and I exchanged suffering glances in the mirror.

Clara knew somewhere to park that was by this bar she knew, and it was free, so I said goodbye to Ted and hopped out, wondering how it was that I never knew any bars when I was seventeen. I left my Nokia in the car. It was useless now, and for once I didn't have my wind-up charger with me. It simply wouldn't fit in the booby bag.

Amber clocked me checking my Siemens phone, just to make sure it still had battery (although there were no useful numbers stored in it) and exclaimed, "How many phones do you have?"

"Oh," I was used to this now, "this is my old one. I'm just running down the credit on it."

Clara led us off to the wine bar, which was big and modern and soulless and expensive. I got money off them all and ordered a round of Smirnoff Ice, and a Diet Coke for myself, then watched the girls clatter off to greet a group of blokes enthusiastically.

"Amber didn't want to bring her boyfriend?" I asked Laurence, who looked singularly unimpressed.

"Didn't she tell you? They broke up on Monday night. She was stringing him along anyway," he said with distaste.

"They broke up? How come?"

He shrugged. "I dunno. Think she has her eye on someone else." But he wouldn't say who.

"Who are those guys she's with?" I asked.

"Rugby team. She trains with them."

I stared. "Amber does rugby training?"

"Yeah. Clara, too. Not properly. They just do it for the boys."

Why hadn't I ever thought of that?

I was beginning to wonder how far away the club was, and if we were ever going to get there. My feet were already masses of pain, no matter how I stood, and enough people had bumped into my leg to make it throb patiently and consistently. The girls had disappeared upstairs, and so had Marc, and I was about to go and find them when Laurence said, "Not a good idea."

"Why not?"

"Well, that skirt...and the steps are open..."

"I'm wearing very pretty knickers," I told him, and he blanched.

"More than I needed to know."

I hung around near the bar while I waited for him—or someone—to come back. If I'd made the knickers joke to Luke or Angel or Ella, they'd have grinned and said, "So show them off, then." But not this lot. This lot didn't get half of my jokes, or they thought my normal comments were hilarious.

Was I that sad when I was seventeen?

I watched the three girls clatter down the stairs in their minuscule outfits, big hair, glittery shoulders, drag queen makeup, shoes they couldn't walk in, and thought, yeah, I was that sad. I thought I looked good in stuff like that. It's only when you grow up and look back that you realise how Godawful you used to be, and you wonder how anyone who knew you then could still even speak to you.

But then I guess that's the point of friends, or family or whatever. They've seen you at your worst and they still love you. People who have never seen you look bad or get paralytically drunk or cry until your face is a tomato are not your friends. They can't be.

"Hey, what happened to your leg?" asked a drunk guy at the bar, pointing and nudging.

"Birth defect," I said, smiling, and he dropped back. The girls came over and announced they wanted to go to the club now. Marc, Laurence and I didn't seem to be included in the discussion.

The club seemed to be not only on the other side of Chelmsford, but the other side of the damn county. It wasn't that I was cold walking around in my teeny tiny little outfit, far from it. For September it was suspiciously warm. It was just that I was wandering around in slightly less than I usually slept in.

Even when I was sleeping with Luke.

Amazingly, no one ID'd us at the door. I wondered why, until I saw Clara hugging the bouncer. It's not what you know, it's who you know, huh? And I had proper ID, too. Damn.

Inside, the club was dark, and cooler than the air outside, thanks to ferocious air-conditioning units that would probably have been deafening were it not for the ear-breakingly loud club beats thumping out. But I've been to a lot of Chalker's gigs, where they play in clubs the size of my living room with a rig more suited to Shea Stadium. And I've been meeting 737s on stand for years. My ears can take a lot.

I was dispatched for more drinks and the irony of my choice of beverage was soundly laughed over. The man at the bar asked me if I had any ID and I thought, oh honey. If only you knew what kind of ID.

I checked my booby bag into the cloakroom and tucked the ticket in my bra and wandered off to find the main dance floor. The club was well into its own happy hour now and the floor was full of boys trying to dance and girls ignoring them. Up on podiums impossibly pretty girls with amazing legs were writhing about athletically, occasionally kicking out a hefty shoe at the guys trying to join them. I found a spot and lost myself in the beat for a couple of songs. It was cheesy time and I danced to S Club and Abba and Gloria Gaynor, revelling in the lyrics. I'd lost sight of the others as soon as I gave them their drinks. My usefulness was painfully obvious.

But not as painful as my feet. I gave up when they started playing Steps and hobbled over to the bar for another drink, then found a seat on a banquette, hauled my feet up onto the table, and glared at people for walking into me.

"Those are great legs," came a voice in my ear, and I whipped round to see Marc there with a bottle of Becks.

"Oh. Thanks." I studied them. They weren't bad.

"Apart from that massive bruise."

"Oh. Yeah. Told you, I fell over."

"Must have been a hell of a fall." He was still looking at my over-exposed thigh.

"Well. I'm clumsy."

"I'm so glad you're driving us home."

God, yeah, driving. My feet could barely support my weight—although, to be fair, there was a lot of me. I'd never get my feet back into my trainers or get any kind of control over the pedals. All the others had been drinking and besides, I couldn't ask them to drive Ted. Poor Ted.

Something slower came on and Marc looked at me speculatively. Uh-oh.

"You wanna dance?"

God. My feet had ears of their own and they were screaming in protest already. But wasn't I supposed to be gaining Marc's confidence?

"I'll warn you," I said. "I'm six foot two in these shoes."

He shrugged. "Doesn't bother me."

Liar. It bothered all men if a girl was taller than them. Even Luke complained when I wore big heels. So I did it to annoy him anyway.

I drained my drink and stood up. Marc looked up at me— then a little bit more—and his eyes widened.

"You weren't kidding," he said, and I wondered how he hadn't noticed before.

I'm not one for slow dancing. I always feel awkward and usually, too hot and sweaty. Despite the heroic efforts of the air conditioning, movement made me sweat, and so did being pressed up against someone else.

Marc was so different from Luke it was like they were a different species. But then, if you gave Marc another ten years, maybe he'd have a hard, moulded body too.

Although there were some parts of him that were coming along nicely. And some that needed no encouragement at all.

The song ended and I peeled myself away, avoiding eye contact, and stumbled off the floor, through the crowd and up the steps to the ladies.

In here it was bright, so bright I could hardly see when I walked in. I hadn't seen the girls since we came in, and I thought I saw Lucy coming out of a cubicle, but when I looked closer it wasn't her. I checked out my reflection. My face looked like it was melting, but otherwise it wasn't too bad. I was glad my hair was up, not hanging round my shoulders like a fur coat. I looked down at my feet, which were once more raw in places, and considered going to get my bag from the cloakroom for some emergency plasters. But nothing short of a full cast would have protected my feet adequately now, and even that would probably rub.

Back in the club, there was no sight of Marc. Or of anyone I knew. I hadn't seen Laurence since I gave him his drink, and I was partly glad now that I was on my own. They'd have to find their own drinks now.

I was bored, though, and the music was improving slightly. I took off my shoes, sighing with relief, and went out onto the dance floor, avoiding sticky patches and anyone with a bottle. A guy who was so very drunk he could barely stand came up to me and started trying to get me to dance with him. I gave him one of my Drop Dead looks and he backed off pretty sharpish.

Nice to know I've still got it.

Pleased with myself for burning off so many calories, I retired once more to my banquette, but found it occupied by an enthusiastically necking couple who seemed completely oblivious to everything around them.

In shock, I realised it was Lucy and Laurence.

Go Laurence, I cheered silently, and moved off to get something to drink before I completely dehydrated.

I found another table and spent an amusing half an hour fending off men who were very interested in the backless nature of my top and kept walking past pinging it. One of them was even quite cute, but I reminded myself firmly that I was a taken woman.

"Are those real?" asked one lad, staring openly at my chest.

"No. I'm a man really," I replied, and he vanished.

I looked at my watch and wondered what time the club closed. I had a feeling the girls wouldn't want to go home any time soon. They seemed the sort of people who love clubbing and wild parties. Me, I'd prefer a night in with the Scoobies any day of the week. Which just goes to show you how very old I am now.

I went back to see if Laurence and Lucy could be separated, and was surprised to find that they'd vanished.

Kate Johnson

"Excuse me," I shouted to the guy in their place, "did you see where the couple here went?"

He shrugged. "Think he went outside. Dunno where she went. Off to the bog I think." He looked over my little skirt. "You can stay if you wanna."

Yeuch, no. He had baggy jeans and a Porn Star T-shirt and his hair was in greasy curtains. *Not* my type.

"I have to go and find my friends," I said, backing away on my bare, blistered feet. He was watching me go, so I approached the bouncer, who was looking bored. "Can I go outside for a second?" I asked, thinking some cool, fresh air would be good.

He pointed to the girl on the admissions desk. "Need to get your hand stamped."

The girl rammed a rubber stamp down hard on my hand and I looked through the redness to see the word TART imprinted on my skin. I scowled. The men got a GEEZER stamp. Not fair.

I stepped outside and breathed in the glorious air. So clean and cold and clear. Ahhh.

"Laurence?" I called. "Are you out here?"

Silence, but something was moving on the other side of a couple of giant wheely bins. "Laurence?"

Foolishly, I stepped around them, the tarmac cold under my bare soles. I was checking the ground for broken glass and other nasties, but at a sharp sound behind me I snapped my head up.

"Laurence?"

And then I tripped over something, someone grabbed my arm and twisted it behind my back, making me yelp, and something sharp pricked the skin of my inner arm.

248

"Fuck," I yelled, thinking, someone's trying to inject me. Someone's stuck a needle in my arm!

There was a plastic crack and something snapped against my skin. My assailant shoved me, hard, and I fell facedown into the grubby shadows behind the bins.

"Hey," I started to shove myself to my feet, aware of footsteps behind me, running away. But then I saw what I'd fallen on, and I forgot about looking for anyone.

I'd fallen on Laurence, and he didn't look like he was breathing.

By the time I'd blown some air into Laurence's lungs and mercifully, spattering him with frustrated, frightened tears, got him breathing again; by the time I'd gone back into the club and requested the phone from the girl at the desk, explained that it was for emergency services and wrestled it from her grasp; by the time I'd called for an ambulance and police too, for good measure; by the time I'd got the bouncer to go and tell the DJ to make an announcement for Clara, Amber, Lucy and Marc to meet me outside; by the time the ambulance had arrived, the club was shutting down, the girls were crying and I had to get Marc to go in and fetch our handbags. The hot, grumbly weather decided to break, smashing great big raindrops down on me as I sat on the ground, holding Laurence's still hand.

I couldn't find my ticket, but I explained what the bag looked like as I handed Laurence over to paramedics and tried to tell the police what had happened. Now, I judged, would not be the best time to tell them I was a government agent and didn't really have to answer any of their questions, so I acted like a normal person (well, as much as was possible) and told them what they wanted to know.

"Something pricked your arm?" the policewoman asked. She was probably only a couple of years older than me but she looked tired, really tired, not just physically, but sick of attending scenes like this in the middle of the night. I couldn't blame her.

"Yeah." I squinted at my arm in the darkness. "A needle or something. But it broke."

"It broke before it pierced the skin?"

"No—well, I thought it went in." I rubbed the vein below my inner elbow. There was something there. "I think it might have broken off...sort of...in me."

She looked horrified, in a weary sort of way. "Mike," she called to the paramedic tucking a blanket around Laurence's body and hurrying him into the ambulance, out of the rain. "We've got another one for you."

I repeated the story to Mike, obviously another veteran of club/drug crises, and he told me I'd better come along to the hospital for blood tests.

"No telling where that needle might have been," he said. "You need to get it out or you could get infected."

What I really wanted to do was go home. Marc and the girls needed me for lifts and I didn't want to leave Ted here. Thoughts of my warm, soft bed drifted by me. And with the immortality of youth, I was sure there was nothing really wrong with me.

And, I needed to keep an eye on Marc and the girls. I wasn't at all happy about the fact that I'd let them out of my sight tonight.

"Can't I do it tomorrow?" I pleaded. "If I don't drive then they'll be here all night."

"We can take them home," the policewoman said, not looking too pleased at the prospect.

"What about my car?"

"I'm sure there must be someone who can bring you back here tomorrow. Where do you live?"

"Stansted. Near the airport."

"Oh." She considered this. "That's quite a way."

No shit, Sherlock.

"I'm not going to the hospital," I said, and finally saw Marc emerging from the club with my bag.

"Had to wait until all the others had gone," he said apologetically, handing the kitsch little clutch over. I glanced at him, then at the policewoman, and lowered my voice.

"Can I speak to you in private?" I said, and she frowned, but led me away to the far side of the ambulance where the rain was coming down harder.

I withdrew my wallet from my bag and pulled out my military ID.

"I don't actually have to do what you say," I said apologetically.

She inspected the card. "Special agent?"

"Uh-huh."

She shook her head. "Damn. Had one of your lot over near the airport a couple of weeks ago. Cocky bugger, he was."

"Tall, blond hair, really good bone structure?"

"You know him?"

Intimately. "We work together." I put my ID away. "Can we go now? You've got everyone's addresses and everything?"

She nodded gloomily. "I suppose this will go to higher powers? Attacking an agent and all that?"

"You'd be surprised," I replied, and we walked back around the ambulance.

"Watch your feet," the policewoman called as I hobbled away, leading the gang through the fierce rain.

Marc walked with me, mostly silent apart from when he pointed out the broken glass or chewing gum on the pavement. The three girls walked along together, all of them competing for biggest diva, but Lucy crying hardest of all, especially when we heard the ambulance whistle past.

The drive home was long and quiet and tense, and for me, really painful. My feet were not only raw, but dirty and hot and prickly. There was dust and dirt in the burst blisters, and they hurt like fuck. Not to mention the broken needle in my arm, which I'd somehow managed to hide from the others.

Luke was going to love this.

Chapter Thirteen

My dreams were distorted, uncomfortable and hot. People in dark cloaks with giant syringes were coming after me, stabbing me repeatedly in the arm until it ached and throbbed, pushing me to the ground where Laurence lay grey and bleeding, then jumping on my feet until the bones crunched.

I felt like I'd hardly slept at all—it was nearly light when I finally fell into bed, naked, my clothes in a wet dirty heap on the floor—and when someone lightly brushed my shoulder I jumped.

"What?"

"You were dreaming," Luke said, and I opened my eyes a crack to see him sitting on the edge of my bed. Sometimes I wish I'd never let him have a key. But then he'd probably have broken in anyway.

"Go away." I yawned.

"That's nice."

"I'm really, really tired. What time is it?"

"Ten."

"Blegh."

"Sophie," Luke chided, "you have to get up and look respectable. Great Aunt Tilda's garden party, remember?"

I put my face in the pillow and moaned.

"How'd it go last night?"

In flashes, I remembered. The rain, the stabbing club lights, the thud of the sub-speakers from outside. Laurence, pale and dead-looking, the jab in my arm—

I sat up. "I have to call the hospital."

"Ah, underage clubbing. Who had their stomach pumped?"

"No one. One of the boys was attacked. He—"

But Luke had grabbed my arm, and I winced.

"Sophie—what the hell—?"

I looked down. The needle was wedged under the skin of my inner arm, just below the elbow. There was a red line scoring down to it, like a track mark. I hadn't even looked at it properly last night. I'd just told myself to take a trip to the doctor's in the morning and I'd be fine.

"Oh," I said. "I got attacked too."

"There's something in your arm!"

"Yeah. I think it's a needle." I tried to think of the right word for it.

He stared at me. "Like a hypodermic needle?"

"Yes!" Clever Luke.

He took a deep breath, still holding my arm under the elbow, trying to look calm. "There is a hypodermic needle in your arm," he said, nostrils flaring.

"Only half of one," I said helpfully.

"There is a hypodermic needle in your arm."

I felt a further correction would not be helpful.

"I was going to tell you," I lied, "but my phone ran out of battery." There. Nearly true.

"Why didn't you go to the hospital straight away?"

"It's not that bad," I said, looking at it doubtfully. The skin around the needle was puffy and pink, my arm throbbed a little, but on balance I think my feet hurt worse.

"Sophie," his fingers were nearly cutting off my circulation now, "do you know where else that needle has been?"

I shrugged. "How would I—"

"Do you realise you could have got hepatitis? Or worse?"

I stared at my arm. That hadn't occurred to me.

"Jesus." He dropped my arm pretty sharpish and left the room. I got up, pulled my dressing gown on—God, I hurt everywhere—and padded out into the living room after him. Tammy was sitting on the kitchen counter, looking plaintive. I put my hand out to her, then withdrew it.

"Sorry, baby. Mummy might be contagious."

"Can you be serious?" Luke snapped. He had my Yellow Pages out and was going through the hospital listings. When he found one he liked, he grabbed my phone and stabbed at the buttons.

"You can use my phone if you want," I said, and he glared at me.

"Hello, casualty? My girlfriend has a needle stuck in her arm, right under the skin...a hypodermic needle. It's broken off. She was attacked," he added sharply.

He listened for a while as I moved over to the kettle and switched it on, examining my arm as I went.

"Right. I thought so. I'll bring her up. Thank you."

He put the phone down and turned to me. "Get dressed."

"Sir, yes, sir."

"And for God's sake take your makeup off."

I looked in the mirror. Blegh. He was right.

I couldn't be arsed with a shower, but I bathed my feet in the sink (Luke decided he was impressed with my agility and said he'd take advantage of it when he was sure I wasn't going to give him anything. Told you he was an unromantic sod) and packaged them up with plasters and thick socks. I pulled on jeans and a T-shirt and added a baseball cap to cover up my hair, which really needed washing after the smoke and sweat of the club. When I was done, I looked like a teenage junkie. Great.

Luke put me in his car and drove me up to the Princess Alexandra Hospital, where we waited for a couple of hours before someone came along with a scalpel, cut open my arm to get the needle out, and promptly hit a vein. Blood gushed everywhere, and the young doctor went pale.

"Right. I'll, er, I'll just sew that up, shall I?"

Luke rolled his eyes at me. He'd tried to blag us to the front of the queue with his Special Agent status, but it hadn't worked. I'd read *Hello!*, *Okay* and *Chat* magazines until I thought my brain might explode. Tired and grubby, and in pain from several sources, I waited patiently while my arm was cleaned and stitched up, and then a needle was inserted into my other arm (check out the irony of that) so they could check my blood for hepatitis or AIDS or whatever other nasty things Luke was convinced I had.

On the way out, I asked the receptionist if she could get me any news about Laurence. To my shame I realised I didn't know his last name, but I gave her admission details and she came back with the news that he was in a coma, following a heroin overdose.

"Will he be okay?" I asked, clutching Luke.

She shrugged. "The sooner he wakes, the better."

"But you don't know when that will be?"

She shook her head. "Sorry."

I walked out, holding tightly onto Luke. Suddenly I realised what someone had been trying to do to me. I was pretty certain Laurence wasn't a user. I don't know why—call it another hunch. Someone had injected him, and then they'd tried to get me, too.

"Heroin," Luke said, looking impressed as he dragged me back to the car. "That could explain why you're so tired. You're still stoned."

"I am not stoned. I don't think any of it went in me."

"You don't feel happy and relaxed?"

"I'm in too much pain to be relaxed." I clutched the bottle of painkillers they'd given me and considered becoming addicted to them.

"Oh. Well, if it hurts, you're probably not stoned. It's supposed to relieve pain. That's sort of the point."

"I'm glad to hear it." I collapsed into the car. "Luke, someone tried to kill me."

"Again." He touched my face. "Remind me not to let you out of my sight."

"It's not as if I've even done anything."

"You're a spy, sweetheart. That's enough."

I thought about this on the way home, drowsy with painkillers and antibiotics and lack of sleep, looking down at my arm which bore a fresh bandage. If this went on any longer I'd soon be totally mummified.

I guess as long as I was trying to find, infiltrate and stop bad guys, then the bad guys would be trying to stop me. And while SO17 might stop people by putting them in jail, nasty people weren't so nice. They preferred to remove you permanently.

Sometimes, I could see how they had a point.

"Luke," I said as we pulled up at my flat, "do you know if it's just Marc and his mother going to this party?"

"I haven't seen the whole guest list. Why?"

"No reason." I didn't want to say it until I'd thought about it some more.

"Do you still want to go?"

I nodded. "I need to."

Luke looked me over and seemed to decide I'd do. "Okay. But please wash your hair."

Out came the clingfilm to keep my bandage dry while I showered. I stood looking at the contents of my wardrobe for quite a while, making faces, until Luke—already looking smart and lovely in chinos and a linen shirt that had somehow escaped my blood fountain, the pristine bastard—asked me what was wrong.

"What kind of party is it?"

"A garden party."

"Yes, I know, but is it the sort of party me and my friends have where we eat pizza and get smashed and listen to cheesy pop?"

Luke shook his head slowly.

"I didn't think so. I get the feeling I should be wearing something floral."

"And...?"

"And I don't feel very floral." I narrowed my eyes calculatingly. "It's not going to rain any more, is it?"

"I don't think so. It's cooler than it was. There's a breeze. Why?"

I pulled out my leather jeans. "I'm *really* not feeling floral."

So my feet hurt and my arm ached and my thigh was throbbing from the effect all that dancing had had on the bruise. So what. I swallowed some more pain pills and swiped on some eyeliner, and felt a lot better for it.

Luke took one look at my outfit—leather jeans, red boots, sheer black top that showed off my DD cup bra—and decided he needed to change too.

"Just no leather," I said, as we got in his car and went back to his place, already running late.

"Why not?"

How could I put this in a PC, non-offensive way?

"You'll look gay."

"That's nice."

"Sorry, Luke, but you would. If you put on leather jeans— don't tell me you still have them?"

"I could still have them," Luke said moodily.

"But you don't?"

"...No."

"If you wore leather jeans, I'd seriously have to call your sexuality into question. Me, the girl you've been screwing senseless for months."

"You never call Spike gay and he's always wearing them."

"That's because he's Spike. He's in his own class. He could wear pink and still look straight."

"Are you saying I looked gay when I wore them in Cornwall?"

"No, 'cos you were dressed up as Spike for the party." And damn, he'd looked good.

"So Spike's not gay, but I am?"

I couldn't help laughing. "Of course not. You're very straight." He'd stopped the car in the yard now, and I leaned across and kissed him. "Very straight."

But Luke pulled back, and I looked at him, hurt.

"You," he began, and looked nervous. "You could be..."

"Contagious. Right. I'll have to carry a warning."

"Sophie, I didn't mean—"

"It's okay." I got out of the car. "I'm all right. If I drop off into a coma I'll be sure to remember as my last thought how glad I am that you didn't get infected."

He came after me, bleeping the car shut.

"It's not funny."

"No." I stopped, annoyed now. "It's not. Blood poisoning is the least of my worries. I could be HIV positive. Fuck knows where that needle'd been."

"Probably it was only Laurence..."

"Probably? Oh, thanks."

I flumped down on his chesterfield and flicked through the news channels on Sky, half expecting there to be something about Laurence on there. But I guess teenage overdoses are too common for ordinary news.

Luke came out, wearing black jeans and a snug, pale blue T-shirt. He had big boots on and he was scowling.

"Mmm," I said, "much better. Are you sure you won't kiss me?"

He looked mardy. "How long will it take for the blood test results to come back?"

"Fuck knows. This is the NHS. Probably about a week."

Luke sighed. "I'll see if Karen can speed them up."

His Great Aunt Tilda's house was about an hour's drive away and I was surprised when he suggested we take my car. And then I realised that Great Aunt Tilda would probably be terribly grand, and that a Defender would look a hell of a lot better than a Vectra, sitting there in the driveway. Or round in valet parking. I didn't know how rich she was.

In fact I barely knew anything about Luke's family at all. I knew they must have had money, to continue sending him to Eton. I knew they weren't close to him. That's all I knew.

Luke insisted I wasn't to drive and I, mindful of all the drugs I was now on, agreed and winced as he thrashed Ted's gearbox around.

"Be nice to him," I said. "He's been through a lot."

"Not as much as you," Luke said.

He turned off the B-road onto a long, straight lane with wide grass verges on either side, bordered by high brick walls. It looked like the entrance to a grand country house, but there'd been no indication it was private at the junction.

And then we came to a road crossing the long lane, and opposite from us was a sign announcing Gravely House. The lane had been part of the drive. Luke went straight over and through the wide, open wrought iron gates, and we followed the long drive up through more carefully tended green lawns until a house came in view.

Well, I say a house. Really it needed its own postcode. It was huge. It would have made Buckingham Palace look like a garden shed. There were wings and crenellations and outbuildings and a flock of gardeners tending the borders. I got the feeling that looking after this place was a bit like painting the Forth Bridge—no sooner had you got to one end than the other needed attention.

Luke glanced over at me.

"You okay?"

I nodded. "It's, uh, impressive."

"Yeah. She opens it up for public viewing most of the year. The party is to celebrate her getting her home back."

"Your great aunt really owns this place?"

He nodded. "Bit of a white elephant. Costs so much to keep she barely breaks even."

But still. I was impressed when my mum inherited her mother's flat. My flat. One bedroom and no garden. You could live a lifetime in this house and never see the same room twice.

"Do we have to go inside?" I asked. "Only my feet still hurt and I think it might take me a week to get from one end to the other of this place."

He grinned. "We don't have to go inside. Unless it rains and we'll go in the ballroom."

Dear God.

"That's good," I said, "because I think I might need Ted to get around this place."

"Well, he's a Defender. He'll fit right in."

"See, my car is very useful."

"Hmm."

At the front door of the house Luke pulled up and a young man in a suit came and asked for his invitation. Luke showed it, and the young man wrote out a ticket which he stuck to the rear view mirror, then he got in and drove Ted away.

I stood, waving. "I do hope that's valet parking," I said, "and he's not stealing my car."

"It's valet," Luke said, slinging an arm around my shoulders, "Ted's gone to meet the Mercedes breeding ground round back."

"So no one will see we arrived in him?"

"They'll see our ticket in the window," Luke said consolingly, and I supposed that would have to be good enough.

I could hear jazz music coming from the back of the house, and expected it to be on a PA. But it was a live jazz band, men and women all in black and white, playing merrily under a white awning. The garden—well, probably one of many gardens, part of the grounds or whatever—was beautiful, sculpted and perfect. The lawns were perfect flat terraces. The edging was hairdresser neat. All the foliage was perfectly symmetrical and there was not one dead leaf or drooping flower anywhere.

It was all a bit intimidating.

"Are you sure Marc's going to be here?" I asked Luke.

"Pretty sure. Why?"

"'Cos I'm nervous."

"Why?"

I looked up at him. He really didn't seem to understand.

"Because..." I tried to choose my words carefully, things about "your world" and "family" and stuff like that, but before I could form a coherent sentence that didn't sound like it was out of a soap opera, Luke nudged me and said, "That's her."

He was pointing to a woman who was probably about the age of my father's mother. Probably. This was just something I worked out based on Luke's age. By her appearance, Great Aunt Tilda could easily have been the same generation as my parents. She was what people call "well-preserved"—and not in the pickled-in-alcohol sense. Her hair was white, immaculately drawn back into a bun. Her skin was good and her makeup invisible. She was wearing a beautifully cut pale pink dress with a matching jacket that I'd bet my flat cost more than my yearly salary. Than both of my salaries. Put together.

Oh, Christ. Suddenly I wished I was wearing something floral.

"Aunt Tilda," Luke said, and the woman turned around, frowning slightly. Clearly, she had no idea who he was.

Luke's expression didn't slip. "I'm your great nephew," he prompted. "Luke Sharpe. Giles and Miranda's son."

Giles and Miranda? How the hell had he ended up with something as normal as Luke?

"Ah." Tilda's face cleared. "Luke. Of course. About time you came to one of my parties. Any more refusals and I'd have stopped inviting you. How's the SAS?"

He nodded easily. "Fine."

"And who's this?"

Beady eyes were turned my way. I smiled hopefully.

"This is Sophie. My girlfriend."

Oh, thank God he'd used the G word. I stuck out my hand.

"It's nice to meet you. Uh," I hesitated, "I haven't really met any of Luke's family."

"That's because Luke never sees any of us," Tilda said with a cut glass smile, which Luke returned. It was easy to see the family resemblance.

"I return the affection I'm given," Luke said, and I wanted to die.

"This is not the time or place for this discussion," Tilda said. Her eyes swept over me dismissively. "I have guests to see to."

And she glided away.

"What are we, caterers?" I muttered. "Nice lady."

"Yeah. One of the nicer ones."

"Seriously?"

"Yep."

"And I thought I had family problems."

"Your family's great."

"If insane."

"Yeah, but that's what makes them great. Look, champagne."

I scowled at the passing waiter. "Look, lots of meds."

Luke gave me a sympathetic smile. "Sorry. How're you bearing up?"

Like I was in labour or something. "I think I'll make it through the day. Is there food here?"

We found some canapés and stood picking spots off people for a while. Most of the people I singled out for ridicule seemed to be related to Luke, which he seemed to find hilarious.

Until I spotted a large woman wearing a too-tight pink dress that made her look like a sausage that had been stuffed back into the tube. Her hair was blonde and piled up fatly on her head. Her legs went straight down into shocking pink court shoes.

I shuddered.

"What?" Luke said, looking over. "Oh God."

"I know. As if court shoes were ever—"

"No, I mean Oh God. That's my cousin Avril."

I gaped. People called Avril should be willowy and pale, like spring flowers. They should not be bright orange and the approximate shape of a lemon. "You're related to her?"

"Yep."

"But you're so fit..."

"Compliments later. Now, run."

But Avril had already spotted us. Screeching "Luke!" so loudly everyone turned to look, she sailed over like an ocean liner, happily unaware of sending ordinary people flying with her bulk. Being towed along behind her was a thin, nervous-looking man. As well he might be. I was starting to worry that Avril might start eating guests if she ran out of canapés.

"Luke darling, I haven't seen you in ages." She clasped him to her, and he hung on to my hand grimly. It was all I could do to keep from laughing. "Mummy, Daddy, come look who I've found!"

While I waited in grim fascination to see who the hell her parents were, Avril shoved forward the thin man.

"This is Howard," she said proudly, fingering his shirt collar.

Howard ducked his head nervously.

"Hey, Howard," I said, feeling a dash of solidarity for someone else involved with this crazy family.

"And, Luke, you haven't introduced me yet! Where are your manners? Who is this charming young lady?"

"Which charming young lady?" I muttered automatically, and Avril was sent into peals of laughter.

"Oh, gosh, you're funny! Mummy, come and meet Luke's young lady!"

Mummy and Daddy were as well-dressed as the rest of the family, considerably thinner than their offspring and noticeably more polite than Great Aunt Tilda.

"Soph," Luke said wearily, "this is my Aunt Bridget and Uncle Quentin and my cousin Avril and her—er—Howard."

I fought to keep a straight face.

"And this," I was pushed forward slightly, as if for inspection, "is Sophie."

No "girlfriend" this time. Huh.

They all said polite hellos. Avril looked me over in admiration. "That's quite an outfit you've got there, Sophie!"

At least I think it was admiration.

"Thanks," I said uncertainly. "I, er, like your, er, shoes..." I stamped on Luke's foot.

"Oh, I know. I adore them. So funky!"

God, this was killing me.

"You're a bit in the wars," Aunt Bridget observed of me. "What happened?"

I took a deep breath. "The graze? Oh, that's just where someone tried to kill me in New York."

Luke had his knuckles in his mouth. The rest of the family stared at me for a few seconds.

"Rough place, New York," Uncle Quentin managed.

"Oh, Daddy, she's joking," Avril said. "Aren't you?"

I shook my head happily. This was more fun than I'd thought.

"And what about the bandage?" Bridget asked nervously.

"What, this?" I looked at it. It was beginning to make my arm cramp. "Oh, this is where someone tried to OD me with heroin last night outside a club. I had to have the needle cut out this morning. Don't worry," I added when they looked alarmed. "I'm not stoned. I don't think."

"And she's probably not contagious, either." Luke slipped his arm around my shoulders. "Probably."

"We just have to wait for the blood tests to make sure I don't have hepatitis."

"Or AIDS."

"Or septicaemia."

"Or tetanus. Or endocarditis."

"What's that?" I looked up interestedly.

"Heart murmurs. If the needle was dirty."

"Oh. But," I added to Luke's shocked relatives, "I'm *probably* clean. And Luke, I'm pretty sure you can't catch it by kissing me."

"Are you sure?"

"Well, not unless we exchange about ten pints of saliva."

I could hardly believe I was saying all this. Aunt Bridget looked like she was about to faint.

"Should we go?" I said to Luke.

He nodded. "Let's."

We half ran to the back of the band tent and Luke had to hold me up because I was laughing so hard I could hardly breathe.

"Oh, God, their *faces*."

"I thought Avril was going to burst."

"I *know*." I pressed my fingers under my damp eyes. "Endocarditis? Is that even a word?"

"Yeah, it's heart murmurs. One of those field training things. Don't share needles. Always use a condom."

"What *is* a heart murmur?"

"Something to do with the lining of the heart. Jesus, Sophie," Luke could hardly stand. "I haven't laughed that hard in—"

"Is it serious?"

"What? A heart murmur? It can spread. Naff up the kidneys and brain and things."

Suddenly it wasn't so funny any more.

"Can it kill you?"

Luke straightened. "I don't know."

I sat down hard on the grass, not caring about my leather jeans.

"Sophie?"

I was trying hard to breathe.

"Look, it's really unlikely. You're healthy, your heart's fine..."

"What if it's tetanus? Or hepatitis?"

"Well, there are treatments for those..."

"What if it's AIDS? What if I'm HIV positive?" I started to shake, cold terror overwhelming me. "Luke, I could *die*."

Luke crouched down beside me.

"You won't die."

"I could get AIDS and die from a cold. I'll be one of those people wearing bad hats who you see outside Tube stations begging for change. My parents will disown me. I'll never have children. I'll get stomach flu and die from it, oh God..."

I was rocking now, well on my way to hysteria. Luke put his arms around me and I pushed him away.

"And you, you'll catch it too. I'll kill you, too. God, Luke, you're going to die because of me."

"No one's going to die because of you."

"Because of some stupid kid with a bloody needle..."

"Sophie." Luke took my face in his hands. "You are not going to die. I am not going to die. No one is going to die."

But they are, I thought. Someone's going to die before this is over.

I sniffed. "I'm really scared," I said in the tiniest voice.

"I know you are." This time I let him hug me. " But you'll be okay. The tests'll come back clean."

"What if they don't?"

"They will."

"But—"

"If they don't you can move in with me and I'll wrap you up in cotton wool until a cure is found," Luke said in exasperation.

"I could be ninety."

"I don't care. Having you safe is what's important."

I felt tears flood uncontrollably out of my eyes. Damn, I wish I wasn't wearing so much eyeliner. I'd look like a panda.

"Luke." I pulled him to me and kissed him. "You're not scared about infection?"

"No."

I sniffed. "Liar."

He held me close against him, stroking my hair, and I thought about what he'd said. What if the results came back positive—now that I'd calmed down I didn't think they would— but if they did, would he renege on his promise?

"Would you really look after me if I was really sick?"

"Course I would." Luke kissed my neck.

"What about if you had a job to do?"

He moved back a few inches and looked at me. "This again?"

I nodded. "I need to know."

"I—well, we'd think of something," Luke said on a sigh.

"If I was really sick and couldn't be left..."

"Then I'd stay with you."

Tears were flowing freely down my cheeks now. I must have looked awful—a good warning for Luke. If I got ill, I wouldn't be a pretty sight.

"Even if the job was really important?"

"Even if." He squeezed my shoulders. "Now what's brought this on?"

You, I wanted to say. You, preferring to spend time with me, rather than go out and do your job. You, acting like you're in love with me. You, placing me above all other things.

"You," I gulped eventually.

"Well, thanks."

I wiped my eyes. "I can't believe I'm going to say this."

"Say what?" Luke looked a little apprehensive. As well he might.

"I wouldn't do the same for you."

Chapter Fourteen

I sat in the boathouse, crying hard. So this was our second break-up. And this time it was a proper one—not just a bit of enforced celibacy for everyone's sanity. This was the real deal. This was it.

It was over.

At first Luke hadn't quite understood. So I'd had to explain, rather spoiling the drama of the moment. I'd had to explain that if push came to shove, the world was more important than him. So saving the world would be my priority.

So I'd have to leave him to die.

So I couldn't be with him any more.

The realisation had been creeping up on me for a while, but right then was when it clubbed me over the head and made its presence known. I was a spy. Maria had told me from the start that Luke was a relationship-free zone, and I'd figured that was just Luke, being a rock or an island or whatever. It hadn't occurred to me that it was a hazard of the job.

If I was ever going to be a halfway decent spy, then I'd have to make my job my first priority. I'd have to concentrate on it totally. Which meant any relationships I had needed to take a backseat.

Only...

Only Luke could never be on the backseat in my life. Luke had to be there right next to me. If I wasn't going to go at this full throttle (where do all these car metaphors keep coming from?) then I'd have to cut him loose. Ejector seat. It would have to be over.

There's a reason James Bond never has the same girl from one film to the next.

When I'd finished explaining, there was a sort of stunned silence.

"Sophie," Luke said, reaching out to me desperately. "Look, calm down, you don't mean—"

"I mean," I said. "I don't want to do this—"

"So don't."

"But I have to. It's like Tara said."

Luke ran his hands over his face. "Who?"

"In Buffy! About not wanting to go, because it'd hurt too much. Even though she really loves Willow..."

There was another awful silence, then Luke said, "You don't love me."

I was crying so hard now I thought my body would shrivel up.

"Don't ask me that."

Luke stood there and watched me cry for a while, my head bowed so I couldn't see him. And I didn't see when he left.

At the bottom of the garden, away from all the noise and music and food and general happiness, there was a picturesque lake, fed by a small river that flowed off into the countryside. A boathouse sat on the lake, silent and dark, shielded from the sun, with a couple of dinghies on the decking and a smart houseboat moored up inside. When I was a kid one of my dad's friends had a houseboat and we went on it for a day. Talk about going nowhere fast.

I sniffed, loudly, and wiped my eyes. If I leaned over I could see my reflection in the water. I looked bloody awful.

I stood up, determined to find Luke and get my car keys back so I could go home. My arm was aching—oh, shit, I couldn't drive. Not like this. I felt okay walking about but I was on such a cocktail right now that if I got dizzy I could crash the car...

Oh well, I was going to die anyway. Might as well go out wearing leather jeans.

I checked my face in my little handbag mirror and wiped away the worst of my panda eyes. Out came the concealer to make me look more human, lip gloss for confidence, a pinch of my cheeks to brighten my face. I couldn't wear an outfit like this and look like hell. It just wasn't done.

I was just about to snap the mirror shut and make my way out into the sunlight when I saw, reflected behind me, someone in a shapeless black hoodie, hood pulled over a balaclava'd face, sneaking up behind me.

Damn, I thought in that split second, I wish I had my gun.

And then I dropped the mirror—bad luck, hah!—and rammed my elbow back. I caught the stalker in the stomach and he—she? it?—doubled over. I glanced around for some kind of weapon and saw a coil of rope on the floor. I dashed for it, but the black figure lashed out and I tripped, my ankle caught, and fell heavy on my face, winded.

I saw the rope come down on me and rolled to the side, desperately trying to breathe. I kicked out, restricted by my tight jeans (Buffy never has this problem) and landed a foot somewhere on a knee or a thigh. My attacker came at me again, this time pulling a spanner from under the big black hoodie, and I suddenly found my breath and yelled, loudly and incoherently, just enough to startle the attacker until I'd scrambled to my feet. But he had a rope and a spanner—a big heavy spanner—and I had nothing. Not even my handbag, which had got flung in a dark corner of the boathouse.

It was so dark in here I could hardly see, but then the hooded figure glanced behind at something, and when the head came back I caught a glimpse of eye, recognised the head movement, and nearly fainted with the realisation.

"You?" I gasped, and the hooded figure came forward with its spanner and rope. I was backed into a corner, no escape, and I was just about to dive into the water, *sod* my jeans, when the door slammed open and Luke came rushing in.

Feeling like the helpless heroine in a film, I let a grateful sigh escape me, a sigh that was rapidly expelled as a scream of horror when the hooded figure lashed out suddenly with the spanner, slamming it into Luke's jaw and sending him crashing hard against the cement wall. I heard a hideous, nauseating crunch, a sound I will never, ever forget, and saw a dark streak of red on the pale wall as Luke slid down it.

He was dead.

"No." Once again winded, I couldn't even move. The hooded figure grabbed Luke's body and shoved it across the decking, kicked it hard in the ribs and sent it sprawling with a boneless thud into one of the dinghies. A second later, the boat hit the water with a splash, and the black figure kicked it out into the water, where the current caught it and snatched it outside.

"God, Luke—" I stumbled towards the water, sniffing and snottering with fear (this definitely never happened to Buffy), but I was caught with the spanner. I went down, my head crashing against the decking, seeing the hooded figure halt and listen like a cat as voices passed by.

"Help," I tried, but my voice wouldn't come. Light was fading. My attacker ran out of the door, pushing it closed and dropping a lock into place. "Help, don't let..."

And that was it. I was out.

Someone shook me awake, someone who was whispering and sobbing my name, crying, "Please don't be dead, Sophie, please don't let them have killed you, please..."

I recognised the voice, and although my head was throbbing like a flamenco dancer was practising his petulant Spanish stamping on it, I somehow managed to drag my eyes open.

"Clara?"

"Oh, thank God you're all right," she wept, throwing herself on me. "I thought she'd killed you."

"What?" I tried to pull myself half upright. I was still in the boathouse, and there was an electric light blaring into my eyes. "Who? Clara, what are you doing here?"

She rubbed her eyes, smudging glittery eyeshadow all over the place. "I came because...I came because I knew what they were going to do. I knew they were going to try and kill you."

"Who?"

"Marc and Amber. I think," she drew in a shuddery breath, "I think it was her who stuck the needle in you. I saw her whispering with Lucy."

"Lucy's in on this?"

"I think they made her. Luce is a bit of a sheep."

I nodded. I wasn't surprised at anything she was saying.

"Is that why she was making out with Laurence? To get him to go outside so they could attack him?"

Clara dissolved into fresh tears. "No," she sobbed, "he just followed her. He really liked her."

I absently put my hand on her shoulder, and through the fog of pain that pressed in on me, I tried to figure it out.

Of course. The needle had been meant for me, but Amber— or Lucy, whoever—had got Laurence by mistake. In total darkness it's easy to blindly get the wrong person. So they'd tried to get me with the same needle, but there was nothing in the syringe. Or if there was, none of it went in because the needle broke.

"How did you know I was here?" I asked.

"Amber. She was teasing Marc about coming here because he liked you." Flattering, but not the time. "She talked him into letting her come. I didn't know why, but I just talked to Lucy and she said she was worried Amber was going to do something stupid and I *knew*..."

Get this girl a badge and sign her up. We need her.

My heart was starting to pump faster now. I forced myself to stand up, holding the wall for help.

"Okay, Clara, what time is it?"

She sniffed and peered at her watch. My eyesight didn't seem up to looking at mine.

"About eight," she said.

Oh fuck. I'd been here for hours.

"Right. Okay. Have you seen Marc or Amber or Lucy since you got here?"

She shook her head. "I think they left. They kept talking about this place in New York..."

I stared. "They've gone to New York?"

"I don't know." Another sniff. "Maybe. Sophie, why do they want to kill you?"

Because they know who I am, I thought. They saw the bruise and the graze and they know from Maretti and Doyle what happened. They knew I'd be here, because I was everywhere Marc went. Dammit! Why couldn't I have been more subtle?

"Okay." I pressed my knuckles into my eyes to try and clear my vision, which still wasn't twenty-twenty. I felt like I'd got a really bad vodka hangover, the worst kind where you're still drunk as well as in pain. "Okay. Do you have a car?"

She nodded.

"Give me the keys."

She looked uncertain. "Why? What are you going to do?"

"I'm going to go after Marc and Amber and Lucy."

"But—they'll kill you!"

Not if I kill them first, I thought grimly.

"I'll be okay," I said, and started looking around for my bag. Christ, my head hurt. She must have hit me damn hard with that spanner.

I located my bag on the edge of the dock, slowly letting its contents slip into the water. I picked it up carefully and checked through. Makeup, check. Wallet, check. Nokia phone...car keys...

Shit.

"Do you have a phone?" I asked Clara, and she nodded and dug in her back pocket for a little Motorola. "Is it prepaid?"

"Contract."

Excellent.

"I'm going to need to borrow this too," I said. She looked reluctant, so I dug in my bag and fished out my wallet. I showed her my military ID, and her eyes widened.

"Special agent?"

I nodded, my head thudding gently with every movement. "I'm not seventeen at all."

"How old are you?"

"Don't be rude." I tried to think. I needed to find out if the terrible three were on their way to New York or not. And then I needed to follow them. God, if only Luke was here to drive me—

"Oh, Christ," I said, remembering, and nearly slid down the wall again.

"What?"

"Luke. He's—" Tears formed behind my eyes, but I made them stop, made myself think and act.

"I need you to go to the house and find a phone and call emergency services. My—" I couldn't say it, "—partner is—he's hurt." The words just wouldn't come. "In a boat down river. You need to find him. Luke, remember, from the bowling alley?"

"I remember. Is—is it bad?" Clara asked, and looked like a frightened rabbit.

"It couldn't be any worse."

I found her car, a rickety Nova, flung at a haphazard angle on the gravel outside the house, looking so at odds that the valet parkers were starting to look uncomfortable.

"Hey," one of them said, spying me. "You can't leave that here—"

"That's okay," I yanked the door open. "I'm just leaving. Tell Great Aunt Tilda she's a cow."

I drove off rather slowly, foot to the floor, begging the car for more power. If I was right, Great Aunt Tilda's family pile was only about twenty miles from Heathrow. As I drove I called

Karen and got her to find out if Marc and the girls had taken a flight to America. They had, two hours ago.

I didn't mention Luke. I couldn't, yet.

She booked me on the next flight, and I left the Nova, shuddering and panting, in the car park while I stumbled down to the terminal and checked myself in.

The security personnel took one look at me and conducted a full body search, but apart from a lot of bandages they found nothing at all. I flopped down by the gate and took some more of my pills—thank fuck they hadn't fallen out of the bag—and waited to board.

I slept through most of the flight, rather frightening the young businessman next to me who took one look at my clothes and messed-up makeup and wild bruises, and obviously assumed I was a junkie whore. When we arrived, I bought a whole load of currency with the company credit card and got the SuperShuttle to take me to the Hotel Philadelphia. It was well after midnight, local time, but I couldn't think of anywhere else to go.

I fell down on one of the seats in reception and hauled out Clara's phone. It searched frantically for signal and found none. Not triband, then.

Bugger.

I hauled ass over to a payphone, ignoring the open stares of the night staff, and dialled my own house number, remembering that Docherty had been about to tell me something, and hoping with every fibre in my being that he'd called my house and left the message there. I hadn't really been in a position to check yesterday.

"You have two new messages. Message one: Soph, it's me. Look, I can't find you anywhere so I'm guessing you must have come home. We really need to talk about this. I—I don't know what to say, except that it's stupid. Please will you call me. I'm coming over when I get home."

Tears filled my eyes and spilled down my cheeks as Luke's warm voice filled my ear. He was gone. He'd tried to save me and now he was gone, and all I had was one hurt, confused phone message.

I was in such an advanced state of misery I almost didn't hear the next message.

"Sophie? I've been trying your damn mobile all day but I can't get through. Focking Yank networks."

I stood up straighter. Docherty was in America?

"I came over to check out Xander's apartment and one of the neighbours said some kids had been coming round here a lot. A boy and three girls. I think they might be your school posse. Anyway there's a possibility they might be coming back over. I'll try the airlines and see what they have to say. Anyway call me if you can, I've got a temporary number..."

I didn't need to check the airlines. I already knew where they were.

I slammed the receiver down, collected my quarters, then stared feeding them back in again.

"Docherty? Thank God I got you. I'm in New York. The kids are here."

"I know," he said. "I'm waiting for them at Xander's apartment."

"I'll meet you there."

The subway, I'm told, is not place for a nice girl after midnight. But tonight I was not a nice girl. Tonight I was bleeding and shaking and numb with every kind of pain, and if anyone came anywhere near me they vanished when they saw my face. So I looked like a hooker junkie. So what.

Walking through the meatpacking district after dark was educational, but I wasn't in the mood to learn. As I approached Xander's apartment, a shadow detached itself from the darkness and held something out to me. It glinted. A gun.

"Glad you could make it," Docherty said, smiling in the darkness.

"Wouldn't be a party without me."

"You look like hell."

"Been there and back. It's fucking freezing out here."

"You want my coat?"

I shook my head. "I want to go inside. I'd rather wait for them."

"The door's been padlocked…"

I gave him a look of contempt and checked out the gun. It was one of his matching Heckler Koch .45s.

It made very short work of the padlock.

No one seemed to bat an eyelid at the sound of a gunshot. The pair of transvestite hookers on the corner made loud dirty jokes about bangs and I ignored them, kicking the door open, shooting off the inner lock, and stalking inside.

"You really do look like hell," Docherty said helpfully as I looked around the place.

"Thanks."

"Want to tell me why?"

I closed my eyes and an image of Luke sliding down the concrete wall made me catch my breath.

"No."

Docherty came up behind me and laid his hand on my shoulder. "Are you okay?"

Not by a long shot.

"I'm fine."

"Why are you here?"

I took a deep breath and turned to face him. I told him about Clara, and about my attacker, and how I was pretty sure it'd been Amber.

"And Luke didn't come with you?"

My insides twisted. "No," I said, trying not to let him see my face in the darkness. "We, uh, we broke up."

"Again?" Docherty sounded faintly despairing, and at that I smiled.

"Yeah. Again."

"Won't last," he said sadly.

Wanna bet?

But we were prevented from any further discussions by the sound of voices outside. I ducked down behind the sofa and Docherty slipped behind the curtain pulled between bedroom and studio.

"Shit," that was Marc's voice, "the lock's been broken…"

"Probably just vandals," came Amber's voice. "Can we get inside? I'm freezing. Unless you want to warm me up out here…"

She sounded drunk. Or stoned. Or both. I wondered if the heroin had been a one-time deal or if she was used to it. I wondered if Marc was. I wondered when the hell they'd open the sodding door.

It felt like hours, during which the most revolting smoochy noises and little girlie moans came from the other side of the door, but eventually it opened, and Amber and Marc fell in, her hand slamming the light switch as she went.

I fired my gun, a split second after Docherty fired his. Neither missed, but unfortunately both had been aimed at Marc.

"Shit," I hissed, as Amber froze in horror. I swung my gun at her, but I'm a dreadful shot, and if it hadn't been for Docherty smacking a bullet into her thigh, she'd have got away.

She crumbled to the floor, falling bit by bit, clumsy and messy and clutching at her thigh, her mascara stark and black against her white face.

"Where's Lucy?" I demanded, and she looked up at me in shock. "Where. Is. Lucy?"

"I don't know," Amber said, clearly terrified. "She—she went off on her own. She said she wanted to see the Brooklyn Bridge..."

"Shit, she's going to jump," Docherty said, and I knew he was right.

"Go," I said. "I can handle this."

"Sure?"

I looked at Marc, sprawled facedown, bleeding from the leg and shoulder, and Amber, sitting rocking on the floor, holding her leg and crying, and knew they were only kids.

And felt really old.

"Sure. Go. You know what she looks like?"

He nodded. "I'll call you on this number."

And then he was gone, and it was me and the murder twins alone together.

"Mind the blood on the floor," I said. "Probably won't bother Marc, seeing as it's his father's, but you don't want to mix blood, do you, Amber? You can get all kinds of nasty things."

She was shaking, looking up at me with mascara stained eyes.

284

"Are you going to kill me?"

"You killed Luke," I snapped, "so it's all you deserve."

Amber cowered.

Yes, I'd known it was her. The balaclava had been a nice touch, but she'd forgotten to take off her amber eyeshadow and mountains of mascara. Bizarrely, I remembered a school play where a couple of girls had painted over their orangey stage makeup with their own foundation because they were too vain to walk around looking like Oompa Loompas, and consequently looked like ghosts under the stage lights. Teenage vanity.

"But I'm trying to be professional," I continued, my voice as steady as I could make it, which was to say not very. "So I'm going to get a confession out of you. And then I'm going to kill you."

I still had the gun aimed at her. If the cartridge was full, and knowing Docherty it would be, then I had eleven more shots. Plenty to keep me going.

"I didn't mean to kill him," she said. "I don't know my own strength..."

"Right," I said, "the rugby training. Thought you'd have gone for someone a bit beefier than Marc. Although it explains how you managed to haul Doyle and Maretti's bodies around. Did you kill them because they knew?"

A pause, then she nodded tearfully.

I needed to start at the top. I probably didn't have too much time before Marc bled to death. "Who killed Shapiro? Who killed Marc's father?"

Amber took a few very pretty heaving breaths. "He did," she said.

"Who?"

"Marc. He didn't mean to."

"How can you not mean to slit someone's throat? Or shoot him?"

"He came over here to see his dad. He was buying this hideous portrait from some gay kid who lives here. Lived here," she amended. "But he was hardly ever here. He was always out at bars and stuff. And Marc's dad kept coming over to see him. I think he fancied him, the kid."

Jeez. No wonder Xander wanted to get his money and get out.

"When did Marc kill his father?"

Amber sniffed. Her mascara was making trails down her face. "I don't know. A week—two weeks ago? He'd just brought the portrait home and he and Marc had this big fight and Marc stabbed him in the neck with the knife from room service dinner. He didn't mean to."

Yeah, 'cos I so often accidentally stab my family in the throat over dinner.

"At the hotel?"

"We hid him there for a couple days." Already inflecting Americanisms. "I went out and got a really big suitcase and wheeled him out and we tried to think of somewhere to put him."

"And this sofa was your best choice?"

"Marc was still mad at the painter guy. He said we should bring his dad over here."

I nodded. Twisted, but in a scary way it made sense.

"So what about the bullet?"

"That was so people would think it was the painter."

"His name is Xander," I snapped.

"Yeah, you were friends with him. Doyle said so."

"When did you meet him?"

She laughed suddenly. "God, it was so stupid. They found out about Mr. Shapiro, so they came here to move him, and they knew it was us... That's why they came to England."

"And why you killed them?"

She nodded. "They thought you and that Xander guy were in on it too." Her face lit up with a sort of sly innocence. "We saved you guys from them."

"No, you didn't. You knew about them hitting me with the car."

"Okay, all right." Amber pouted. "So we figured that out."

"Did you do it? Kill them?"

She hesitated. "Marc and Lucy helped."

No wonder Lucy wanted to top herself.

"Who put Maretti outside my door?"

"That was Lucy. But it was my idea," she said proudly. Stupidly.

"Well done. But I'm not so easily scared, Amber, it's not the first time I've come home to a corpse."

She looked exasperated. "Look, who are you?"

"I'm doing the questions," I snapped.

"You're not a sixth-former."

"No, I'm not," I agreed.

"You or your boyfriend. Did you have to follow us *everywhere*?" she whined, petulantly, and I decided I really didn't like Amber. Sometimes I respected criminals a bit. The first time I even quite liked the girl.

But I still shot her.

I ran through my head any other business I had with her. Oh yeah.

"Laurence," I said.

Amber shifted her leg, which was bleeding copiously all over her skirt. "I thought he was you," she admitted.

"There's not much difference."

"It was dark, okay, I had a bloody scarf over my head. A person is a person."

Well, yes. In some respects. "Why did you try to kill me?"

"Because you knew."

Not really. But I wasn't going to tell her that.

"You were always *there*. You were up to something, always asking all those questions. And driving that car, God, what are you, a farmer?"

I narrowed my eyes at her for that, and she looked away. Her eyes fell on Marc's body.

"Did you have to kill him?" she asked, sounding more like her age.

"Check his pulse."

I followed her movement with the gun, my arms aching horribly. She held his wrist with a bloody hand, and then she looked up at me in amazement. "He's still alive!"

"Oh, well, never mind. Be careful about mixing blood," I told her again. "Or do you already know about that?"

She looked away. "It's dangerous."

"Do you always use clean needles?"

"Yes," she said defiantly, and I breathed an internal sigh of relief. "Usually."

My finger nearly squeezed the trigger. "*Usually*? Was my needle clean?"

"It was supposed to be killing you, I didn't—"

"Do you realise you could have given me *anything*?" I yelled. "I could have hepatitis or fucking AIDS and it's all your fault." I felt like one of those Victorian rape victims who is punished for what happened to her.

And just like that, I understood *Tess of the d'Urbervilles*.

"I'm sorry," Amber was sobbing. "I'm so sorry. This is all a horrible mistake. It's all horrible..."

Maybe Shapiro was a mistake, I thought grimly, but the rest weren't.

Not moving the gun from its position, I reached over for the phone by Xander's sofa, praying there'd be a dial tone. I dialled 911, and waited.

Chapter Fifteen

As so often, there was a soundtrack in my head as I turned around and said good morning to the night. Elton John again. Mona Lisas and Mad Hatters—well, right now, I wasn't much of an oil painting. I guess that made me a mad hatter.

It figured.

The NYPD had taken quite a lot of convincing that, although I was the one holding the gun, I was the good guy in this equation. It had taken most of the night to explain the over-complicated situation to them, and by the time Marc and Amber had been fitted into an ambulance and driven away, and I was released (without the gun; Docherty would not be pleased), the sky was getting light.

"Hey," a voice stopped me as I trudged towards the subway on 14th and 8th. Didn't know if it'd be open; right then, didn't care. "Subway's no way for a good man to go down." Docherty paused. "Or a good girl."

"Do I look good to you?"

He hesitated.

"No, I don't," I answered for him. "Did you find Lucy?"

He nodded. "She wouldn't have jumped. She's in custody now. With her friends."

I felt sorry for Lucy. I had the feeling she'd been swept up a bit. Like Clara had said, she was a sheep.

Poor Clara. What would she do now, all on her own?

"Where are you headed?" Docherty asked.

"Hotel."

"Why?"

I blinked. "To sleep. I've hardly slept in days."

"So sleep on the plane." He looked at me for a moment, unruffled and dark and handsome in the early morning light. I must have looked like a train wreck, yet here he was, just as sexy as ever. It wasn't fair. "They'll manage without you. Do they have SO17 contacts?"

I nodded. "I told them to speak to Harvey."

"Good girl. So go home. There'll probably be a flight out soon enough." He stepped out in the street and raised his hand, and a yellow cab came to a halt not far away.

"How much to JFK?" Docherty asked the driver.

He shrugged, looked me over. "Fif—seventy dollars. Plus tolls."

Docherty handed me a couple of hundreds, like Monopoly money. "Don't spend it all at once." He pulled me towards him and kissed the top of my head. "Safe journey."

I sniffed and nodded. "I'll pay you back."

He gave me a slight smile. "You will," he said. "You will."

Uh-oh.

I dozed off in the back of the cab, and then again on the flight home. When I landed it was dark, and I couldn't remember what Clara's car looked like. God knows how I made it home without collapsing at the wheel, but I eventually did, and fell into bed, exhausted.

I was woken in the morning by the phone ringing. Groggily, I ignored it and let it go to answerphone.

Karen's voice rang out.

"Sophie Green, you will answer your phone! What's wrong with your mobile? When you get home, call me."

And that was it. Karen wouldn't leave a message that would get her in any trouble.

I looked at the clock and was surprised to see it wasn't morning at all. It was nearly three in the afternoon.

I pulled myself out of bed and made some coffee, and when I felt I could stand up unaided I made myself stand under the shower until all the travel dirt had gone down the drain.

Dressed, fed and made up, feeling a little more prepared for the world, I heaped loads of food into Tammy's bowl (thank God she's a vicious little killer, or I'd worry about her starving) and replayed Karen's message. Then I called her.

"I'll need a full report," she said. "I've been contacted by the New York police, who are not happy that you left Manhattan—"

"Bully for them," I yawned. "If I stayed there any longer I might never have got out."

"Can you come in now?"

"It's Sunday."

"Your point being?"

My point being, my plans for today involved sitting around crying into my cat's fur, then going to Luke's house in order to smell his pillow and clothes, staring at pictures of him, and sobbing uncontrollably.

"I have plans."

"You're going to see Luke?"

I blinked. I wasn't that macabre.

"I—she found him, then?"

"Yes. And just in time."

The world sort of whooshed to a halt around me, as if the earth had stopped spinning and everything was still.

What?

I forced myself to breathe, and it sounded very, very loud, even over the pounding of blood in my ears.

"Just in time?" I said, and my voice sounded surprisingly normal.

"He woke up this morning. I—well, I was quite worried. There was a subdural haematoma, but they've operated and apparently the outlook is good."

Outside, a tree swayed.

"And I have to say I was surprised at you leaving him, Sophie. I'm not sure if I'm impressed or not."

I dragged in a wheezy breath. "He's alive?" I croaked.

"Well, of course he is." Karen sounded puzzled. "You thought he was dead?

Duh.

"I—I saw him die, she smashed his head. There was blood..."

"He's alive," Karen said more gently. "And I think he'd like to see you."

I needed no second bidding. I was back in Clara's poor little Nova in a shot and up at the hospital as fast as the one litre engine would allow me. I swear, that car's only horsepower was supplied by old nags. I rushed along the corridors, getting lost several times, hot and flustered, knowing I looked a wreck. And when I found the ward, I was stopped by a nurse who said I couldn't go in.

"But I *need* to see him," I said urgently. "Luke Sharpe. I have to see him."

"Are you family?"

"His family hate him," I said dismissively.

"Then I'm afraid—"

"Please, can't you go in and ask him?"

"It's really not up to him."

I sniffed.

"Look, can I take your name," the nurse asked, not unkindly, fetching a clipboard, "and we'll see what we can do."

"Sophie," I told her. "Sophie Green."

She stopped, and looked up in surprise.

"What?"

"You're Sophie?" She put down the clipboard. "Why didn't you say so? He's been asking for you."

"He has?"

"Yes. Even in his sleep. You're his girlfriend?"

I was too tired to lie. Adrenaline had drained me completely. "Ex."

"Oh." She looked surprised. "Not very ex?"

"No. Not very."

She led me to a private room—lucky Luke—and I stood in the doorway, looking at him for a while.

He looked appalling. I don't know what kind of shoes Amber had been wearing when she kicked him across the dock, but it looked like they'd broken his ribs. His bare chest was crisscrossed with wires and he was hooked up to a lot of things. One of his hands was wrapped tightly in a splint and the other had a drip feed stuck in it. I winced at the thought of the needle, but not as much as I winced at the sight of Luke's face.

For a start, his head had been shaved, and there were several rows of stitches running across his scalp, along with the mother of all bruises. His face was bruised too, badly, one side of his jaw and cheekbone almost deformed.

He looked to be sleeping, so I said a very soft, "Hey," and prepared to leave. But his eyes opened, he looked at me, and one side of his mouth moved in a tiny smile.

He lifted a hand and waved.

"You okay?"

Yes, I know it was really stupid question. Luke's look said he thought so too.

"How come you're so talkative?"

He tapped the air above his bruised jaw.

"Is it broken?"

He shook his head and pointed to a pad and pen by his bed. I handed them to him, and he looked at me patiently, waving his splinted hand, until I realised he wanted me to hold the pad so he could write. I sat on the edge of the bed, feeling surreal.

"Not broken," Luke wrote. "Fucking hurts tho."

I smiled. "And the rest?"

"Dunno. All hurts. Lost teeth."

A wound more to his vanity than anywhere else, I guessed.

"I'm sorry," I said.

"Y?"

Good question.

"Because I left," I said. "I should have stayed."

There was a pause, and I thought Luke was going to tell me to go. But then he wrote, "Did you get them?"

I nodded. "Uh-huh. They're in custody. Marc and Amber and Lucy."

"Lucy? Surprised."

"Me too. She tried to top herself."

"You stopped her?"

"Docherty did."

Luke said—or rather, wrote—nothing. The silence went on too long, and eventually I blurted, "I thought you were dead."

He blinked. "Really?"

I nodded. "I saw her hit you—"

I broke off, because Luke's pen was tearing through the paper: "It was a *girl*?"

I laughed. "Amber. She played rugby, if that's any consolation. And she had a spanner."

He looked sulky under his bruises. Finally he scribbled, "Bloody girls."

I laughed again, and it felt good. "Hey," I tried out a Buffy quote, running my fingers along his arm, "you're all covered in sexy bruises."

Luke scowled. "Not going 2 dignify with answer."

I smiled.

"Girl helped me," he wrote. "Blonde dreadlocks. Who she?"

"Clara. She helped me out a bit too. She even let me nick her car."

"What car?"

"Nova."

Luke winced, and I smiled. Then I remembered something, and my smile faded.

"What?" Luke wrote.

"I left you."

"Yeah, and still mad at you. Even if did only just find out."

There was that half smile again. It was heartbreaking.

"I left you to do my job," I said, and I know I sounded heartless for it, but I meant it. And I even hated myself for it, but it was true. "And I'd do it again. I had to stop them. It was more important than..."

Luke dropped the pen and covered my hand with his. There were tears pricking my eyes and I sniffed.

"God, I'm such a bitch."

He nodded sympathetically, making me laugh, then he picked up his pen and wrote, "Is OK. Did right thing. I'm OK." Was he really? "Mostly."

There could be complications, I knew. Massive head trauma was never a good thing. It was only because of his unusually thick skull, I surmised, that he'd survived at all. But then there were complications for me, too. I was still awaiting the outcome of blood tests. Then there was Laurence, probably still in his coma. If he died it would bode even worse for the terrible trio in New York.

Luke was writing more, but he wasn't looking at me as he did.

"Would have done same."

"Oh, cheers."

Half of me wanted to believe I was more important to him than his job. That was the heart part. The head part of me said, of course his job's the most important thing to him. He doesn't need to choose. That's why he's such a good spy. You'll never be heartless enough, Sophie.

But didn't I dump my boyfriend and leave him for dead? Isn't that heartless?

My head had no answer.

"I should go," I said, and Luke grabbed my hand again.

"Don't," he wrote.

"I have a million things to do. I still have to talk to the police in New York. They don't believe I'm a spy."

Luke rolled his eyes. He twirled his pen for a few seconds, thoughtfully, then wrote, "Are we" and stopped, frustrated. But I knew what he meant.

I took a deep breath. "I think we're over," I said carefully. "I think neither of us can do our jobs properly if we're thinking about each other."

"Will still think about you," Luke wrote, and there was a note of pleading in his eyes. I nearly cried.

"Bye," I said, and slipped out before I said anything I didn't mean.

I went to the office and made out a report, or half a dozen. I spoke to fast-tempered NY cops on the phone. I called Clara and arranged to return her car. The school was on hiatus now that parents and teachers had been informed of the trio in America.

And then I went home, feeling lost, nothing to do and no one to do it with. I thought about going up to Angel's to see how Xander was getting on, but I couldn't work up any enthusiasm for the idea.

I couldn't even really be bothered to watch *Buffy*.

So I fed Tammy and cleansed my poor grubby face of all the New York dirt my shower didn't seem able to clear, and I massaged my feet and I rubbed arnica into my bruises.

And then, for want of anything better to do, I went to bed.

It was late when the knock came. A sure, hard knock. Not someone who was going anywhere without me answering.

I tried to peek out of my bedroom window but it was raining and dark, and I could see nothing. So I got my gun and rearranged my pyjamas into something more respectable, and I went to answer my door.

Docherty stood there, tall and dark, his eyes all over me.

"You're back," I said, stupidly.

"I am."

His shirt was plastered to his body. His excellent body.

"You're wet," I stood back to let him in, wondering when my brain had gone on strike.

"I'm that, too."

We stood and looked at each other for a while. My gun was loose in my hand and my heart was thumping.

"Did you want something?" I asked, knowing the answer.

Docherty nodded, and moved closer, and cupped my face.

"I came to get my apology."

Oh, boy.

About the Author

To learn more about Kate Johnson and Sophie Green, please visit www.KateJohnson.co.uk or visit Sophie's MySpace at http://www.myspace.com/sophiesuperspy. Send an email to Kate Johnson at katejohnsonauthor@googlemail.com.

Look for these titles

Now Available

Never underestimate the blonde.

I, Spy?
© 2007 Kate Johnson

"The British spy is elegant, suave and sophisticated. The British spy is not blonde, built, and confused."

But Sophie Green is, and she's just been hired by a highly secret government agency. She drives a car the colour of bile and is obsessed with Buffy the Vampire Slayer. She doesn't know which end of the gun to fire from and her hair hasn't been natural since she was twelve. But that's not going to stop her from trying to save the day, once she figures out who to save it from.

Sexy spies, plane crashes, firebombs and multicoloured cocktails—they're all in a day's work for Sophie. Roll over, Bond, there's a new bombshell in town. And it's got Sophie's name on it...

Available now in ebook and print from Samhain Publishing.

While investigative reporter Catherine Steel looks for Mr. Right,
she tries to learn if someone murdered the janitor
from her old high school.

A Fiery Secret
© 2006 Diane Craver

Catherine Steel is an investigative reporter for a newspaper in Ohio. To supplement her income so that she can buy clothes and gifts for her small godchild, she writes fluff pieces for women's magazines. Two recent articles are: "What To Wear to Get Noticed" and "Catherine's Ten Simple Dating Rules."

When Jake Michaels fills a sports editor's spot on the paper, Catherine wonders if he is man enough to fulfill her fantasy. And does she want him to be the one? After all, he broke her heart ten years ago in high school when he failed to show up for their prom date. And now that he's back in town, he wants to date her. Catherine refuses to go out with him but he keeps asking. Should she give Jake another chance?

When it appears the high school janitor, Max, was murdered, Catherine is determined to learn the truth about his death. Catherine's list of suspects for Max's death include: the school secretary with her intense dislike of Max, the charismatic mayor, the mayor's unbalanced girlfriend, the angry school principal, and a strange math teacher.

Available now in ebook and print from Samhain Publishing.

Printed in the United States
149062LV00004B/21/A